COFFIN MORNING

Rosie Neale

CHAPTER 1

Coffee Morning

Organised coffee mornings are not my idea of a good time, much as I enjoy a nice piece of cake. I have never been the 'earth mother' type and I don't have a passion for natural childbirth. Nor am I obsessively worried about which brand of nappy or approach to weaning is best. I hope never to indulge in competitive parenting. Local gossip tends to pass me by. I am not even very sociable.

So how did I end up at a coffee morning, listening to Charlotte rather loudly explaining to poor Emily how brilliantly her daughter Clemency was doing learning the piano, and just how vital it was to give children the chance to shine at an early age?

It was all Deborah's fault. She would not take 'no' for an answer.

"Look, Sam, I understand how you feel about this, but it is time for you to stop being a hermit. We're finally allowed to meet in person instead of on Zoom and you need contact with other adults. It's in Beth's enormous garden, everyone will do a lateral flow test and there'll be plenty of room for social distancing. It would do you so much good..."

Then came the clincher:

"You owe it to Chloe to come. She's nearly six months old now and she needs to learn to socialise with other children and adults. You know how crucial that is ..."

So here I was, a safe distance from Charlotte, Emily and the others, with Chloe on a blanket in front of me. She had her own toys, since sharing was not allowed yet, but actually she was looking round intently at all the other people. She was not the shy child I feared she might have become. She was fascinated with the other children and adults she could see. Deb was right. She was lapping it up. There was no excuse to keep her safely at home when she was clearly enjoying it.

"Sorry, do you mind if I sit here?"

The voice, slightly nasal and hesitant, came from behind me. I turned awkwardly to look up over my shoulder and saw a face I vaguely recognised from Deb's Zoom meetings. I had a moment of panic, while I tried to remember her name, and then it came back to me: Lesley.

"Of course, not, Lesley. There's plenty of room."

Lesley had two children with her: a very solemn three-year-old girl, who looked at me with enormous, slightly scared eyes, and a chubby baby boy, who was about the same age as Chloe. She struggled to put out her blanket and snapped at her daughter to help, then managed to put down her heavy burden of baby, changing-bag and toys.

"It's a struggle managing everything, isn't it?" I ventured. "I had never realised how much equipment you have to transport when you have children. Luckily I live round the corner, so I was able to use the buggy."

Sweating a little in the hot June sunshine, Lesley managed a smile.

"You'd think having an older one would help, but Jackie is such a dreamer. Just drifts along like her father," she remarked acidly. "Now that I have to manage everything on my own, I really need her to be more useful."

Suddenly I remembered why Deborah had talked to me about Lesley in particular. Her husband had left the family suddenly several months ago and now wanted a divorce. Lesley had been heartbroken at the start, since her whole focus was on husband and family, but over time the sadness had fermented into anger and bitterness.

"She was always a bit possessive," Deb had said. " And when lockdown came along, Mark just couldn't take being with her twenty-four hours a day, not ever having a moment to call his own. She even resented him working at home and kept coming in to interrupt him when he was on a Zoom call. Terrible thing to do, leaving young children like that, but you can kind of see where he was coming from…"

Lesley finally had the children settled and heaved a great sigh of relief.

"I'm really sorry – I know I've seen you on Zoom before, but I don't remember your name, although your face is very familiar …"

I couldn't help reddening. I had hated my fifteen minutes of fame, as the pregnant widow of the first doctor to die of the Delta variant, but my face had been plastered all over the papers and television for a few days and was now all too recognisable. That was part of the reason for staying at home, even after the rules were relaxed. I took a deep breath and hoped that I could avoid going through my story all over again.

"Don't worry – there were so many people at those Zoom meetings, it was really hard to keep track of names and remember who was who. My name is Sam – Samantha Elsdon."

I need not have worried. Lesley was far too bound up in her own grievances to be interested in me.

"I've only been part of this group for a little while – I didn't feel the need until my selfish husband decided to walk out on us. Can you imagine – leaving us at a time like this? How am I supposed to manage Jackie and Charlie on my own?"

The little girl was staring at her mother with a strangely adult look of long-suffering and intelligence. Stupidly, it brought a lump to my throat.

"How awful for you and the children," I mumbled, embarrassed by my emotion and not knowing what else to say.

"Oh, the kids are OK," she said airily. "They're too young to understand. That's the only comfort – they don't know what a pig their father is."

This really was too much for me. I could not take any more bile, and did not want the little girl to hear that kind of attack on her father.

"Do you want to take Jackie to get a drink and biscuit? I can keep an eye on Charlie for you if you like. They have a table over there with drinks and things and paper cups if you haven't brought your own."

"That's so kind of you. Are you sure? Come on, Jackie – let's get something to drink."

Lesley stomped off, pulling Jackie along with her and scolding her for dragging her feet. I heaved a sigh of relief and smiled at Charlie, who was lying on his front, looking over at Chloe. Impulsively, I hugged Chloe tightly, somehow wanting to make sure that Lesley's sourness hadn't affected her.

"I'm so lucky to have you," I whispered in her ear.

Charlotte was still droning on at poor Emily and anyone else who was within earshot.

"I don't ever allow myself to feel down or depressed, you know. I just count my blessings whenever things go wrong or I feel a bit shaky. That's the right thing to do, isn't it, vicar? Don't you think that's the best thing to do, Lesley? I just go over in my head how extremely lucky I am to have such very intelligent, talented and beautiful children, a wonderful husband who earns enough for me to stay at home, a fabulous house…"

And on and on she went, smug self-satisfaction radiating through every syllable.

"But you don't have to rub other people's noses in it!" muttered someone from behind me.

I looked round and saw a slight, fair woman in a carer's uniform, sitting on a deckchair, bouncing a baby on her knee. She looked exhausted and there was a rather bitter twist to her mouth. Her eyes brightened as she saw me and she gave me a weary and slightly apologetic smile.

"Sorry, I shouldn't have said that. But it's sometimes a bit hard to take Charlotte. Not all of us have everything given to us on a plate like that."

"I know, don't worry. I was feeling much the same. I don't think we've met before, have we? My name is Sam and this is Chloe."

"Nice to meet you, Sam. I think Deb did mention on the phone that you would be here. I don't do Zoom. I'm Annette and this bundle of wind and energy is my son Simon."

Time for the conventional questions.

"How old is he? He looks really big and strong."

"He's actually only just five months old, but he gets such a lot of colic and wind that he's never still for long. I'm sure it's made his back stronger, though."

"There have to be some compensations, I suppose! Poor you, that must be quite a handful. Does he sleep well at night?"

Possibly the most important question for any parent. I know I cannot survive on minimal sleep and felt really fortunate that Chloe was a good sleeper, on the whole.

"He's not bad, actually, my partner says. I mostly do evening and night shifts at the care home, so I'm not often there to settle him. Mind you, I sometimes think John wouldn't hear him if he was crying – he seems to be able to sleep through anything ... Typical man, but there you are – he is very good with Simon, so I'm pretty lucky."

Half of me wanted to laugh lightly and say, "Just like Charlotte!" But from nowhere I had a powerful urge to cry, and scream out that she did not know just how lucky she was. It took me completely by surprise. I looked up at the blue sky through the leafy branches, breathing deeply, and tried to get hold of my emotions. All I could hear, echoing weirdly through my head, was Charlotte moaning about her coffee...

"I'm really not enjoying this coffee – it's really bitter. Did you find yours very strong, Lesley? Annette, Annette – you had the same coffee as me. Did it taste bitter and grainy to you?"

"It tastes fine to me," soothed the vicar, peaceably. "Perhaps you're used to instant? You - er, you could put some sugar or extra milk in it."

And breathe. Coffee and chat, that was all. Nothing to get upset about.

"I'm so sorry, Sam. Did I say something to upset you? You looked so strange. Are you feeling OK?" Annette sounded worried. It was perceptive of her to notice.

"It's fine, Annette. Don't worry. I'm just feeling a bit emotional today. It's my first time out with people after so long."

"I understand. It can be quite stressful coming out and meeting people. Obviously, I see people all the time in my work, but it's not the same, and doing social things certainly comes as a bit of a shock."

Still feeling rather fragile, I have to admit that my heart sank when I saw Lesley making her way back to us, her mouth pursed angrily. I just was not sure that I had the energy to cope with her bitterness right now. I looked rather desperately around the garden, seeking a discreet way out.

Suddenly Deb was there, right beside me.

"Oh, there you are, Sam. I've been looking for you. The vicar wants to talk to you about Chloe's christening. Can you come and speak to him now? You bring Chloe and I'll carry your things for you."

Trying to hide my relief, I mumbled apologetically to Annette, smiled and waved at Lesley, who was back with Charlie now, and stumbled off after Deb.

"Thank you so much! I was pretty close to a meltdown there. It's stupid really, but I don't know if I could have managed Lesley again ..."

"I could see you were struggling and came to rescue you. I know it's a lot to take in on your first proper trip out. The vicar isn't really looking for you, but come and sit in this nice quiet corner and I'll go and fetch him for you. I'll bring you a cold drink too."

Sitting under a shady tree, watching Chloe pulling at a piece of long grass, I began to calm down. What an overreaction. I really had to get out more, if I could be so disturbed by tiny things. Just avoiding people and difficult situations was no solution. Maybe I needed socialisation as much as Chloe did.

Gradually I became aware of a strange choking sound from the bench by the fence, in the corner behind me. I looked round and saw Beth sitting there, stiff and rigid, her hands on her ears, rocking backwards and forwards. Her eyes were full of panic and she was clearly struggling to breathe. Symptoms I recognised only too well – she was on the verge of a full-blown panic attack.

I put Chloe down carefully and knelt in front of her (socially distanced of course), speaking calmly to her.

"Beth, darling, you can tell me what's wrong in a minute. For now, just focus on breathing as I count. In through the nose, two, three and out through the mouth slowly, two, three, four and five. In through the nose, two, three and out, two, three, four, five."

After a while, she had herself back under control and the colour began to come back into her sweet round face. Beth was one of the nicest people I knew. She never had a bad word for anyone and she seemed to positively take pleasure in obliging people. Living on her own, in a large inherited house, she had always been very hospitable and enjoyed entertaining, especially in the lovely big garden, full of mature trees and quiet corners.

"I'm so sorry I gave you such a fright, Sam. I don't quite know what came over me. I think it was just all the loud voices, so many people around and some of them complaining. I've got so used to being on my own most of the time. I just can't seem to manage adjusting back again."

"Charlotte certainly doesn't keep her voice down, that's for sure. All that moaning about the coffee – ridiculous."

"Oh, but she's such a kind and generous person. I know she doesn't mean to upset me. She does an amazing amount of charity work for people, behind the scenes. It's just that she can be very loud and a little overwhelming ... But it isn't just her. It's having so many people around and so much going on. I can't be sure everyone is going to be safe and if anyone catches it, it will be my fault ..."

Beth's voice was rising in panic and she was speaking faster and faster.

"Honestly, Beth, you don't have to – "

"Beth, darling, what's going on? What's wrong?"

Deb had returned with the vicar in tow. She quickly took charge and calmed Beth down.

"Right, I am going to take you upstairs for a lie down and a quiet cup of tea away from everyone. You don't need to worry about anything. I will keep things going and clear away when we finish. No, there's no point in arguing. It's no problem at all. Come on, you need to relax right now."

"Wow, that was impressive," said the vicar, as the two women went into the house through the back door.

"Deb's amazing," I agreed. "You can't say no to her – hence why I'm here, in fact!"

"Mmm, yes, er ... I think that's why I came too. I ... er ... don't really ... er ... have the time..." His voice trailed off in a morass of hesitations.

I turned and smiled reassuringly at him. He was tall, and much more good-looking than seemed right for a vicar, with lots of unruly wavy dark blonde hair, which still bore the marks of lockdown neglect. I had watched some of his online services and been impressed with how effectively he had managed them. But of course that was all planned and controlled. I had forgotten that Deb had said that in person he was very diffident and sometimes almost paralysed by social anxiety. Not the best characteristic for a vicar, you would think! But apparently he was much more confident with the older congregation members and very good with children, especially for a man who was unmarried and childless.

"It's nice to see you in person, anyway, Reverend. I wanted to tell you that I have enjoyed your online services very much."

A painful flush stained his pale skin.

"Th - that's so kind of you. Pl - please call me Stephen. Everyone does."

There was a somewhat uncomfortable silence. I knew I needed to break it for him.

"So, Chloe's christening?"

"Ah, yes." He was more at ease on familiar ground. "We can do a christening with social distancing, but, to be honest, I have been recommending a service of blessing at the moment, as it is much easier to manage. What would you like to do?"

"I've never been to a service of blessing, but that sounds more like what I want, in fact. I have always felt a bit uncomfortable about the baptism service and making promises for a baby."

Stephen's eyes brightened and suddenly he seemed to be able to express himself with real fluency.

"That's very interesting. So few people actually think about the promises they are making. Of course, in many churches adult baptism is preferred and the biblical sources are unclear about - "

He was off, on what was obviously a subject of real interest to him. I am afraid that I zoned out a little, but I was fascinated with the change in him, when he was talking about something he had a passion for. His voice was firm and confident, he was gesturing with his hands, speaking powerfully and persuasively. Like a completely different person, and much more engaging.

I was nodding and smiling in response to his arguments, when a somewhat piercing shout rang out across the garden, high-pitched and urgent.

"Stephen, where are you?"

He stopped abruptly, seemed to come back down to earth, and looked round towards the house.

"I'm coming, Celia. Sorry."

He looked back at me apologetically and the familiar anxious look had returned.

"I'm so sorry for boring on like that ... I don't ... er ... usually ... My sister is reminding me that we have to get to a ... er ... a meeting in the church with a new ... er ... member of the parish council. Sorry..."

"Don't apologise, it was really interesting. Perhaps we can

meet again or email about Chloe's service. I hope you aren't too late."

Mumbling uncomfortably, he rushed off towards the house to meet his sister.

Charlotte was still complaining loudly, this time about a headache and feeling light-headed. Someone offered her a paracetamol, but that didn't stop her listing all her symptoms, as if we were interested in exactly how she felt.

"What have you done to the vicar?" Deb sounded amused.

"Celia called him. He's a strange one, isn't he? But when he's really interested in something, he's like a different person."

"To be honest, I've never seen him like that," Deb responded. "I think he's scared of me. And Celia keeps him on a pretty tight rein. She probably has to. He's certainly not the most organised of people."

Deb sat down near me and explained that Beth was feeling better, but lying down upstairs, leaving her in charge.

"I'll have to go and check on the refreshments in a minute. Oh, it is so lovely to see you face to face, Sam. It's been much too long."

"I know, I'm sorry. It just felt as if I had to get through everything on my own. I can't - I can't even explain why."

My voice trembled suddenly and the emotions welled up again. I hugged Chloe tightly. Deb looked affectionately at us both.

"I so want to give you a proper hug. And Chloe too! She's simply gorgeous, bless her. Better not just yet though, I suppose. I'm so sorry that Kate wasn't able to be here too. She really wanted to see you, but she had a bad reaction to her last treatment and had to stay in bed."

Kate was the third member of our tight little group. We had all met in school at the start of year ten, having chosen the same option subjects quite by chance, and had been inseparable from the second day. We called ourselves 'The Three Amigas', which somehow seemed incredibly funny and clever when we were fourteen.

I had always felt amazingly lucky to have two such wonderful friends. Deb was confident, popular and sociable and, even back then, the organiser. Kate was tall, beautiful, serene and elegant. And then there was me: studious, often clumsy and anything but elegant or confident. But for some reason we all just clicked.

Even in later life, after university and very different work, family and social lives, we were really close and slipped back into our old comfortable relationship, even if we had not met for some time. But when Thomas died and Chloe came along, somehow I had shut everyone out, even my best friends, even my parents. I had actually insisted on giving birth on my own in the hospital. It was only now that I fully realised what I had done, and still I did not really understand why. But I suddenly felt guilty about it. I had only been thinking of myself, not the hurt to others.

Even more so, because Kate had been diagnosed with breast cancer and having treatment, and I had not been there to support her. Not that anyone could do much supporting with lockdown and social distancing, but I could have been in proper contact with her, done regular Zoom calls or something. As a very private person, she had not even told most people that she was ill, so it felt even worse not to have helped in some way.

Deb looked at the tears now streaming down my face and took charge, as usual.

"Time for you to get home and have some quiet time on your own, I think," she said briskly. "It's quite a shock to the system to see so many people after such a long time isolated. You need a rest, and it looks to me as if Chloe does too. We'll all meet up next week at coffee morning, hopefully Kate too, and I'll ring you tomorrow so that we can arrange a walk together. Come on, I'll help you get your things into the buggy and walk you out, so that you don't need to talk to anyone. It's so frustrating not to be able to give you a hug ..."

I sniffed and smiled gratefully at her through the tears. You never had to explain things with Deb. She just understood.

CHAPTER 2

Fallout

That afternoon, I messaged Kate with a photo of Chloe and asked her how she was. As usual, she did not give any information about her health, but she commented on the photo (which was particularly cute) and we chatted about meeting up next week at the coffee morning, and then for a walk together, as soon as Kate felt up to it.

It felt as if I had broken the ice wall I had built up around me and I decided, without giving myself a chance to have second thoughts, to ring my mother.

"Hello, is that you, Sam? What's wrong? It's not Chloe is it?" My mother sounded anxious. She was not used to me ringing up out of the blue.

"No, Mum, nothing's wrong. I just wanted to hear your voice and to say - ," my voice started to shake but I ploughed on, " that I'm really sorry for pushing you away ... I'd really like ..."

But it was no use. My voice wouldn't hold out and I ended in a sob.

"Sweetheart, don't. Dad and I understand. Look, we can't do this over the phone. Shall I come over now, or do you want to bring Chloe here for tea tomorrow?" Mum sounded pretty emotional too.

We agreed that I would take Chloe to their house on the

following day - actually the first time she would go into someone else's home, even though, as a single mother, I could have made a bubble with my parents. Somehow, it had just felt wrong and simply impossible to me. I had justified it to myself as protecting my father, who had high blood pressure, but in reality I had wanted to isolate myself, just me and Chloe, to cope with my loss on my own terms.

Exhausted by all the emotion, I slept heavily that night and fortunately so did Chloe. Planning what I needed to put in the car to take to Mum's took most of the morning. I actually felt shaky, nervous and excited all at once.

Deb rang, as she had promised, just before lunch. I told her about contacting Kate and going to see my parents.

"I'm so pleased, Sam. It's just what you and Chloe need now. A big step in the right direction. So I don't know if I should tell you, but ..." She hesitated. Most unlike Deb.

"What is it?"

"I suppose you will just hear it from someone else and probably a garbled version. I just don't want to seem as if I am gossiping..."

"Now you'll have to tell me," I laughed. "I can't bear the suspense."

"Well, but actually it is really something quite serious. It's about Charlotte."

"What about her?"

"She's in hospital."

"Not Covid? Please tell me it's not that..." Panicky, I looked down at Chloe playing quietly on the floor. It would just be too much if we all had to isolate, just as I was finally making contact with family and friends again.

"No, nothing like that. It seems she must have taken an overdose of paracetamol. She was unconscious when her older daughter got home from school. They called 999 and the ambulance got her to hospital in time, but it looks as if there will be lasting liver damage. Apparently she is insisting that she didn't intend to do it, that she didn't take an overdose, but the amount

13

in her blood was far too much to be accidental ..."

I sat down in a state of shock. Of all the people to attempt suicide, Charlotte would not have been the one I would have picked. She seemed so happy with her life, to the extent of being, in actual fact, rather smug and self-satisfied.

"I just can't believe it. Not about Charlotte. Some of the others are showing signs of strain, but Charlotte seemed so sure of herself. Did she leave a note?"

"It's a puzzle to me as well. Of all the people ... No, apparently there was no note at all. Strange, I suppose. Oh well, I guess you never really know what is going on in someone's head. But it must be a dreadful shock to her poor husband and the children, especially Clemency. Finding her in that way."

"I just can't imagine. It's going to be difficult for them all to get over something like that and they'll need a lot of support."

Apparently Charlotte had been quite close to the vicar, spending quite a lot of time with him, discussing a charity she was involved with, so Deb thought he might be able to help.

"And I'm sure Michael will get her some counselling or therapy. Hopefully it'll all be OK, and, in any case, it's nothing for you to worry about, but I didn't want you to hear it from someone else."

As it happened, I ran into several people that afternoon, when I walked into town to buy some flowers to take for Mum. All of them wanted to talk about what was fast becoming the main local scandal, and it was hard to avoid the sense of us all gossiping about someone's misfortune. Lesley was particularly strident in her condemnation of Charlotte's selfishness.

"What an awful thing to do! Leaving her daughter to find her. And she kept going on about how lucky she was and how she never got depressed like the rest of us. There was obviously something going on we didn't know about. I wonder if she'd been having a secret affair or something. That might explain it, if he dumped her suddenly - and she talks so much I wouldn't blame him!"

"Oh, Lesley, you mustn't say things like that. I know she can be a bit irritating, but she has a kind heart and we don't really know what was going on in her life - or in her head."

"Well, all I can say is that I have managed to cope with a lot more than her! And I wouldn't do something like that, however hard things get."

"I know, you've been very brave and strong. Not everyone can do that." I tried to placate her. "I'm really sorry, Lesley, but I have to get moving now. Chloe needs a feed before we go to my parents' house."

With relief, I escaped and hurried home. There seemed to be a lot more schadenfreude and prurient nosiness in the local reaction, rather than sympathy for Charlotte and her family. She seemed to have rubbed a lot of people up the wrong way.

It was better discussing it with my parents that evening. They were so much more balanced - shocked and sympathetic, but not speculating on the background to Charlotte's troubles. It was good to have something less personally emotional to talk about, and it helped us to become more comfortable with one another again. By common consent, we did not mention Thomas, or anything which might make the atmosphere too fraught. There would be time enough for that. Babies are great ice-breakers, and there was plenty of detail on Chloe's progress to catch up on. I had sent the odd photo and email, but really kept my parents at arm's length.

It was not until I was about to leave that the tears welled up again. Thank goodness the rule against family hugging was gone. A bear hug from Dad and an emotionally restorative embrace from Mum did me more good than any words of comfort. They could hardly bear to let me and Chloe go, and we arranged to meet up again at the weekend.

The suicide attempt was a real nine days' wonder locally, with everyone trying to analyse the situation and what might have caused it. Poor Michael came in for a lot of ill-informed criticism, as people guessed that he might be a secret abuser or philanderer. Even the vicar's reputation came in for a bit of a battering.

"You would think he would have noticed that there was something wrong. Either that or somehow he was involved..."

Celia was furious about it.

"That stupid woman! Not content with wasting hours of Stephen's time (because, of course, he can never bring himself to say 'no' to anything), she does this. People are even asking me if they were having an affair! It's totally ridiculous. And you can't blame him for not spotting that she was depressed. He's not a counsellor or a therapist - although some people seem to think he should be. No one else realised she was so desperate either. But, obviously, it has to be the vicar's fault ..."

After a few days, Charlotte was allowed home, but she was never left on her own or alone with the children. She was a shadow of her former self, according to Deb, who had been to visit.

"You would hardly recognise her, Sam. She looks anxious, and haunted, and her skin has a yellowish tinge from the liver damage. Michael has been told to keep a very close eye on her for the moment, and not to leave her alone. They are especially worried at the hospital, because she hasn't admitted that she took an overdose. They think she is still a serious suicide risk. I've agreed to sit with her tomorrow, so that Michael can get some work done."

Deb was clearly very disturbed by the state Charlotte was in.

"She hardly says a thing apart from 'I didn't do it'. Mostly she just sits there staring out of the window. It's really uncanny. Michael hasn't managed to get any therapy sorted yet, as they all say she needs to be seen by a psychiatrist first. Anyway, I've said I'll take her along to our coffee morning this week, and stay close to her. It might distract her a bit and take her out of herself."

I ran into Annette in the park one morning, and she seemed genuinely shocked by what had happened.

"I just can't quite believe it! I know I found her really infuriating, but she always seemed so happy with her life - a bit too happy, to my mind. I can't imagine what must have been going on in her head, and now I'm really sorry that I resented her so much."

"I suppose anyone can get depressed, however comfortable their life is," I responded. "But I agree, she didn't show any of the usual signs. In fact, of all of us, she probably seemed the most stable and confident."

I was looking forward to seeing Kate at the coffee morning and I was also, I have to admit, interested to see Charlotte after hearing so much about her. But on the morning itself, I was woken up early by Chloe screaming, obviously in pain. A hurried video call with the doctor diagnosed an ear infection, and it was immediately obvious that there was no way I would be able to take her out that morning.

I was worried about Chloe, who was running a temperature and not taking her milk normally, but also desperately disappointed not to be able to go to the coffee morning and see Kate.

Kate reassured me on WhatsApp that it wasn't a problem, she would come round in a couple of days for a garden visit, if Chloe still wasn't up to going out. "We have plenty of time to catch up," she wrote.

Deb was understanding.

"That's the trouble with planning things when you have small children - it just doesn't always work. Look after yourself and Chloe. I'll ring later or tomorrow to see how you are, and let you know what happens with Charlotte."

CHAPTER 3

Horror

Chloe began to pick up quite quickly that day on the antibiotics from the doctor, and had a good sleep in the late afternoon. Feeling relieved that she was starting to recover, I dozed a little myself, but was woken by a sudden ring of the doorbell. No online orders were due, and I never had unexpected visitors, so I was puzzled, as I hurried to the door.

It was Deb, looking more dishevelled and distraught than I had ever seen her.

"What is it? What's happened? Is it Charlotte?" The questions tumbled out.

"Worse than that," Deb managed to say. Her voice was quavering.

"Come in quickly and tell me what it is." What could be worse? I began to feel shaky as I led her into the house.

"It's ... I have to tell you, but I don't know how. It's Kate."

My eyes opened wide with horror.

"What's happened?"

"Oh Sam, I can't believe it myself, but she's - she's dead. Martin found her lying dead on the sofa a few hours ago. He rang me as soon as he had called the doctor - he's totally distraught. I rushed over, but there was absolutely nothing I could do. The doctor came straight away and he was shocked too. They all thought she was doing well on the treatment. She seemed fine this morning, a bit tired and subdued, but fine. And suddenly she's gone..."

For a moment, the shock was too much. I stood there staring at Deb, unable to take it in. Not my beautiful friend Kate. I was going to see her soon, she couldn't be gone. Life wouldn't be that cruel. Then it hit me.

"Nooooo!" It was more of a whisper than a scream. I couldn't get my breath.

Deb and I clung together, sobbing hysterically. All thought of social distancing was gone. Chloe woke up and began crying again, adding to the feeling of utter chaos and despair.

This time, there was no thought of me coping on my own. I called Mum, barely able to get the words out, and she rushed over and took Chloe home with her for the night. To start with, the moments of gasping hysteria were hard to cope with. Deb stayed and we wept and talked and wept again.

It was as if all the pent-up grief after Thomas' death was released at once in my anguish at the loss of Kate and I just couldn't hold it back. The dam had well and truly burst, and I could hardly breathe through the pain of my suffocating emotions. The doctor, prompted by Deb, prescribed some tranquillisers, but I did not want to take them. I needed to feel the pain.

Over the next few days I gradually grew a little calmer. Deb and I went for long long walks, whatever the weather, sometimes in silence, sometimes able to talk about Kate, Thomas and our memories of them both. Mum took charge of Chloe each day, pushing away my thanks.

"She's my granddaughter. I love to spend time with her. I can't do anything else to help, I can't take away the pain, but I can do this."

She called Stephen, the vicar, who was quite helpful. He would just sit with me, make endless cups of tea, not even flinch, when I railed at the cruel God who had taken my husband and my best friend from me. He never tried to give me easy answers or mouthed empty platitudes. Once, when I was crying inconsolably, and verging on hysteria again, he held my hand and stroked it gently, until I came back to the surface and looked over at him. He dropped my hand abruptly and turned away to get more tea, embarrassed by the gesture, but I was grateful to him.

Eventually, I began to feel slightly more normal. I could smile at Chloe and hug her without breaking down. I could taste my food again and sometimes even sleep peacefully for a few hours. I felt as if I had swum back up to the surface, I was not quite drowning any more. Combing my hair, putting make-up on, enjoying a shower, these ordinary things came back into my life, along with the routine tasks of looking after Chloe and the house. I was not over it, not the anger, nor the grief, nor the aching loss, and I knew that I might never get over it fully. But life had crept back into my heart and I began to treasure the moments with Chloe, time with my parents, and with friends, especially Deb.

However, there was another shock to come.

CHAPTER 4

Murder

It was Wednesday morning, and I was just thinking of taking Chloe out to the park, when my phone rang. It was Deb, sounding strangely distracted and unlike herself.

"Glad I caught you before you went out. Ummm," she hesitated and I could hear her drawing in a long breath shakily. "This is a big shock, and there's no easy way to tell you. I haven't got long and he'll be there soon."

"What on earth is it, Deb? Who'll be there? What's wrong?"

"There's been a post-mortem and it shows that Kate didn't die of the cancer, or the treatment. She was - murdered."

"You can't be serious!"

"I'm afraid I am. I can't tell you all about it now, but he wanted me to ring and let you know before he arrived, once he knew how close you were to her."

"Who is this 'he'? What are you talking about?"

"The police, of course. They are investigating. I've just had them with me for over an hour. A Detective Inspector Morton and Sergeant Evans. The sergeant is coming to see you now, while the inspector deals with some of the other interviews. He should -"

She was interrupted by the sound of my doorbell ringing suddenly, loudly.

"That'll be him. I'll go now, Sam. Get in touch later, when he's gone."

Rather slowly, I laid Chloe down on her playmat and walked to the door, just as the bell rang again, insistently. I opened it and saw a youngish man in a suit and tie, his thick dark hair cut short but showing its curls, brown eyes bright above a black face mask.

"Mrs Elsdon? I'm Detective Sergeant Evans. Your friend Deborah should have let you know that I would be coming round."

"I was just speaking to her when you arrived. Do you want to come in?"

"Please. I do need to talk to you. Ideally without a mask on, so if we could sit outside or in a well-ventilated room that would be best."

"Come on through. We can sit in the garden if you like. Is this likely to take long? If so, I'll just call my mother to come and look after Chloe."

His eyes crinkled in a smile as he looked down at her, rolling on her mat.

"What a cute baby! Well, I think, if it is at all feasible, it would be a good idea if you could get your mother to look after her, so that I can have your full attention."

This was sounding scary. I felt confused and disorientated. Kate murdered and the police interviewing me? It was surreal. We sat mainly in uncomfortable silence until Mum arrived and whisked Chloe away. She didn't ask any questions, it was obvious that there was no time for that, but she looked curiously at the policeman.

"Come over and get her whenever you like, Sam. You know she'll be happy with me and your father."

By now feeling a considerable degree of anxiety and trepidation, I took the detective into the garden and we sat on the patio. The sun was strong and the air was full of pollen. A large bee buzzed slowly past. He carefully took off his mask and used hand sanitizer.

"Sorry, I should have offered you a drink or something."

"We're not supposed to accept food or drinks at the moment, thank you - Covid regulations."

"Of course, I understand."

There was a silence, which seemed interminable to me. He took out a notebook and pen and put them on the table in front of him. Just get on with it, I thought.

"How much did your friend tell you?" Finally he spoke.

"Only that Kate's death was - was murder." It seemed strangely theatrical and unreal to use the word in real life.

"Mmmm, yes, I see." Another long pause. Was this some type of interviewing technique? It was certainly unsettling.

"OK, then, I think, under the circumstances, I need to put you fully in the picture."

Under what circumstances? I couldn't help wondering. He opened his notebook, as if to refresh his memory.

"Right. As you know, Mrs Elsdon - "

"Sam, please - no one calls me Mrs Elsdon any more, not since I stopped teaching." Why on earth had I interrupted him just as he was about to get going?

"Sam, then. If you're sure you are comfortable with that. As you know, your friend, Kate Rigby, was found dead just over two weeks ago. It looked like natural causes, given her medical history, but her GP was surprised that she had passed away so suddenly and he and her hospital consultant ordered a postmortem to see what had caused it. To everyone's astonishment, it showed that she had died due to an overdose of co-codamol."

"But that can't be true! I know she had a condition which meant she could not take it. Her liver turned too much of it into morphine or something. She was never allowed to take it and she knew how dangerous it was for her."

"Very true, her husband and her doctor also told us that. There was none in the house for that reason. Obviously we considered accident or suicide, but it was clear that she had never bought any or used it."

"Suicide? Oh, definitely not."

"No, we rapidly came to the same conclusion. Normally, in this kind of case, we would look first at the husband, but due to the nature of the medication, it was possible to pinpoint the time of taking it pretty accurately. It was taken, or rather I should say was given to her, during the coffee morning. So her husband was out of the frame."

I sat there open-mouthed. How could he be calmly talking about such things? It felt increasingly unreal, sitting there in a hot garden, with birds singing, as if nothing had happened.

"Out of the frame? But - I just don't understand any of this."

"I can imagine that it must be a shock to you. Anyway, to begin with, we considered a racial motive, as your friend Kate was black and some people do have an irrational hatred of people of colour. But looking at the previous attempt, we soon realised that it could not just be that."

"The previous attempt? Had someone tried to kill her before?" My brain just wouldn't work, it felt thick and woolly. What did he mean?

"Oooh! You can't mean - you do mean Charlotte. She kept saying she hadn't taken an overdose. Was it true? Was she the first - victim?" Again, I felt uncomfortable using the terminology. I loved murder mysteries, but this was supposed to be real life.

"Clearly. Once we heard about this and looked in detail at the hospital records, it was obvious that she had also been poisoned, and at the first coffee morning."

"I remember she kept moaning about the taste of her coffee."

"Exactly. When we interviewed her, it became clear that she had noticed something amiss with her coffee, and actually began to feel unwell while at the coffee morning. Unfortunately for her, she then took more paracetamol when she got home, so it looked as if she had deliberately, or accidentally, taken an overdose."

"But this is awful, unbelievable. We can't have a killer running round poisoning people at coffee mornings. It's like something out of *Midsomer Murders* or Agatha Christie!"

He smiled ruefully.

"It does seem a bit far-fetched. To be honest, it is not at all the kind of case we normally have to deal with. We do have to investigate murders, but usually it is domestic violence, or related to gangs or organised crime. This kind of thing is just not what we are used to. No proper forensics, no witnesses, nothing to get hold of."

"But - why have you come to talk to me? I was there when Charlotte was poisoned, but I was here with Chloe when someone, when someone killed Kate ..." My voice trailed off. I could not believe that anyone in their right mind would want to kill Kate. But that was the issue, wasn't it? The killer probably was not in their right mind.

"You're absolutely right. And that is why I have come to talk to you, and hopefully to rope you in, to help us in our investigation. You are the only one to have been missing on the second occasion, so you are the only one who cannot be a suspect."

"You can't be suspecting everyone at the coffee mornings, surely? They are just nice normal people."

"One of them isn't," he said, soberly.

I stopped short and took that in. He was right, of course. One of those 'nice normal people' was a murderer, and had killed one of the friends I held most dear. Someone surely no normal person would want to hurt, let alone kill.

"But how can I help? I wasn't even there the second time. I don't have any useful information or insights. I don't even know all of them very well - most of them I met for the first time that day."

"I understand that. But you are an insider. They will all talk to you. My boss, DI Morton, is amazing at interviewing gang members - she can have them eating out of her hand and even giving up friends or enemies. But this is not her type of case. She has nothing in common with these people and she doesn't know how to open them up. As for me, I don't think they will talk to me much either. I don't fit into their world at all. But you know that this is going to be the main topic of conversation in the area for the next few weeks. You will hear the gossip, see the people who are reacting oddly. And you can pass that on to me."

"You are asking me to spy on my friends and neighbours! I'm not sure I can do that ..."

"I'm asking you to help us to find the killer of one of your best friends, before they kill someone else."

He spoke simply and directly and it went right to my heart. He was right. I would not want Kate's killer to escape justice, but even more than that, I could not let anyone else die, if I could help to prevent it. Who would be next? There was no way to know, without understanding the motive of the killer.

He could see from my face that his words had hit home.

"I'm not asking you to pretend to be a private detective and go around interviewing people. I will do that, and hopefully it will shake some of them up a bit, and they will let out more than they realise, either to me, or later to a friend. But I do want you to keep your eyes and ears open, to take any chance to talk to the group from the coffee morning. And to pass everything, however trivial, on to me."

"But how will I do that? I don't think I could put it all in an email."

"No, we need to meet, so that you can talk freely. But I don't want the whole town gossiping about it, and I don't want the suspects to know that you are talking to me. So although I can come here once more, I think, as it will seem to be a normal part of the investigation, we will need to find somewhere else after that."

"Perhaps at my parents' house? It's only about fifteen minutes away by car and it won't cause any talk for me to go there regularly."

"That sounds perfect. I don't mind you telling them what is going on, but apart from them, this must be kept secret. You understand that."

"Even from Deb? You surely can't suspect her."

"She seems unlikely, at this stage, but she certainly had

opportunity, even if there is no obvious motive. I am also concerned that she won't react naturally around others if she knows what you are doing. I know it's difficult, but I think it is essential that this remains secret. For your safety, apart from anything else."

"My safety? You think this could be dangerous?"

"I don't think so, and of course I hope not, but we cannot be sure. There is a dangerous person out there, possibly a sick mind. I don't want to take chances."

"What shall I tell Deb later about this interview then?"

"Just say I was looking for information about the first coffee morning, and your impressions of the people there. You could say that you found it too difficult to talk about, so I am coming back the day after tomorrow to take your statement."

"I could do that, I guess," I said reluctantly. "It will be very strange to keep things from Deb, and I know she isn't the killer, but I do understand that it might affect the way she behaved around me and others if she knew."

He smiled understandingly.

"I knew you would be able to be sensible about this. I understand that it is asking a lot of you, but it really could make all the difference here. I'm going to leave you my card with all my contact details. The mobile number will get a message to me at any time. Please do use it if you feel the need. I really am very grateful for your help."

And with that, he stood up and put his mask back on. I led him out to the front door and let him out, then walked slowly into the living room, shaking my head a little as if to clear it. What had I got myself into?

CHAPTER 5

More questions than answers

The whole situation felt completely unreal. I could not even remember the policeman's name. I looked down at the card he had given me: Detective Sergeant Daniyaal Evans. I had noticed a slight Welsh lilt to his voice - reassuring to me, as my favourite grandmother had been from the Valleys. Maybe that was why I had agreed to his crazy idea. It all seemed impossible to me, now that he had gone.

Surely it must have been some kind of accident. Murder simply wasn't part of real life. But Kate - suddenly I stopped myself going down that track. If someone had killed my precious friend, and tried to kill Charlotte, then I would definitely do what I could to bring them to justice, whatever that looked like. It seemed to me that it must be someone who was mentally disturbed, and that ought to be relatively easy to spot.

The difficult thing would be keeping my role from Deb. Rather than waiting for her to call back, I decided to grasp the nettle and give her a ring, before going over to my parents' house.

"Hello, is that you Sam?" Deb still sounded shaken. "How did it go?"

"I don't know, really," I responded. "I was so shocked, I couldn't think straight. He just wanted to know what I had seen, when I was at the coffee morning, but my mind couldn't get past that word - murder. It doesn't make any sense to me."

"I know, I was flabbergasted as well. Still am, to be honest."

"He was a bit irritated with me, I think, but he's coming back the day after tomorrow to take my statement. I'll have to get it clear by then. Maybe we can meet up and talk it through first. As you know, I wasn't exactly at my best that day. He didn't say I couldn't talk about it."

"That sounds like a good idea. I just can't get over it. It would definitely help to talk to you properly."

"I'm just going over to Mum's to pick up Chloe and will probably stay there this evening, but what about meeting for a walk and a coffee tomorrow morning?"

Deb agreed, still sounding rather listless and unlike herself. It was not at all usual for me to be suggesting the time and place - Deb, the arch-organiser, usually did that. Feeling rather worried and definitely uncomfortable about the whole situation, I drove carefully over to pick up Chloe, concentrating hard because everything felt so abnormal.

It was so good to hug Mum and Dad, and hold Chloe. At least I did not need to play a part with them.

"What's going on, Sam? What did the police want with you?" Dad was clearly concerned and full of questions.

"You're not going to believe this, but Kate didn't die of natural causes. She was - she was actually murdered." Saying it out loud was so strange. I still could not feel that it was true.

Mum and Dad were as astonished as I was, and made me go over what Sergeant Evans had said several times. They quickly came to some disturbing conclusions.

"It must have been premeditated. No one goes to a coffee morning with a bag or pot of powdered or liquid paracetamol or co-codamol in their bag!" I had not thought of that. It must have been done (both times) very quickly and discreetly, so the murderer had to have been prepared.

"But would they have known that Kate would be there? She missed the previous one and had been unwell." Mum was right. That did not fit.

"They must have been preparing to kill someone. What happened on that second morning to make them pick Kate?"

Suddenly I could see where I needed to begin. I had to find out, probably from several people, but starting with Deb, whose account I knew I could definitely trust, what had happened during that second coffee morning. I really could not imagine what could have been said or done to make Kate a target - she was never one to take the limelight or put herself forward. Obviously with the news of her death coming later that day (I still felt the tears starting immediately at the thought), I hadn't heard anything about what had happened.

"Why Charlotte then? You were there that time, Sam. Can you think of a reason why she might have been picked out?"

"Well, - nothing that would trigger murder, I would think, but she was honestly very annoying that day. You could hear her voice all over the garden. Talking at the top of her voice about whatever went through her mind."

"Yes, you told us that after her so-called suicide attempt, but what did she actually talk about? It could be really important."

I racked my brain.

"First of all she was showing off to Emily about how brilliant her children are, especially Clemency and her music, and giving her a lot of useless and no doubt unwanted advice! Then what? Oh, I know, she spouted a lot of platitudes about always looking on the bright side of life and counting her blessings. She insisted on saying how fortunate she was to be well off and to have such a beautiful house and such amazing talented children. It was very irritating! I remember it really annoyed Annette, who isn't nearly so lucky. What next? She moaned on and on about how bitter and grainy her coffee was, asking everyone else if their coffee was horrible as well - Oh!"

I stopped suddenly, realising what I had just said.

"That must be exactly when she took the paracetamol. In that specific cup of coffee."

Mum nodded, but Dad suddenly looked very anxious.

"Listen, Sam, this person, this killer - yes, I know you don't like the word, but it is true - is very dangerous. Especially if they were prepared to kill, but then acted impulsively. That's a bad combination. This is extremely serious. You are going to have to be very careful indeed not to let anyone - anyone at all - know that you are helping the police, and you need to take real care over what you eat or drink with these people. You could be next. You could have been the victim instead of Kate or Charlotte. This is a big risk to take."

I stared at him, open-mouthed. I just had not thought that I could genuinely be in danger. I knew it would be uncomfortable, spying on friends and acquaintances, but still had not properly accepted that one of them was, as Dad said, a killer.

"Even without helping the police, you could be in danger from this person, since we have no idea why they targeted Charlotte or Kate. I'm not asking you not to do it, not to help the police. This killer has to be caught and you are in a unique position to make a difference. I know that you're not the kind of person to shrink from a task just because it is hard or dangerous. We're so proud of you, you are an amazing daughter. But I am asking you, in all seriousness, to think carefully about what you say to anyone who was at the coffee mornings, and to avoid eating or drinking anything they could have touched or interfered with."

Mum nodded her head vigorously. She looked rather white and frightened, but she reached out her hand to clasp mine.

"Please, please be careful, Sam. Can you say that you're on a diet or something? Just drink water, and use your own bottle? Even a café will let you use your own cup these days."

That was a really good idea. After so long at home with Chloe, I could stand to lose a few pounds and people would understand that.

"You are both brilliant - what would I do without you? I will do that, Mum, and I'll tell Deb tomorrow that I am going on a health and fitness binge after everything that has happened. Oh, and I forgot to tell you. Sergeant Evans wants to meet me regularly but privately, so I suggested he came here. Is that possible?"

"It certainly is," said Dad. "It will enable us to keep an eye on what he is asking you to do!"

Driving back with Chloe, I struggled to keep my mind on the road, with so many thoughts whirling around. I put her to bed and then just sat, unable to focus on anything, feeling totally exhausted. But after dragging myself sleepily to bed, as soon as my tired head hit the pillow, my brain woke up and refused to let me sleep, constantly going over what had happened, with dreadful repetitive words like 'murder' and 'killer' bouncing around my head. Every time I did manage to drift off, Chloe, who was also restless, would cry out and wake me up again. The night seemed interminable.

CHAPTER 6

Deb and Kate

I was positively glad to get up early in the morning, completely unrested, but prepared to take on whatever the day had to throw at me. The familiar routine of showering, getting breakfast for Chloe, and chatting away to her about nothing, just to hear her gurgle of contentment, was reassuringly normal. She was starting to be a real companion now, communicating her feelings with a range of interesting sounds and warming my heart with her gleeful smiles and giggles. Mum had offered to have her today, but I had decided that it would be better to have her with me. Focusing at least partly on her would hopefully help me to deceive Deb, a task I was not looking forward to.

She messaged at around ten o'clock to arrange to meet me at the park for our walk and talk. Mixed feelings and some apprehension gave me butterflies in my stomach, but once we met up I was able to relax. I realized that she genuinely wanted to talk about the murder and the coffee morning, and that it was not going to be at all difficult to get her to open up about it. She seemed more herself this morning, although, like me, she had not slept.

"It's just so weirdly surreal, Sam," she said. "Murder just doesn't happen to people you know, certainly not around here.

It feels as if we are in the middle of an *Inspector Morse* episode! I half expect Lewis to walk round the corner..."

"I know exactly what you mean! It's just not like real life at all. In a strange way, that almost makes it easier to deal with, you know? If it isn't real, it isn't so scary. And it helps you to keep the emotions at bay."

"I agree, but actually, it is quite scary, isn't it? That someone we know is a killer."

"You are so right! Talking to Mum and Dad last night, it came home to me that the murderer must have planned it in advance, in order to have ground-up, dissolved or powdered medication on them ready to use, but at the same time they can't have known for sure that Kate would be there, so they must also have acted on impulse to a degree. But what made them do it? Why Kate, of all people? It just doesn't make sense."

Deb stopped suddenly and looked at me in shock.

"I hadn't thought of that. So it could have been anyone, any of us, and that must go for the attempt on Charlotte too. Wow - that really is a frightening thought!"

"Can you tell me what happened at the second coffee morning, Deb? Was there something which might have made them choose Kate as a victim?"

"Well, not really, I would have said. It was a bit of a different atmosphere though. Because of what had happened with Charlotte, everyone was very careful around her, and somehow we became one larger group talking together, rather than splitting into smaller groups, as we did when you were there. But we were all keeping social distancing, of course! In fact, Beth was still so anxious about Covid that she insisted on wearing a mask, whenever she wasn't eating or drinking. She kept looking reproachfully at me, because I wasn't wearing mine."

"What did you all talk about?"

"Oh, you know, this and that. Covid restrictions being lifted, maybe, plans for the summer, whether we would try going abroad or not … Oh, I remember. Sophy (I don't know if you noticed her the previous week, she was unusually quiet that day, and was sitting over with Emily and Charlotte) asked Kate about her career as a model. As you know, Kate doesn't like to talk about herself normally, but Sophy seemed genuinely interested and I think it was easier for Kate than facing questions about cancer and her treatment."

Kate's modelling career had been short but really quite spectacular. She had taken fashion as one of her sixth form courses and had been 'spotted' at an exhibition they had visited, where they were showing student work. No one had been surprised that she had been picked out in that way, as she truly was elegant, graceful and beautiful.

She quickly became very successful and spent her time travelling the world, in what looked from the outside like a highly glamorous lifestyle, but which was actually, according to her, a life of boring drudgery, surrounded by obsessive, ambitious and often unpleasant people. Naturally slender herself, she was shocked at the fat-shaming, bullying and disordered eating she witnessed. Deb and I knew that she had hated the way of life, but carried on with it, because the money she was earning made such a difference to her mother.

Kate's mother had struggled financially ever since her partner left her, shortly after Kate was born, and had worked several jobs to keep her head above water. Kate was always loved and looked after, but food was scarce and new clothes were a very occasional treat. Sewing and altering clothes for herself and her mother had introduced her to fashion in the first place. As a model, Kate was so pleased to be able to help her mother to move to a comfortable flat and support her to give up her cleaning jobs. She even paid for her to train as a nurse, which had always been her dream.

But only five years into her modelling career, Kate met and fell in love with Martin Rigby and left the work and the success without a backward glance. Fortunately, he was extremely well-off, not to say rich, and wanted nothing more than to look after Kate and provide for her mother. Two beautiful children soon followed and Kate found deep satisfaction in looking after them and volunteering with local charities.

Everything in the garden seemed rosy, until Kate was diagnosed with breast cancer, an aggressive form, which required punishing chemotherapy as well as an operation. And now she had been murdered.

"Most of the people there didn't know Kate's story and were amazed. You know she never normally talks about it. But Sophy is something of a fashionista and she knew how to ask the right questions about designers, shows, and fashion houses. Kate actually told us more that morning than she had previously said to you and me. Everyone was fascinated, especially by how it had all happened so easily, just by chance, as if it was always meant to be."

"I know what you mean - it always felt to me a bit like a dream or a fairy story: the beautiful girl who became a princess."

"Mmmm. There were one or two rather sarcastic comments, I have to say. I can't remember from whom. But mostly people were just interested."

"I can't see anything there to make someone want to kill her. It really is puzzling. How did it all work with drinks and things? Apparently the police know she was definitely poisoned at the coffee morning, in a drink."

"There was a table with hot and cold drinks, a tea urn, a coffee machine, all that sort of stuff. You could bring your own cup, or there were some paper cups and reusable ones that you could use. But because everyone was listening so intently to Kate, we did also make drinks for other people and pass them round. I really did try to keep it as safe and organised as possible, but you know what people are like."

"I know you will have done that, Deb - no one can organise better than you! I guess it must be impossible to work out who touched which cup, or the police would have gone down that road. What did Kate have to drink?"

"She had several cups of some sort of medicinal herbal tea that she liked to take during her treatment. Very bitter, apparently - even with honey in it, but she insisted that she liked the bitterness, as it made her feel it was really doing her good and helped with the nausea. It has to brew for at least five minutes, which makes it impossible to say who was, or was not, near enough to it to put the drugs in it. Everyone was, at some point."

"That's so frustrating. But whoever it was, was still taking a terrible risk. Anyone could have seen them."

"That's true, but generally your back would be between the group and the cup, so I suppose it could be done. Anyway, it was done! But I still can't believe it or understand why Kate would be the victim, unless she was just the easiest one to poison."

"The policeman mentioned something about racism, but I don't see how that fits with the attack on Charlotte. In fact, I don't see that Kate and Charlotte have anything much in common at all. You know, it would be even more alarming if the whole thing was just random. Then it could have been any of us!"

"That hadn't occurred to me until just now. I think as we go forward, if we have another coffee morning (and I don't want this tragedy to stop us meeting and supporting each other), I'll have to ask everyone to bring their own drinks, just in case."

"You're absolutely right, Deb. It's just too much of a risk."

We walked on in silence for a few minutes. I felt better than before. It seemed to me that Deb would want to find out who the killer was just as much as I did, and that she would be helping me, even without knowing that I was reporting back to the police. It no longer felt as if I was spying on her, or deceiving her.

"You know, Sam, I think the police are going to struggle with this one. You and I will have to keep our eyes open and see if we can spot someone who is behaving strangely, or showing signs of being disturbed."

Deb had obviously been thinking along the same lines.

"I agree. We could make a list of everyone who was there and then keep a close eye on them. Although probably the most important thing is to listen to what they are saying..."

"Great idea, Sam. Let's go and have a coffee in the park café and make our list."

CHAPTER 7

The suspects

O nce she started something, there was no stopping Deb. "I'll put it into a spreadsheet when I get home, but let's just make a quick list on paper first of who was there."

"Are you going to put everyone down?"

"Of course! Oh, I suppose that means it includes me. Oh well, that's fine. I'm at the top of the list."

"It seems ridiculous, but the others are mainly nice people too. No way would I believe Beth was a killer, but I suppose she has to go on the list."

"You're right. As soon as you start, it gets difficult, so we'll just have to play fair and put everyone down."

"Do we put Charlotte down, even though she was the first apparent victim?

"I suppose so, Sam - it doesn't make much sense, but she was at both sessions and - you never know, I suppose. Although I hardly took my eyes off her at the second coffee morning, as we were all so worried about her. I don't think she ever left her chair, unless I was beside her."

"It would have been very difficult for her to do it. But we do want a complete list. Emily was talking, or rather listening, to

Charlotte for ages the first time - was she definitely around when Kate was -"

My voice trailed off. It was still so difficult to say it aloud. But making it an academic exercise like this did actually help. It was so much less personal.

"Oh, yes, Emily was there. She sat with Charlotte, when I had to go and get things organised. She's a really practical, reliable person. And of course Sophy was there too, as she was asking most of the questions. I don't think you know her, Sam, but she's been part of our online group for a while. She has an adorable baby, Elise, just a month or so older than your Chloe."

"It would be nice to meet her properly, then. Annette was there, you said, and so was Lesley. I did find Lesley quite difficult, to be honest. I am a bit worried about her daughter Jackie, hearing all that resentment and bitterness all the time."

"I know what you mean. But you have to remember that Lesley's husband did walk out on her and the children at a very difficult time. I don't know how patient or forgiving I would have been under those circumstances."

"Too true! But that little girl looks so sad."

"I know, that's partly why I have encouraged Lesley to come along. Being with other people can only help her to get over it, I think."

"Hopefully. Who else?"

"Oh, of course, the vicar and his sister, Celia."

"He's been really good to me in the last couple of weeks. I didn't think he had it in him, to be honest. I've been so grateful for his support. But I don't much like Celia, I must say. She's always nagging him and putting him down."

"I know, she can be difficult. But he is a bit scatty, so I guess he does need someone to keep him on track. There's more to being a vicar than taking services and writing sermons."

"I suppose so. Is there anyone we have missed?"

"I don't think so. Oh dear, looking at these names, I can't possibly think one of them is a murderer!"

"No, but someone did kill our precious Kate - and attack

Charlotte. I can only think it must be someone with a mental health issue."

"In books and on television, it's always the vicar," said Deb, mischievously. "Especially if he's not married."

"Oh, Deb, that's mean. He's a very kind man, and not a bit like the obsessed fanatics they like to put in those programmes."

"I thought you would defend him," teased Deb. "Still, he's the only man on the list, and men are statistically more likely to be murderers, they say."

"Well, in books they always say that poison is a woman's weapon, so that should rule him out," I retorted.

It felt wrong to be having a 'normal' conversation about such a serious thing, and so soon after losing Kate, but at the same time, it was good to smile again. Chloe gurgled away cheerfully, as if she was joining in; she seemed really happy to see us talking together like this.

"What do we do next then, Deb? Talk to people? See if any of them shows signs of being disturbed?"

"I don't see what else we can do. They are all going to want to talk about what has happened anyway. I'll put some columns on the spreadsheet so that we can add in any motives, or odd behaviour or reactions we discover. But we will have to be really honest about this. It's not going to be easy to put in suspicions about people we know and like."

"I know," I responded, seriously. "But it has to be done. It'll definitely make it easier to work on it together. Let's agree on total frankness about anything we hear from the others. We're not judging them. But we have to be fair to everyone, and not play favourites."

Back to her normal business-like self, Deb agreed, and we arranged to meet, in a couple of days time, in order to compare notes.

CHAPTER 8

Daniyaal

That evening, Sergeant Evans rang to arrange when to come and see me. I suggested just after lunch, when Chloe would be napping. I felt rather anxious about it all morning. I was not used to strangers coming to the house, had never had personal dealings with the police before, and really did not know what to expect. Since the start of the pandemic, my routine had been so fixed, my world so narrow and everything so carefully planned, that even small changes set off anxious feelings, and the events of the last few weeks, whatever else they were, were not small.

To keep myself occupied in the morning, I cleaned and tidied the living room, while Chloe kicked happily on her playmat. Then we went for a walk into town, ostensibly to buy some biscuits, but really just to work off some of the stress hormones. Chloe loved being outside and I always pointed out any birds, cats or plant life to her. She especially loved cats and would point and gurgle at them. I rather expected her first word to be 'cat'.

In the shop, we saw Sophy (I did recognise her from the coffee morning as soon as I saw her again), who came straight over to introduce herself to us. Deb was right, her daughter Elise was really cute and very communicative, smiling and laughing

41

when I spoke to her. Chloe was fascinated with her and, before we parted, we agreed to meet for a walk in the park on the following day. I immediately felt comfortable with Sophy, and it was nice to think that Chloe and I might both make a new friend. We both had masks on, of course, but it is so easy to see when someone is genuinely smiling from the eyes.

After lunch, with Chloe settled for her nap, I walked up and down the living room restlessly, until the doorbell rang, making me jump, even though I had been expecting it. I took a few deep calming breaths and went to let the policeman in. He was on his own again, and wearing a mask, so I put on the one I kept by the front door just in case.

"Please come in, Sergeant Evans. Would you like a cup of tea or coffee?"

"Still not allowed at the moment, Mrs Elsdon. Much as I would like one. Do have one yourself though."

Thinking of the new biscuits, I decided that I would make myself a cup of tea.

"Please do call me Sam, though. Mrs Elsdon makes me feel as if I am back in front of a class!"

"OK, then, Sam. You are welcome to call me Daniyaal or Dani if you like. Sergeant Evans is a bit of a mouthful, and we are going to be seeing quite a lot of each other in the next few weeks, I think. No one calls me 'Evans' - it's not like on the television."

I laughed rather nervously. Was he a mind reader? I had been thinking of Sergeant Lewis from the *Inspector Morse* series.

"Which do you prefer, Daniyaal or Dani? From my experience in school, most people have a preference."

"You know, people almost never ask that. It's very sensitive and considerate of you. I actually do prefer Daniyaal. As you will no doubt have realised, I have Pakistani as well as Welsh heritage, and my mother always insisted on using the full name, so I just find it more comfortable. But I know that Dani sits better with some of my colleagues, as it sounds like an English name."

"Do you - no, sorry, that is none of my business." I had instinctively wanted to ask him if he encountered much racism in his job. As a teacher, I had always tried to look at things from an anti-racist perspective, and had been shocked by recent revelations about the prevalence of racism everywhere, from cricket to the police. But it was definitely not my place to ask questions like that.

"Don't worry, you can ask me anything you like," he responded with an understanding smile in his eyes. "I need you to feel comfortable enough with me to be able to pass on really personal, and sometimes confidential information about your friends and neighbours, so I am happy to reciprocate and answer your questions too. But maybe not today, if that is OK with you. I only have an hour before another interview, and we have a lot to get through."

I was rather embarrassed, but his smiling eyes put me at my ease.

"That's fine. Let's get this over with."

"First of all, did you discuss my request with your parents? Are they willing to help us to meet regularly?"

"Oh yes, that's no problem. They are keen to help - they knew Kate well and loved her almost as much as I did. They adore spending time with Chloe too, so more regular visits from us certainly won't be a chore! In fact -"

"Yes, what is it?"

"In fact, to be honest, Serg - Daniyaal, they want to make sure that you are not putting me in too much danger."

I blurted it out rather breathlessly, and looked away.

"You don't have to worry about telling me that, Sam. I am glad that they were able to assess the situation so quickly. They are right, you are in danger, but not only you, your friends too, and you would still be in danger, even if you were not helping the police."

I looked hesitantly back at him, seeing concern in his eyes and hearing it in his voice.

"That's rather the conclusion we came to. Someone I know, someone I am probably going to spend time with, is a killer and quite possibly mentally disturbed as well. So the more quickly we can find that person and get them some help, as well as taking them out of society, the better and safer for me and all my friends."

We talked through the issues I had discussed with Mum and Dad and the idea that the murderer must have been prepared to kill, but probably then acted on impulse, as they could not have known that Kate would be there.

"That seems quite likely," agreed Daniyaal, "although it could be that they would just have waited for another occasion, when Kate was present."

"But I can't see any connection between Kate and Charlotte and I really don't understand why anyone in their right mind would choose Kate as a victim anyway. Oh, I guess that is the problem - they probably are not in their right mind."

"Given the nature of the murder and the other attempt, and the people involved, that is possible, but in my experience, even people who are disturbed usually have some kind of rationale behind their actions, even if it doesn't make sense to you or me. We have had to deal much more with victims, witnesses and perpetrators with mental health difficulties in the last few years, as you will have heard, and although their behaviour may seem irrational to you or me, when you dig a bit deeper, there is usually some logic to it."

Daniyaal's rather formal voice and way of expressing himself was quite calming.

"That actually helps a bit, Daniyaal. It means I can look for motives which might seem too small to me to warrant murder, but which could be the killer's justification for their actions. I'm not just looking for some kind of 'maniac' - sorry to use that word, I know it's offensive. But what I mean is that I don't need to be on the lookout for a stereotypical 'mad' person."

"Exactly, Sam. They may seem very reasonable and may well have some motive which you can pick up for us. They are certainly rational enough to plan to kill, and then to cover it up afterwards."

"I've already spoken to Deb. I did as you asked, and did not tell her I was going to help you, but she is as keen as I am to find the killer, and is going to keep track of what everyone from the coffee mornings says to her as well. We've - you will think this is funny, I guess - we've made a spreadsheet of all the possible suspects and we are going to use that to try to work out who might have done it."

"It's not funny at all, it's a great idea. As long as you remember that, strictly speaking, your friend Deb is a suspect too."

"I know that, and she insisted on putting herself on the list. We decided that we couldn't leave anyone out without being unfair to the others. We even put Charlotte on the list."

Daniyaal looked rather amused at this evidence of our detective efforts, but he encouraged me to keep talking to Deb about it, especially since I had not attended the second coffee morning.

"She did tell me something important about it, I think. I was puzzled by Kate becoming a target, as she is normally very quiet in company, but she told me that, on that day, she had actually become the centre of attention for the whole group."

I repeated as accurately as I could what Deb had told me and gave him some extra information about Kate's past history.

"This is really useful, Sam. Would you mind going through it all again? I would like to record you, if you don't mind. I think it is more accurate than using a notebook with things like this. I will get it transcribed later."

I found it rather intimidating to be recorded to start with, but as Daniyaal asked me questions and prompted me, I relaxed and forgot about the recording.

"This will really help me with interviewing the suspects, Sam. It's just the kind of thing I need to know. Please try to keep a note of important things like this, so that we can go through them when we meet."

"I will," I promised. "When do you want to meet again?"

"In all honesty, I think I need to see you again really soon. The day after tomorrow? Would that be possible?"

"I will check with my parents, but I should think I could

take Chloe over for tea and you could come over then."

I told him that I would be meeting Sophy tomorrow and would see who else I could catch up with, and then he said briskly that he had to go.

"Thank you so much for your openness, Sam, I really appreciate it. I know this isn't a normal or easy thing for you to do, but it could make a huge difference to our chances of catching this character, before they hurt someone else."

"Thank you for making it relatively painless," I responded. "See you on Thursday afternoon."

I had already given him my parents' address. Closing the door behind him, I suddenly felt a bit shaky. I wasn't used to so much adrenaline. But it was true, Daniyaal had definitely made what was happening seem really normal and nothing to worry about. It was just that, every so often, a wave of anxiety, sadness and, let's be honest, fear came over me as I thought about what was a truly surreal situation. But I pushed it away and tried to focus on the practicalities. I had a job to do, and that was that.

CHAPTER 9

Sophy

Meeting Sophy in the park seemed like a nice patch of normality in a rather threatening and ominous landscape. We hit it off immediately, in a way that was rare for me, especially when the main thing you have in common is having children of a similar age. She was chatty, humorous and intelligent, a pleasure to talk to. I even felt reasonably comfortable speaking about Thomas, and what had happened the previous year.

"Deb told me a little about your husband's death - I was so sorry to hear about it. That must have been so difficult to deal with on your own, let alone in a pandemic."

"The worst thing for me was all the publicity. The papers seemed like vultures, hovering around, wanting me to cry for them. I felt numb and lost, and actually being angry with reporters was the only genuine emotion I could cope with. But, after that, I shut myself away and didn't even accept the help from my family I could have had. Not even when Chloe was born. I don't really know why, even now."

"It seems like quite a natural reaction to me," said Sophy. "You shut everything down and want to process it all undisturbed. And it's hard enough to deal with grief when you're looking after a baby, at the best of times. My friend's mother died when she had small children, and she said it wasn't until later that she realised that she hadn't grieved properly at all. It all came out years further down the road."

"I think you're right. I couldn't face the grief, just turned away from it and anyone who might remind me of Thomas and what we had. But then when Kate died, it hit me so hard ..."

Even thinking about it brought a lump to my throat. It was all so raw still. I could not believe that she was really gone, and somehow it exposed the deep loneliness I had experienced after I lost Thomas.

"I'm so sorry, Deb told me how close you three are - were. It must have been a dreadful shock."

"It really was. And it felt worse because I had just got back in touch with her, and I was so looking forward to seeing her that morning, to having a regular friendship again."

"What was she like? Do you mind telling me? I didn't know her very well, had only really seen her on Zoom meetings - and in magazines years ago, of course. She was so very beautiful and stylish."

"She was amazing. Such a caring person. She didn't have a lot of close friends, she was quiet and could seem withdrawn in a group, but when you became her friend, there was literally nothing she wouldn't do for you. She always remembered what you had told her and would ask about it the next time you saw her, even if it was months later. She had a brilliant dry sense of humour and could imitate people really well - she used to have us in stitches in school imitating the teachers. And she was very passionate about causes she cared about like the environment, poverty, and sweatshops. She would research really carefully and then persuade you to change your mind or your behaviour, even when you didn't intend to. I - I'm going to miss her terribly."

It was true. It was not until then that I fully grasped how deeply I had loved Kate, and what a hole she would leave in my life, despite not seeing her for so long. It left such an ache in my heart.

"Wow, she sounds like a wonderful person! No wonder all her friends and family are so devastated. What I don't understand, is how she could become a murder victim. In books and television programmes the murder victim is usually hated for some obvious reason."

"I know, that puzzles me too. Who could possibly want to hurt Kate? Was anything said at the coffee morning? Was there any kind of argument?"

Sophy paused, thinking back.

"Shall we sit here, Sam, and let the girls watch the ducks? I hadn't thought of that. Do you mean that she might have been killed because of something that was said at the coffee morning?"

"Well, the police know she was poisoned there, so it has to be a possibility."

"What a horrible thought! You mean, if I had said the wrong thing, it might have been me?"

"I don't really know, but I can't see any reason for someone to have a long-term grudge against Kate. Not unless they were a climate change denier or a racist, and then why would they have gone after Charlotte? She doesn't fit that profile at all."

"You're so right. I really hadn't thought it through. Let me just think for a minute and then go back over what was said. I don't know about you, but my memory isn't what it was before I had Elise!"

"I know what you mean - there's a kind of baby brain fog, I think."

Sophy took the time to think carefully, looking out over the pond at the trees beyond.

"Mmm. Well, the main thing we talked about as a group that day was actually Kate's career as a model, and how that came about, as well as how it ended. I used to write on style and fashion for a newspaper before I had Elise, and was really interested in her story. It's actually really rare for someone to be 'discovered' like that and to have such a stellar career. And even rarer for them to give it up so suddenly at the height of their success. I'm afraid I asked her lots of questions about how the different fashion brands were to work with and what she thought about fast fashion, eating disorders among models and, oh yes, even about sweatshops. You're right, she spoke really passionately about that, and about what we can do as consumers to make a difference."

"But I can't see anything in that to make someone want to kill her."

"No, indeed. If anything, it should make people admire her, not just for her achievements but also for her principles. I actually found it quite inspirational."

"How did other people react? Do you remember?"

Sophy shook her head ruefully.

"I was trying to think, but I didn't really notice. You see, I was so absorbed in Kate's story, that I didn't really pay any attention to the others. I was kind of hoping that I might be able to persuade her to let me write a long article about her for my newspaper, so you see... I realised later that I had even forgotten to drink my coffee, and had to go and get another one because it had gone cold and horrible. The police asked me about that when they came round, but I couldn't give them any help - I didn't notice Kate's tea at all."

"I understand. If you could get her talking, she was so articulate, and persuasive as well, especially when she got onto one of her hobby-horses."

"I do remember someone, I think it might have been Celia, the vicar's sister, asking her some kind of slightly hostile question, something about it being immoral to make money out of other people's slave labour. But of course, Kate completely agreed about that, and talked about a charity she worked with, which tried to make a difference in that area."

"I know she had a lot of moral objections to parts of the fashion industry, and she had no hesitation in walking away from it, when she fell in love with Martin."

"That's what I found so fascinating. She was such a natural

for modelling and had been so very successful across the world, that it was a shock to everyone when she just gave it all up. I guess the fame and fortune just didn't mean anything to her."

"She was very glad of the money in the early days, so that she could support her mother, but she never wanted money for its own sake, and I think fame was something she actively disliked. She really made an effort to avoid anything related to her public life when she was here, and much preferred not to be recognised. She always dressed very casually to avoid looking like the photos in the magazines. And over time that became easier, of course, as people forgot about her."

"She was a very unusual person, it seems. But such a positive one. I just don't see why anyone would want to kill her."

"Me neither. I have been thinking about that a lot in the last couple of days. No disrespect to Charlotte, but she did put people's backs up and you can imagine that someone, who is mentally disturbed, might possibly find a motive there. But not Kate. I suppose it can't have been a mistake?"

"That's a thought. You mean they might have intended to kill someone else? But - no, I don't think so. Kate had special tea, she mentioned that she couldn't have caffeine, and was taking a special kind of infusion as a boost to her immune system. She said it tasted horrid, but it was worth it, because it definitely made her feel better. I can't remember what it was called, but it would have been really obvious which drink was hers. I think she had honey in it as well, although she said it didn't actually mask the taste."

"Oh dear, that does make it pretty clear that she was the intended victim. And how she didn't notice that her drink had been spiked. Deb said everyone was back and forth to the drinks table and it wouldn't have been difficult to put something in her tea as it took so long to brew..."

"It's a puzzle, that's for sure. I don't know how the police are going to sort it out, but I hope they are quick about it. It's a strange feeling, thinking that there is a murderer among us."

Suddenly Elise started coughing and spluttering, and by the

time Sophy had dealt with the problem, the subject had been changed and we carried on our walk. Once I reached home, I mulled over what Sophy had said and made a few notes to remind me when I reported back to Deb - and Daniyaal.

Later that day, I rang Deb to talk things through.

"I knew you would hit it off with Sophy," she said rather smugly. "She's just your sort of person."

"You're right, Deb. I think we could be good friends."

"Did she say anything helpful about the - the murder?" Evidently Deb was also finding it difficult to say the word naturally.

"She mainly said what you had already told me. She didn't really notice how other people reacted, because she herself was so interested in what Kate was saying. And she agreed that it would be impossible to work out who had tampered with Kate's tea. But she did say that someone, Celia she thought, had said something critical about it being immoral to make money out of people's slave labour in the fashion world, having a dig at Kate of course."

"Mmmm, I think she is right that it was Celia. You know she has that rather sarcastic tone of voice. Kate dealt with it really well, but it wasn't a nice thing to say."

"What is Celia like? I don't really know her."

"She's a strange one. Works very hard in the parish, as if she were a vicar's wife rather than his sister. Doesn't have a separate job, so I guess he supports her. She does a lot of good works, like visiting the elderly or people in hospital, but she's not what I would call a natural 'people' person, and I can't say she's very popular around here."

"I noticed that she seems to nag Stephen a lot."

"Yes, she keeps him in order. But she's a bit possessive of him too."

"She said to me that she resented Charlotte taking up so much of his time …"

"Actually, I don't like to say this, but she was a bit annoyed about him spending so much time with you after Kate's death. She said he was neglecting his other work, and didn't you have other people who could support you, especially as you aren't a regular churchgoer."

"That's nasty. I didn't ask him to come, Mum did, and he was so kind and supportive. I really appreciated it. But I wouldn't have wanted him to neglect his other work."

"I don't suppose he actually did neglect it. I think she just likes to have him at her beck and call."

"Oh dear, do other people feel that I was monopolising him?"

"Not at all. Everyone knows how upset we both were, and understands that it brought out all your stored up grief. Don't worry, she doesn't represent what anyone else thinks."

"I wonder if she and Stephen are the next people to talk to. I still need to sort out Chloe's service of blessing, so I do have an excuse to go round."

"That sounds like a good idea. What about me, who shall I talk to next?"

"How about Beth? She's always glad to see you and I was worried about her the other week. She seemed almost like a different person, really anxious and stressed."

"That's a good call, Sam. I'll see if I can pop round tomorrow."

"I'll message Stephen and ask if I can go and see him in the morning as well."

CHAPTER 10

Stephen and Celia

S tephen said he was free at half past ten, so I walked round to the vicarage with Chloe that morning, after doing the regulation lateral flow test. Infection rates were quite low at the time, but I was trying to be careful and keep everyone safe. Stephen had said that we could talk in the garden.

Celia's mouth was tight with disapproval when she opened the door to me.

"He's in the garden, waiting for you. He has another meeting at quarter to twelve in the church hall, so please don't take too long."

"Morning, Celia. Don't worry, I just need to sort out the arrangements for Chloe's service of blessing next month," I said, soothingly.

"Well that shouldn't take too long, I suppose," she said, grudgingly. "Come on through."

She led me through to the back garden, a beautiful space with birch and beech trees giving shade, and a naturally laid out, but very well-tended, set of colourful flower beds, grasses and shrubs. There was even a small wildflower meadow in the corner, with a bird feeder and bee house.

"Why, Celia, this is gorgeous! What a fantastic garden. Is

this your work or Stephen's?"

Celia coloured and her face softened.

"I love gardening," she admitted. "It's been my sanctuary during the pandemic."

"I'm really impressed. I'm not an expert, but I know just how much time and hard work goes into making it look so natural."

For once, Celia looked pleased. She led me over to a shady spot, where Stephen was sitting.

"Here she is, Stephen. Don't forget you have another meeting at quarter to twelve. Please try not to be late again. I'm going to go and make cakes for the old people's coffee morning tomorrow. Have you managed to find any volunteers to help me?"

Stephen looked guilty and mumbled something non-committal.

"I don't suppose you could help, could you, Mrs Elsdon? I need someone to help make tea and coffee and welcome people."

My instinctive reaction was to refuse, as it was not at all my type of thing. But then I realised that it would be a great chance to talk to Celia and find out more about her.

"Please call me Sam, Celia. Well, I think, possibly, I could help you out, this time," I said, smiling at the surprise on her face. "Mum would love to look after Chloe for the morning, and you and Stephen have been so kind. What time would you need me?"

"Oh, if you could be there by ten o'clock that would be really helpful. We start at half past ten, but there is all the setting up to do. Are you sure? I know you don't normally attend our church services."

"I've been watching the online services for quite a while now, so I feel I do know what the church is about. It would be good for me to help out and do something different."

I was not really sure that it would be good for me, but if it would help to find Kate's killer, I was game for anything.

"I'll see you tomorrow, then," said Celia. She looked a little uncertain, as if I had changed her view of me. "Thank you." She still sounded slightly grudging.

Stephen looked grateful.

"That's very, er, kind of you, Sam. Don't feel you have to if you, um, you are not up to it tomorrow. Celia manages very well. But - I was supposed to ask for volunteers and it, er, I'm afraid it slipped my mind."

Somehow Stephen had relapsed into his old social anxiety. I had not noticed his hesitancy at all, when he had been comforting me last week. I introduced the topic of Chloe's blessing service, to give him back his confidence, talking about something he found interesting, and we soon had all the arrangements made.

"I was actually wondering if we could do a service of remembrance some time for my husband, Stephen. I haven't discussed it with anyone yet and, to be honest, haven't really thought it through at all, but since we couldn't do anything when he died..." My voice faded out as the tears came again. My shell of protection had well and truly cracked, but at least I did now feel able to talk about Thomas again, and Stephen had seen me in tears often enough already, so I was not too embarrassed about my show of emotion.

"That is a really good idea, Sam. No rush, but, when you are ready, I would be happy to help you plan it."

"I would like that. Not until all the trouble around Kate's death is finished with, though. I don't suppose Martin will be able to have a funeral for her yet, either."

"No, as I understand it, there won't be a death certificate for quite a while. It makes it even harder for him and the children. Such a tragedy."

"I just can't imagine who could have wanted to kill Kate. She was such a lovely person and I don't think she had an enemy in the world. I know people often say that about someone who has died, but it really was true about Kate."

"I know it was," Stephen responded seriously. "I didn't tell you before, but we got to know each other quite well during her illness. I used to try to be in touch with her at least once a week, even if it was only on Zoom, or on the phone. Even when she was really suffering, she was always thinking of others. She was really worried about you, I know that."

I gaped at him in surprise. I had felt guilty about not being there for Kate in her cancer, but I had not had any idea that she had been concerned for me.

"I, er, I just shut everyone out, even Kate and Deb, and even my parents. I'm so desperately sorry. And I can't undo it with Kate. I must have hurt her so badly."

Stephen shook his head firmly.

"Not at all. I think she really understood what you were going through. She never felt hurt or left out, just knew that you needed support, but weren't able to ask for or accept it at the time. Don't worry, Sam - she knew you loved her. She had a capacity to love and understand people very deeply."

"You must have got to know her really well, Stephen. You are absolutely right, but most people didn't see that in her. She could seem very withdrawn at times and some people thought she was rather aloof."

"I, er, actually, I found her very easy to talk to. Like you. I can talk to you in a way I can't with most people."

He looked away, perhaps embarrassed at what he had revealed. But it was true for me too. I felt that, once he relaxed and lost his anxiety, he was very easy to talk to.

"Did you notice anything strange about how people reacted to her at the coffee morning, Stephen? Deb told me that Kate was, for once, the centre of attention. Did anyone seem resentful or angry about that?"

Stephen looked puzzled.

"You mean that the killer might have decided to murder her during the coffee morning? But, Sam, that's a dreadful thought. I find it hard enough to reconcile myself to the idea that I have spent time with someone who had such black thoughts in their heart. The idea that some innocent conversation could have triggered it is horrifying!"

I nodded, understandingly.

"I know, it came as a shock to me when I realised. But the killer can't have been sure that Kate was going to be there - no one knew for certain - and yet came prepared to kill."

"I am trying to pray for the, er, I suppose I have to call them the killer, but I must admit that I am finding it difficult at the moment. Such a cruel end for a much-loved person. But surely the killer must be very disturbed to have acted in such an impulsive way."

"That's what Deb and I think. So please, if you can, think back to any odd reactions you may have noticed, even a look or a facial expression, that might give away what was in their head."

Stephen looked appalled.

"I will try to go back over it in my mind. But I have to warn you that I am not at all good at interpreting other people's body language or facial expressions. Celia is always telling me that I have misinterpreted signals from people."

"I don't think you need to 'interpret' as such. Better just to be factual, if you can."

"Everyone was watching Kate most of the time when she was answering Sophy's questions, I know that. Celia - well, Celia is a little jealous of people who are really attractive, and Kate was quite beautiful, as you know. She was staring at her, and I couldn't really say that she looked happy. I don't know what she was thinking. I looked away. It was - embarrassing."

"I'm sorry, I know this is difficult and very personal."

"Yes, it is, but it is also important. Whoever it is, that person is both dangerous to others, and in need of help. If I can do anything to speed up the process of catching them, I will."

I smiled gratefully at him, a little surprised at what I had discovered about him during this conversation. He was a more perceptive and sensitive person than I had imagined.

"Was there anything else you noticed?"

"Well, Beth was sitting next to and slightly behind me (distanced of course), so I couldn't see her face. But I did hear her making little exclamations, little noises, from time to time. She was probably just extremely interested in Kate's story, but some of them were quite odd sounds."

"I know she's been having some anxiety issues recently, so that could be it."

Stephen suddenly looked at his watch and looked panicky.

"So sorry, Sam, I really have to go. I can't be late again!"

"No problem at all, Stephen," I soothed. "Just let me know if anything else occurs to you."

I quickly gathered up Chloe, who had been quietly enjoying playing with her toys, and we hurried back through the house. I started to walk home, watching Stephen running towards the church, his hair flying in all directions. He was certainly not a natural runner. His arms and legs did not seem to be coordinated at all. I smiled at the image. Not your typical vicar.

CHAPTER 11

Progress report

I rang Deb before going over to my parents' house to report
back to Daniyaal.

"It's interesting that even the vicar thought his sister
looked a bit hostile. I'm glad you are going to be able to talk to
her tomorrow. She is a bit strange and can be very intense, and
sometimes rather negative, but I imagine it'll be easier to talk to
her when you are doing things together."

"Like the washing-up! I hope I haven't let myself in for a
horribly stressful time. You know I'm not really a coffee morning person, let alone a church coffee morning."

"You will be fine," soothed Deb. "I went to help at one of
those sessions for the elderly and Celia had it very well organised. And the old people are lovely, honestly."

"OK, I'll take your word for it. Not looking forward to it,
though."

"You might find out a bit more about Stephen from her. I
hadn't realised that he was so friendly with Kate - she never
mentioned him at all, and he didn't say anything to me about it."

"I do think he's a bit scared of you, to be honest! You are so
organised and prepared, and he really isn't."

"Ha, ha - no one is scared of me! You are the scary one, when you put on your 'teacher' voice. But seriously, it would be good to find out more about him. The murderer is almost always the priest or vicar in fiction, and he isn't married or anything. He could have all kinds of repressions and psychological hang-ups."

"Deb, that's just not fair, and you know it. He's not like that at all. He's been so kind to me."

I actually felt quite angry on Stephen's behalf and Deb could hear it in my voice.

"Oh well, you may be right, but someone did it, and we are friendly with most of the suspects, so we have to think the un-thinkable. You really like him, don't you?"

I had not thought about it, but in fact it was true. I did like him a lot, odd creature though he was.

"Oh, I don't know - he's a bit strange, but yes, I do like him. I think he could be a good friend."

"Or something more?" teased Deb. "Oh, don't worry, I'm only joking. It is good to see you finally out and about, making friends like him and Sophy. It's been so long."

"I know. I've suddenly become aware of how lonely I have been in the last few months. Chloe is wonderful, and having her to care for absolutely saved me at the darkest of times, but it's not like talking to an adult."

"I know. You definitely need to spend more time with friends, as well as seeing more of the family. But it is a bit diffi-cult and uncomfortable, until we know for sure who killed Kate."

I agreed wholeheartedly. The sooner this mess was cleared up, the better for everyone.

"How did you get on with Beth, Deb? Is she feeling better? Stephen did mention that she had a rather odd reaction to Kate's story at the coffee morning."

"I really don't know what to tell you, Sam. She's not in a very good state and as soon as I started to talk to her about the murder, she burst into tears and started hyperventilating. She said she felt responsible, as it was her garden, but I just couldn't get her to calm down enough to talk properly."

"Oh, poor Beth. Of course it's not her fault."

"Mmmm. I couldn't help wondering if she was making herself upset to avoid talking to me about something. I can't be sure, but it just didn't feel quite normal, and it didn't seem to me as if she was reacting entirely naturally. I know she can't have anything to do with the murder - we've known her for years, and I just can't believe that she would do something like that. But I felt as if she was hiding something from me."

"Oh dear. Do you think I ought to try to talk to her?"

"If you would, Sam. I need to know that it is all my imagination. And if there is something upsetting her, we need to try to find out what it is and clear it up."

Typical Deb, always wanting to solve everyone's problems and fix people. But she was right, and I agreed to try to see Beth in the next few days.

During the fifteen minute drive to my parents' village, I ran over things in my mind. I was a bit nervous about talking to Daniyaal about what I had discovered. None of it seemed very helpful, it was just a few impressions and nothing at all provable or concrete.

He arrived very punctually, which was much better for me than having to hang around waiting for him. Mum was giving Chloe her tea in the kitchen and Dad answered the door and brought him in, looking somewhat sterner than usual.

"I hope that you are aware, Sergeant, that you are putting my daughter at risk by asking her to report back on her friends like this. If she says the wrong thing or upsets the wrong person, she could be your next victim."

Daniyaal answered him directly and very seriously.

"I know that, Mr Hambledon. We did discuss it. But that could happen, even if she wasn't reporting back to me, and at least this way we have a better chance of catching the killer and making everyone safe again. I don't want Sam to take any risks. If a conversation is getting fraught, she needs to back off and leave. And she definitely mustn't accept food or drink from anyone at the moment."

Dad was obviously relieved that Daniyaal was taking the

danger with appropriate seriousness. He offered him tea or coffee, but as usual Daniyaal refused, saying that he preferred to keep his mask on.

"Do you want us to wear masks too?" I queried.

"It's up to you. I know you are testing regularly and being careful. But it's part of our Covid regulations from work to keep the mask on, and I am hopefully protecting you by doing it. Obviously I have a much wider circle of contacts than you do at the moment, not all of whom are taking appropriate precautions."

"We're grateful for your consideration," Dad responded. "It's worrying to see how lax some people are being and obviously my wife and I are in a more vulnerable age group."

"You are right to take care, Mr Hambledon," said Daniyaal. "I've seen first-hand the results of not taking Covid risks seriously. If people really knew what the virus can do, they would be much more careful."

Dad nodded sympathetically and went to see how Chloe was getting on with her tea.

There was a short silence, a little uncomfortable on my part.

"OK, then, Sam, let me know what you have found out. Please try not to leave anything out, even if it doesn't seem important to you. Even small indications can help to point us in the right direction."

Using the notes I had made, I gave as much detail as I could about my conversations with Sophy, Stephen and Deb. As before, Daniyaal made a recording of what I said and asked plenty of questions which helped me to keep on track.

"I'm sorry there isn't more, Daniyaal. It doesn't seem much at all."

He smiled reassuringly, his eyes crinkling up at the corners above his mask.

"Don't worry, this is exactly what we need. There is no way that I or the Inspector could get half of this information. It certainly gives me some idea of who to interview next, and what kind of questions to ask. The only thing I would ask, is that you remember the first attempt on Charlotte, as well as Kate's murder."

"You're right, I have been only focusing on the second coffee morning because I wasn't there and it was easier to ask about it. But I will see if I can talk about Charlotte as well and watch how people react."

"That's the way to do it. Did you say that you are spending time with Celia tomorrow?"

"Yes, the dreaded old people's coffee morning! Not my kind of thing, but I guess it will show me Celia in her natural element."

"Indeed. I'm very grateful to you for thinking of it. Can we meet again in a couple of days to follow up on what you have found out, if anything?"

"I was planning to spend Sunday afternoon here - is that any good to you? I don't know when you work."

He laughed.

"Easier to say when I don't work! My hours are quite flexible and I can certainly pop in on Sunday afternoon, if you are sure your parents won't mind. Around half past three?"

"That would be perfect. I'll walk you out."

Keeping our distance and with no handshakes, it was a little awkward saying goodbye. I caught myself wanting to give him a wave as he walked back to the car and gave myself a little shake. He was not a friend, just a policeman with a job to do. But he was certainly very pleasant about it.

He had obviously made a good impression on Dad. They were discussing him when I went into the kitchen, where Chloe, having finished her tea, was sitting on Mum's knee looking from face to face as they spoke.

"Well, he seems like a sensible young man, Sam - I liked him. I think he will do his best for Kate and also try to keep you out of trouble."

"I'm glad you got on with him. He is coming back on Sunday afternoon at half past three. Is that a problem?"

"I'd like to meet him as well this time," said Mum. "Just to be sure. Not that I don't trust your judgement, but I can't help feeling a bit anxious about the situation. I want to make sure that he is keeping your contribution to the investigation entirely confidential."

Chloe yawned suddenly and I decided it was time to take her home and get her settled. And I was feeling really hungry myself. Being involved in all this, had definitely improved my appetite.

"Can I eat with you on Sunday evening, Mum? I know it's a bit late for Chloe, but I can bring the travel cot you used before. It will be the first time I've had the chance."

"Of course, darling. You can stay overnight if you like. It would be more relaxing for you."

"That would be lovely," I responded. "It's been so long since I stayed with you. Are you sure you don't mind having Chloe to-morrow morning?"

"Of course not, sweetheart. We'll have a lovely time to-gether, won't we Chloe? I'll come and pick her up straight after breakfast."

Hugs all round and then we left. I felt nearly as tired as Chloe was. It had been quite a draining day, one way or another.

CHAPTER 12

Another coffee morning

Everything felt rushed in the morning. Chloe had slept later than usual and I only just had breakfast finished and her things put together by the time Mum rang the doorbell.

"I'll have to get a key copied for you, Mum," I said.

"We'll see," she responded. "I think it does you good to have your privacy, your own space. You don't want us popping in on you all the time. How's my lovely Chloe? Coming to see Grandad? Oh, she's so cute, Sam. You are lucky."

She was right. I was really lucky, in spite of all the bad things which had happened. My family was definitely something to be grateful for. I gave Mum an impulsive hug and kissed Chloe goodbye.

Celia looked mildly surprised when I arrived at the church hall five minutes early. She was already putting out chairs and tables in groups.

"What can I do first?" I asked.

"Can you please put out the cups and saucers on the table over there? They're in the large cupboard in the kitchen, next to the sink."

Relieved to have something so straightforward to be getting on with, I collected the cups and saucers and started laying them out.

"Those cakes in the kitchen look amazing, Celia. Did you make them all?"

"Most of them, but old Mrs Winston made the shortbread

and Mr Patel always lets us have a few fresh doughnuts from the bakery. Those are very popular!"

"I can imagine. It all looks delicious. Shall I put out some plates as well?"

"Yes, please. It's a big help having you here this morning. People just don't understand how much work goes into something like this."

"You are so right. It's like teaching, people think you just go into the classroom and teach a lesson. They don't realise how much preparation goes into even one session."

"I didn't know you used to be a teacher. That was always my dream - to teach."

"But it didn't work out?"

Celia's mouth tightened.

"No. I had gone off to university doing a teaching degree, but I had just turned twenty, when my mother had a sudden stroke, which also caused dementia. She needed a lot of care, which my father couldn't give her as well as working, and Stephen was only thirteen ... So I went home to care for her. She lived for another twelve years, needing constant care. By then, it was too late to go back and train."

"That's really tough," I responded sympathetically. "You can train in later life, you know. Even part-time now, I think. Especially in a shortage subject."

"But I don't have a degree, and that means the training would be really long. I did think about doing an Open University degree, but - well, it's difficult to find the time and the motivation. It's so very long since I did any real studying. And I'm happy enough with my work now."

She certainly did not sound happy. There was an edge of bitter disappointment in her voice. Not surprising, really. She had spent all her youth caring for someone and, over the years, her hopes and dreams must have died a slow, lingering death. The raw emotions, which I could sense within her, made me feel uncomfortable.

"What will you do if Stephen marries?" I asked, just for

something to say. And wished I had held my tongue - that was a tactless thing to ask.

Celia turned and looked at me, her eyes bright and hard.

"That won't happen. Some people find the idea of an unmarried vicar tempting, and try to get close to him, but it's not right. At his last parish, I - I had to contact the bishop about a divorcee who was really pursuing him. It was disgusting, causing gossip in the parish, bringing the church into disrepute. So we moved here to get away from it. I won't let that happen again."

Wow, that was quite a revelation. The absolute determination in Celia's face was slightly disturbing.

"Oh, I see," was all I could manage. Surely Stephen had a right to have a relationship, settle down, have his own family? But I could not say that to Celia. In a rather awkward silence, we finished setting up, ready for the old people to arrive.

Deb was right - the old people really were lovely. I chatted to them as I served the tea or coffee and cake. Some of them obviously recognised me and called me by name, but they were all very careful in what they said, and avoided upsetting me. The cakes were disappearing fast and most of the tables were occupied, when Annette arrived with a group of very elderly and frail-looking wheelchair users.

"How nice to see you again, Annette!" I said. "I was hoping that I would run into you soon."

"It's an extra shift," she responded, sounding exhausted. "I don't normally do daytime as well. But the usual carer is ill - probably Covid - and my manager was desperate. I managed to find a neighbour to take care of Simon and here I am. I am qualified to drive the minibus, so I was the obvious choice."

"Oh dear, that doesn't sound so good," I sympathised. "Never mind, you sit down over there, and I will bring you tea and some cake, and you can relax while your residents have a good time."

Annette brightened a little, as I led her over to a seat at the back of the hall, and looked positively happy, when I brought her some hot tea and a plate of carrot cake.

"Thank you so much, Sam - you don't know how much I needed that."

"I can imagine. Cake really helps when you are exhausted! Just take the chance to rest a little, while you can. I'll keep an eye on your residents. But, to be honest, they look as if they are enjoying themselves."

It was true. The people she had brought were evidently very infirm and needed a lot of physical care, but they were clearly delighted to see old friends. One was playing dominos and the other two were talking away, ten to the dozen. What I also noticed was how good Celia was with the old people. She was like a different person - chatting, cajoling, smiling and relaxed. So full of life and so caring. It was clear that the older people adored her.

I helped out as much as I could, but then went back to sit with Annette for a few minutes.

"It would be lovely to chat to you properly," I ventured. "I don't suppose you would like to come out for a walk with me and Chloe some time soon? There's no chance to talk properly here."

Annette looked round at me, puzzled but grateful.

"I would love that. But are you sure? You've had such a difficult time recently, and you must have plenty of other things to do."

"I would honestly love to meet up with you," I said firmly. And was slightly surprised that it was actually true. I did want to meet up with Annette, and find out what made her tick. She wasn't your normal coffee morning attendee and I felt that we might have that in common at least. "When are you off?"

"I could do Monday morning, if that is any good to you. I have Sunday off for once, so I shouldn't be too tired."

"Perfect. Ten o'clock by the park entrance? Have you got my mobile number just in case?"

We swapped numbers. Annette got up to see to her residents and Celia called me over to offer tea and coffee refills. I could see that she was a bit irritated that I had sat with Annette, but I ignored it. I felt that I had made another step forward, arranging to meet up with her on Monday.

The time flew by, and before I knew it the guests were leaving.

"Now for the washing-up, I suppose," I said.

"Yes please, Sam. If you can wash, I will dry, as I know where everything goes."

"That sounds sensible. How did you feel it went?"

"Pretty well, I think. We haven't been back up and running for long, but they all seemed more relaxed this week."

"I must say, you are very good with them all, Celia. You are a natural."

Celia coloured and shook her head bashfully.

"It's just that I have had a lot of practice. But I do like them, you know. They are interested in the same kind of things that I am, and I seem to fit in much better with older people. They seem to appreciate me more."

I mumbled something non-committal. It was true that Celia was not exactly popular with the younger people I knew.

"Not like you and your friend Deb, you fit in so easily. And Kate, she was a friend of yours too, wasn't she?"

There was a note of jealousy in her voice, which had flattened and had a sour edge.

"Oh, Deb is a real social animal, and a great organiser. Always has been. I'm not naturally outgoing, but you have to learn to get over that, when you go into teaching. But Kate, no, I wouldn't say Kate was like that. In spite of her career, she was more of an introvert really, and she almost never talked about herself."

"Well, she certainly was the centre of attention at that last coffee morning. People were hanging on her every word." The envy was obvious and bitter now.

"She was probably glad not to be answering questions about her health - that is something she really tried to keep private. Most people didn't even know that she was ill."

Celia turned round to me, looking shocked.

"You mean she really was seriously ill? I know I heard

something about her having been ill, when she first died, but -"

"She had cancer, a very aggressive type, and had been having powerful chemo. That's why everyone assumed that she had died from complications."

Celia's hand flew to her mouth.

"Oh no, I feel terrible! I - I never thought there was anything wrong with her, and I had a go at Stephen for wasting so much time with her. He was seeing so much of her, and I thought it wasn't right and there might be more gossip, especially as she was so beautiful…"

I looked at her seriously.

"You really can't judge by appearances, Celia. Even if she hadn't been suffering from cancer, she might have had mental health issues, or spiritual problems, you wouldn't know about. And I don't suppose that Stephen is supposed to talk to you about those things."

She had the grace to look shamefaced.

"You are right, Sam. I'm sorry."

"I don't suppose that Kate noticed how you felt, Celia. I hope not, anyway."

She began to justify herself.

"I certainly didn't say anything to her about it. I do feel that I need to protect Stephen, and to try to manage his time. He is so soft-hearted, and spends far too long talking to people when he should be getting on with his job. Look at all the time he has wasted on Charlotte."

"I thought that was something to do with a charity she is involved with."

"Oh, that's her excuse, but she seems to be one of those people, who think the vicar has nothing better to do than to listen to them."

I could tell that Celia thought that about me, too. Hence her irritation when I came round yesterday.

"Well, now that people know Charlotte wasn't attempting suicide, things should be easier for her, at least."

"But she's loving it! Keeps on and on about it. She just has to be the centre of attention. I tell you, it drives me mad," said Celia, eyes kindling. I could see that she was still her judgemental self, in spite of her shock at the news of Kate's cancer. We soon finished the washing-up and I was glad to go home. Too much Celia was hard to take.

CHAPTER 13

Beth

I noted down as much as I could remember of Celia's revelations when I got home, before picking Chloe up. I felt very sorry for her, in the abstract. Giving up your youth to care for a parent like that must have been very difficult and it was not surprising that she was jealous of people who appeared to have life so much easier. Yet that didn't make it any easier to like her. Her prickliness, obsessive 'protection' of her brother and tendency to judge people were not appealing, but did they make her a potential murderer? On the other hand, it had been good to see her interacting so well with the elderly people. Still, fortunately I only had to report back, not make decisions on who was a likely suspect.

Walking through the town with Chloe later on, I passed Beth's house. Suddenly, I felt that I could not leave that unfinished business. Best to get it over with. I turned and rang the doorbell, before I could have second thoughts.

"Hi, Beth - I hope you don't mind, I just wanted to see how you are. Last time I saw you, you were really struggling, and I know how that feels."

Beth looked anxious and a little wary, but she opened the door wider and invited me in.

"I know you've been through a lot, Sam. As for me, there's nothing really wrong with me - I know how lucky I am. Would you like to come through to the garden? I don't like to have people in the house yet."

I agreed and followed her out into the sunshine. We found a shady spot under a tree, to keep Chloe cool.

"Do you want a drink, or something to eat?"

Even though she was clearly not herself, Beth was still a very hospitable person and the offer was more than a gesture.

"I'm fine, thanks, Beth. Trying to lose some weight! I have definitely put on a few pounds, so I am trying to stick with water to stay hydrated."

I was astonished to see Beth's eyes fill with tears.

"What's wrong? What did I say? I'm so sorry, Beth."

"It's not your fault, Sam. It's just that, well, I know I need to lose a lot of weight and I just don't have the willpower to do it. I simply can't resist eating at the moment, and I don't get much exercise at all to use up all the extra calories."

Beth had always been naturally plump and rounded, but I could see that she had put on more weight, even though it was hidden under a voluminous flowery dress.

"Oh, Beth, I am sorry to have mentioned it. You look fine, you really do. But I know that doesn't help, when you don't feel fine. Would you like to come on some walks with me and Chloe, or even with Deb as well? Would that help a bit?"

Beth looked even more troubled.

"You don't understand. I don't go anywhere any more. I've just lost my confidence in going out. I never got it back after lockdown. And Deb, well, Deb always makes me feel so guilty, for being lazy and disorganised. She is so strong, and so full of energy. When I'm with her, I feel as if I need to pull my socks up and get busy, but I just can't at the moment."

She was almost wailing and I felt really concerned for her.

"Don't worry, Beth, I do understand. I've only just started going out properly myself. I shut myself away for so long that meeting anyone else just felt impossible. I wasn't even seeing my parents."

"I know, but you had a good reason for it, Sam. You had lost Thomas. That was such a terrible loss. But I am so fortunate. I have this house, a lovely garden, enough money to live on, if I am careful, with a bit of data entry work from home. But I don't do anything to help anyone, I am just a waste of space, a nobody. I sometimes feel it would have been better if I had never been born."

Now she was sobbing, and Chloe was looking up at her, puzzled and a bit anxious.

"Look, Beth, none of that is true, and you know it. You're scaring Chloe. Try to calm down and breathe. You are a genuinely lovely person, one of the sweetest people I know. We all love you, you should know that. But the pandemic has affected you more than some, probably because you were on your own so much during lockdown."

Beth gulped and made an effort to calm herself.

"I did feel lonely at the start, but I got so used to being on my own. Now I can't face seeing people, even my friends. I don't even know if I have friends any more. Maybe a few online."

"I'm your friend, Beth, and you have lots of others. But I understand that it doesn't feel like that at the moment. Have you spoken to the doctor about how you are feeling?"

Beth shook her head firmly.

"Oh, no, I certainly couldn't waste his time with this. The NHS is overloaded, they keep saying that. It's nothing. I just need to get hold of myself, that's all. I can do it, I'm sure I can."

Her voice trailed off into an uncertainty which contradicted her words.

"OK, Beth, we'll try to cope with it together, but you have to promise me that if it doesn't work you will speak to the GP. Please."

She looked at me with her eyes full of tears and fear, but she did nod in acceptance. Then it all poured out.

"I've been feeling so guilty, Sam. I just have to tell you. When Kate was here, the other week, and Sophy was quizzing her about her modelling career, I felt so worthless, but I was also really angry. With Kate, although she hadn't done anything wrong. It just seemed so unfair, that she had so much simply drop into her lap and she didn't even want it! She gave it up! And she's got a lovely husband and two gorgeous children. And me, I have nothing and no one. It made me so cross. I suppose I was cross with myself, for wasting my life, but at the time I felt more angry with Kate, for having so much that I want."

I had not realised that Beth felt that way about her life. She had previously seemed so contented with her stable, if not exciting, way of life. But she obviously wanted, or needed, something more.

"I so much want a family of my own. I don't even have parents or siblings, only a few distant cousins I don't really know. And I feel so bad that I had such angry, envious thoughts about Kate on the day she died. It feels as if it is my fault somehow. I wished her ill, and now she's dead."

Beth's voice was rising again, hysteria not far away.

"It's not your fault at all, Beth. Some horrible person chose to kill Kate, it wasn't an accident, or anything you could possibly have influenced. That's just superstition. It's like kids feeling that somehow they are responsible for their parents' divorce. Not real, just a deep sense of guilt. You have to let it go. Have you spoken to Stephen about it?"

"Oh, I couldn't possibly do that. He would know what a terrible person I am. I'm not a good Christian at all. I should never have such mean thoughts and feelings…"

"I don't think that's what it's all about. He wouldn't judge you. I don't think being a Christian means that you have to be perfect. He was really supportive to me recently, and I don't normally go to church."

"I know, but I really couldn't do it. I couldn't tell him about it, let alone ask him for help."

Beth sounded really panicky.

"It's OK," I soothed, "Don't worry. You don't have to talk to him. I just thought he might be able to help. He was so good the other week, when I - I fell apart. But don't worry, we'll find another way to sort things out."

My mind was racing. Beth needed help so urgently. What could I do? I wasn't trained for this.

"Hey, Beth, let's try a walk around the block now. Right now, before you change your mind." If we could just break the pattern, get her out of the cocoon of her house, start her moving in the right direction, it might help.

"I don't know... It's scary being out there." Beth's tragic eyes brimmed with tears. I did not know if I could help, but I had to try.

"I understand. I felt exactly like that. But you won't be on your own. Chloe and I will be with you."

Beth looked at Chloe and the buggy. She seemed to make up her mind.

"OK, if I can be with you, I will try." She tried to sound determined, but only succeeded in sounding desperate.

"Come on, then. Right now."

I managed to shepherd her out of the house. She hesitated as we started down the road and I asked her to push Chloe, while I answered a message from Deb on my phone. That helped. Holding tightly onto the buggy, she managed to walk slowly down the lovely tree-lined street. I did not take over with the buggy when I finished my message (which was nothing important but had been a good excuse). Pushing the buggy helped, I knew that from my own experience. I kept up a fairly meaningless flow of conversation, mainly focusing on keeping my tone of voice calm, soothing and even. After a while Beth began to breathe more easily and unclenched her hands on the handle. She kept her eyes on the pavement in front and wasn't able to join in the conversation, but she was managing to keep relatively calm and push Chloe along steadily.

We turned the first corner into Steadman Rise. A quarter of the way round. I was starting to feel confident that we would make it.

"Hi Sam! Hello Beth!"

Oh no, it was Lesley's loud voice coming from across the road. Not at all the right person for Beth just now. She had Jackie in tow, and Charlie in the pushchair, and was waving eagerly, looking to cross the road towards us.

"Beth, would you mind staying here with Chloe for a minute, while I go over and speak to Lesley?"

Beth's wide scared eyes swung round to me. I thought for a moment that she was going to bolt. But she took a deep breath and nodded, turning straight back to the buggy to fix her eyes on the pavement.

I trotted quickly across the street before Lesley could start to come over to us. Not ideal, but the best solution.

"Hello, Lesley. How nice to see you. Hi Jackie, and hello, young Charlie. You look happy today - that's a very cute smile."

Before Lesley could suggest joining me and Beth for the rest of the walk, I jumped in.

"We're just on our way back, Beth is very tired as she hasn't been well, so I can't stop and talk. I know you will understand. I'm so glad to see you. I've been dying for a catch up with you after everything that has happened."

How could I lie so fluently? Lesley was actually the person I had been dreading meeting up with.

"What about a coffee tomorrow? The forecast is good, so you are welcome to come and sit in my garden with me if you like."

Lesley, who had been looking disappointed, brightened at the thought.

"That would be great. Are you sure? You are welcome to come to me if you would rather."

I thought quickly. It would be good to see her in her own environment, but the issue of not taking food and drink from someone would be complicated by the fact that I had inadvertently already mentioned having coffee. It would be easier to handle on my own ground.

"That's really kind of you, Lesley, but Chloe and I have been all over the place this week, and I think she just needs some time at home. I'm actually going to stay with my parents on Sunday night, so I desperately need to get some washing done. Shall we say ten thirty? Great. See you then. Sorry, I must dash - I don't want to leave Beth standing any longer."

Lesley smiled. "I will look forward to it. Come on, Jackie, we're going home now, and you can help me tidy up before tea. You left things in a real mess when we came out."

I hurried back to Beth. I had kept an eye on her while I was talking to Lesley, and she seemed to be calm enough, but when I reached her side, I could see that her hands were trembling pitifully and her lip was quivering.

"Thank you so much, Beth. That was a big help and you did so well. I find Lesley quite hard to take, to be honest, and I don't think she would be the best person to chat to on your first trip out. She's such a gossip too. Let's get on now, so that we can get you home."

While I was talking, we had already started to move, with Beth now almost scuttling along. No point in going back from here, it would take just as long and bring her back into Lesley's path. Without stopping, we whizzed round the rest of the block and arrived back at Beth's house. I opened the door for her and handed her the key.

"Would you rather be on your own now, or shall we come in with you?"

Beth looked so relieved to be back in her sanctuary.

"I think I need to be on my own for now, Sam, thanks. That was - that was a challenge, but we did it. Now I need some space to calm down. I'll have a cup of tea and watch something silly on the television to distract me."

"I'm so proud of you, Beth, and you should be really proud of yourself. When shall we try again?"

She immediately looked anxious once more.

"I - I don't know," she mumbled. "Do we -"

"Yes, we really do have to. I'm sorry to push you like this, Beth, but I know what it is like. I can do a quick stroll on Sunday morning before going over to Mum's."

She looked relieved that it was not going to be tomorrow.

"OK," she agreed. "I think I can maybe manage that. At about eleven? I don't find it easy to get up and moving in the morning."

I was concerned about that too, but we had to address one thing at a time. I had thought of possibly attending the service in church for the first time, but that would not be possible now. Never mind. Helping Beth was more important for the moment. Without stopping to wave us off, Beth darted back inside, obviously delighted to be home again.

I felt shattered, after dealing with all that emotion. I was no longer used to being the positive one, to helping others to feel better. I was glad that I had been able to do it, but felt utterly exhausted.

"An easy tea tonight, Chloe, and an early night for me, I think."

My gorgeous daughter gurgled happily. I was so very lucky to have her.

With Chloe safely in her cot, I slumped in front of the television. I knew I should write some notes about my meeting with Beth for tomorrow's report to Daniyaal, but I just did not have the energy.

Suddenly my phone rang, jerking me out of my stupor. I kept meaning to change the ringtone to something gentler, but never got around to it. It was Deb, wanting to know how I had got on at the coffee morning with Celia. I fetched my notes and told her what I had found out.

"Wow, you did get a lot of information," she said. "I always wondered why she was living with Stephen. But to contact the bishop about that poor woman in her old parish - that was really bad. She sounds a bit obsessed."

"She really is," I agreed. "But I do feel sorry for her all the same. It can't have been easy, giving up uni and a career like that. And caring for someone with dementia is not something I think I could manage easily, even if I loved them."

"Definitely not - I have so much respect for care workers like

Annette, who choose to do it as a job."

I told her some of what had happened with Beth, taking the opportunity to jot down some notes while I talked.

"Oh, poor Beth. She is in a real state. I think you did just the right thing. I'll back off for now, if you think she finds me too bracing, but later on I can help and take her out."

"I'm certain she didn't kill Kate, despite feeling so hostile towards her that day. But I don't know what the police will think…"

"No, if they find out how she felt and how unwell she is currently, they might see it as a motive."

I suddenly felt extremely guilty. I was going to have to betray Beth's confidence to Daniyaal.

"You're right, Deb. But at the same time they surely can't convict her of something she didn't do. There wouldn't be any evidence."

"I don't think there's much evidence at the moment anyway. But hopefully you are right, and they will know how to weigh up people's motivations and behaviour rationally."

Deb did not sound too sure. We agreed to talk again soon. I told her that I had arranged to see Annette on Monday, and Lesley on Saturday morning.

"Not looking forward to that one, I can tell you. As you know, we didn't exactly click when we first met, and every time I've seen her since, she's set my teeth on edge with how she treats her daughter."

"I know you didn't hit it off straight away, Sam, but you have to remember that she's had a really tough time too, with her husband walking out on her, and two little ones to bring up on her own. Her parents live at the other end of the country somewhere, so she doesn't have much support at all. I think we owe it to the children to try to help her through this. She's not as bad as you think - she can be quite good fun when she's in the mood."

That was again typical Deb, seeing the best in everyone.

"You always want to help people, Deb. I just find it tough

to be sympathetic to Lesley, but you're right, of course - I should give her a chance. I'll try to keep an open mind."

"I'm going to see Charlotte on Sunday," mentioned Deb. "I know she isn't really on our suspects' list as such, but you never know. She might say something useful."

"You're right. I've tended to concentrate on Kate's murder, but we mustn't forget the attack on Charlotte. I still can't see much they have in common, but there must be something, I suppose. Or she might remember something about who was near her coffee."

Talking to Deb had given me a bit of an adrenaline surge, but after a quick shower I fell into bed and slept soundly, though my dreams were troubled by horrible images of Beth being dragged off and arrested by Daniyaal.

CHAPTER 14

Lesley

Saturday dawned, bright but breezy, perfect for getting the washing out, and also for spending time in the garden. If only it was not Lesley who was coming round. Chloe was in a good mood and settled quickly to play on her mat in the garden, while I hung out the clothes. I often felt guilty that I was not a better housewife, but tried to reassure myself that caring for her was the most important thing, not dusting. But Lesley would probably judge me for it. Oh well, the garden was reasonably tidy, even if it couldn't compare with Celia's work. Thomas and I had set it up to be low maintenance and wildlife friendly. My throat tightened as I remembered working on it with him before the pandemic took him away. He had been living near the hospital for weeks before he died, because he did not want to risk passing it to me while I was pregnant.

"I've seen too many pregnant women and young mothers getting seriously ill and dying, Sam. I know it's horrible being apart, but it won't be for long, I'm sure, and I can't risk you or the baby."

And I had agreed, it was not worth the risk. But, in the end, he died before Chloe was born, and I was not with him when he went. I could see his face so clearly, when he said goodbye on that final video call, before they intubated him. Trying to look positive, trying to comfort and reassure me, but desperate sadness and, yes, fear in his eyes. Asking me to keep praying for him.

They said he died peacefully, but how could I possibly know that? I was not allowed to be there. At least the nurses with him were his friends and colleagues, so in a way he was not alone. Danielle, who gave me the bad news, and was in tears herself, said she had been with him, holding his hand. But it was not the same. Not for him, and certainly not for me.

Tears were streaming down my face, and my body was shaken with aching sobs as the feelings overwhelmed me. I had pushed that memory away, deep down inside, because I could not face up to it. Somehow the garden, where I had spent so much time in the last few months without any problem, had brought it back to the surface. I still could not deal with it, but the flood of emotion felt right in a strange way. I owed it to Thomas to mourn him properly.

Suddenly, jarringly, the doorbell rang. Of course, Lesley. I sniffed, gulped back the tears and tried to wipe my eyes and nose, but I knew that I would look a mess.

"Just a moment, Lesley," my voice quavered a bit, but years of teaching had taught me to hide my emotions pretty well. "I'll come and open the side gate."

Grabbing extra tissues from inside the patio door, I scrubbed at my face and went to let her in. Luckily I had no make-up on, so at least there would be no streaks of mascara. Pinning a false smile on my face, I opened the gate.

Lesley was not the most sensitive or observant of people, but even she noticed that I had been crying. Red eyes, blotchy face and a red nose probably gave it away.

"Are you OK, Sam? I hope I haven't come at a bad time?" The type of question which invites a negative.

"Not at all, Lesley, I'm sorry. I was just - just remembering ..."

"Oh dear, " Lesley filled in. "Deborah did tell me you had a bad time when you lost your husband."

There was an edge of morbid curiosity alongside the sympathy in her voice, a sense that she would enjoy hearing all the gory details.

"Yes, it - it was very difficult. I'll tell you more about it some time, but not today, if that's alright with you. Come and make yourself comfortable. Did you bring some toys for the children? I've put a picnic blanket out for them near the table. I'll just go and make you a drink. What would you like, tea or coffee, or a cold drink?"

Lesley opted for coffee and I escaped inside to calm myself. I caught a glimpse of my face in the mirror as I walked past, and decided to have a wash and put on some lipstick at least, before going back out. It would not have mattered to me with Deb, or even with Sophy or Stephen, but I did not want to seem vulnerable around Lesley, for some reason.

A few minutes later, restored to some semblance of calm, I walked carefully out into the garden with a tray of coffee, biscuits, and juice for Jackie. She was playing quietly with Chloe, hiding her face and then revealing it suddenly, to gurgles of delight from the baby.

"Thank you so much for playing with Chloe, Jackie. There's some juice for you here, and a biscuit too, if you would like one."

"You are very privileged, Sam," said Lesley, in a sarcastic tone of voice. "Jackie never takes the time to entertain Charlie when I need her to. I wish she was more helpful, but she seems to drift along in her own little world."

"She's only young, " I defended the little girl, who was suddenly silent and still. "Come on, Jackie - come and get your drink and biscuit."

Hesitantly, the child came to take her beaker and reached for a biscuit.

"Take a plain one, Jackie," commanded her mother. "I don't want chocolate stains all over your clothes."

Looking at me warily, Jackie took her biscuit quickly, and hurried back to sit down. My heart went out to her.

"Bless her, she's such a lovely little thing, Lesley. You must be very proud of her."

Lesley looked surprised at my words.

"Well, she'll never be a beauty, that's for sure, but I suppose she could be quite cute, if she can ever bring herself to smile."

I felt sick to my stomach. That kind of destructive, off-hand remark could cause untold damage later to the little girl, I knew that all too well from my teaching career. I hurried to change the subject.

"She looks very intelligent. And Charlie seems very strong for his age."

"He's quite placid, thank goodness. Doesn't need too much attention. He sleeps well too. I don't know what I would do, if he kept me awake all night as well."

We chatted for a while in a desultory fashion about sleeping and weaning. I managed to bring myself to ask for advice on the latter, although, to be honest, I would take anything she told me with a large pinch of salt.

Suddenly the tone of the conversation changed. Lesley mentioned Charlotte and her voice sharpened with dislike.

"She's so full of herself now. She seems to think it makes her special, to have been the killer's first intended victim. She goes on and on about it. Personally I still think she might actually have tried to kill herself just for the attention."

"Oh Lesley, you shouldn't say that. The police seem certain that she was drugged. I just don't understand why."

Lesley tossed her head and her eyes narrowed.

"I don't like to speak ill of people," she said, untruthfully, " but she certainly isn't very popular. She is so smug and self-satisfied. Everything is ideal in Charlotte-land: rich husband, huge house, perfect kids, no need to work or worry about money. No one is ever that perfect. I bet her husband only works such long hours, because he can't stand spending time with her."

Shocked at the venom in her voice, I was unsure how to respond.

"But I thought she did a lot for charity," was all I could find to say.

"Charity! I'll give her charity. She has no understanding of those of us who find life more difficult, that's for sure. Not a word of sympathy to me, when Mark left. She could have offered to help out with the kids, as hers are older and she has plenty of time, but no, she is far too selfish for that. You'd think as a so-called Christian, who spends so much time in church, she would be happy to help other people, but I think it's all a front. I don't think she cares about anyone but herself, or even notices when people are struggling."

"People often don't see things clearly, Lesley," I tried to soothe her. "They are so wrapped up in their own lives, their own problems. It doesn't necessarily mean that they don't care. I'm sure if she had known, Charlotte would have -"

"She did know. I asked her for help one afternoon. I needed to take Charlie to the doctor and asked her to pick up Jackie for me and look after her, just for one little hour, but oh no, she was too busy taking Clemency to her piano lesson on the other side of town. Your friend Deb helped me out in the end."

"Deb is so obliging. And she knows Jackie's school because her children went there."

"But Charlotte wouldn't put herself out for anything or anyone. Missing one piano lesson would not have been a disaster, not if she's as gifted as her mother always says. But no, darling Clemency must have everything she wants."

I struggled to think how to stem the flow of invective. I did not know Charlotte well, and she had not made the best first impression on me, but this level of personal rancour was unsettling. I offered Lesley another coffee, and escaped for a few minutes.

Changing the subject on my return to the garden, I asked what Lesley thought about the murder. Her eyes lit up with a sort of ghoulish excitement.

"I know it's not nice, but it is kind of exciting to have something like that happen here. Nothing interesting ever happens in this dead little town. I do feel sorry for Kate's family, of course, but I can't help being fascinated by the murder. I just love crime thrillers and it feels as if we are in the middle of one."

Rather taken aback by her unashamed enthusiasm, I probed a little further.

"I really can't see any motive for killing Kate, though, Lesley - can you? She was such a lovely person and so beautiful."

"Did you find her beautiful? I'm afraid I didn't think she was all that good-looking. When she was talking about her career as a model, I couldn't help thinking it must have been, what do the Americans call it, 'affirmative action'? You know, feeling that they needed to have more black models to meet some kind of quota."

I was genuinely shocked at this. It sounded like naked racism.

"But she was incredibly successful. Everyone was struck by her beauty." It was inadequate, but better than nothing.

"Oh, I don't find that black appearance very attractive myself. I am not a racist, but I just find their hair and that dark skin off-putting. I'm entitled to my opinion, aren't I? Now I think Asians are often quite pretty, although Emily's skin is just a shade too dark, don't you think?"

I was flabbergasted. I had never heard such racist nonsense in person. How could I have invited this woman into my garden? I had to say something.

"Lesley, please don't say things like that to me. I'm afraid it definitely is racist, and I just can't have it. You really need to think about your opinions very carefully."

Lesley bridled angrily, her face flushed with annoyance.

"How dare you call me a racist! I'm no such thing. I just have my own opinions about what is beautiful and there's nothing wrong with that, is there? I suppose as a teacher you were trained to shut down people's genuine opinions by calling them racist, but I don't see anything wrong in saying what I think."

"I'm sure you don't mean to sound racist," I said, calmly. "But I'm afraid that is how it comes over. But I'm sorry, I don't mean to offend you. I'm just very sensitive to anything which sounds racist. Kate was one of my best friends."

"I know that, and I don't mean to upset you. Lots of people like the black appearance, I just don't happen to. But her story was amazing - she had so many lucky things happen to her."

I decided to accept the small olive branch, if only for Kate's sake, so that I could hopefully find out who had killed her.

"Her life always seemed a bit like a fairy story to me." I responded quietly.

"Yes, but with a black princess! A rather strange fairy story."

Lesley saw my eyes flash and backed down.

"OK, OK, I'm sorry, I didn't mean it. You are right though, she was incredibly lucky in life. I wish I had her luck."

"You do know that she had a very poor background, don't you? That she didn't always have enough to eat when she was young?"

"No, I didn't know. She never said. Is that why she was so thin?"

"I think so, yes. She never had to starve herself like most models. But maybe that is also why she got cancer later on."

Lesley looked shocked.

"Did she really? I never knew that. What kind?"

Lesley couldn't help asking personal questions, it seemed.

"Breast cancer, a very aggressive form. She had been having chemo."

"Well, I'm surprised. She didn't even look ill. I suppose she was not so lucky after all."

There was a strange look on Lesley's face. I could not work it out at all. Was she ashamed of having envied Kate, sorry that she had felt so hostile, or secretly glad at her misfortune? I really was not sure.

We talked a little more, mainly about relatives who had suffered from cancer, and then it was time for them to leave. Thank goodness.

"Thank you for having us, Sam," said Lesley. Jackie, prompted by her mother, also mumbled a word of thanks. "We must do this again sometime soon."

I smiled at Jackie and Charlie and murmured something non-committal. I was not eager to spend any more time with this woman, but did not want to burn my boats with her, in case I needed to do more investigating.

"Bye! Enjoy the rest of the weekend."

I was so relieved when she had gone, that I picked up Chloe and gave her an enormous hug. Kissing the top of her head, I silently gave thanks for my own family and my friends. I had not realised just how lucky I was to have them.

This time, I rang Deb straight away. I had to let off steam about Lesley. As I expected, she was shocked.

"I've never heard her saying something like that before, Sam - that's horrible. It sounds as if you said the right things, but it must have been really difficult."

"I couldn't believe what I was hearing. It made me feel quite sick. She was so prejudiced, and so unashamed about it. Scary really. I know there's been a move recently towards people feeling able to say this kind of thing openly, but honestly, I was shocked to the core. I know how I would have handled it in school, with a pupil, but for an adult to say it in normal conversation - I really didn't know what to say to her."

"But you have to say something, otherwise they think it's OK. I know, it's tough to know how to respond."

"She was actually really horrible about Charlotte too."

There was a short silence, and then Deb and I tried to speak at the same time.

"Do you think ...?"

Deb carried on.

"Do you think it is possible that she is the - the killer? She's the only one we've heard really saying negative things about both of the victims, isn't she?"

"Well, I guess there is Celia as well. And would she be that open about how she felt if she was the murderer? Surely she'd be hiding those feelings?"

"You'd think so, but maybe it doesn't work like that, Sam.

How could we know? I would say she certainly merits further investigation."

"You're right, Deb. I was so upset by her racism that I just couldn't face asking her more questions about the murder and how she felt about Kate. I still don't think I could do it. Would you mind following up with her? I can take Emily next week instead."

Deb agreed, almost eagerly. I could tell that she thought we might finally be getting somewhere in looking for motives for murder.

"The only trouble is, I really don't know Emily at all. I don't know how to arrange to meet up with her."

"Mmmm. Yes. Oh I know, dogs."

"Dogs! What on earth do you mean?" I was really puzzled.

"Emily is mad keen on dogs and knows all about them. I can ring her and say that you would like some advice on getting a dog, when, what breed, that sort of thing. She'll be happy to meet you and talk about that, no problem."

"Oh, I had no idea she was into dogs. I guess I could make something of that. See if you can arrange something for me, Deb. I can't do Monday, because I'm meeting Annette, but any other day is fine."

"I'll get on to it this afternoon. Try to get some rest, Sam. You sound emotional today."

"I have to admit that doing this is bringing a lot of emotions to the surface, but that's not always a bad thing. But you're right - it is exhausting, really draining. Chloe and I will have a quiet walk and take things easy this afternoon. Good luck with Lesley - I don't envy you one bit."

"Well, I won't try to see her until after the weekend. I've got Charlotte tomorrow, if you remember."

Chloe started whingeing more loudly, reminding me that it was time for lunch.

"See you soon, Deb - I must go and sort Chloe out. Thank goodness I have you to talk to and keep me sane. Love you."

"Love you too, Sam."

CHAPTER 15

Sunday interlude

I deliberately took a different direction for our afternoon walk, to avoid meeting anyone. I really needed some time on my own with Chloe. As usual, walking and chatting away to her about the birds and plants we could see was very healing. Somehow it switched off some of the jangling thoughts, and the intrusive memories, emotions and anxiety. We went further than usual, and I felt so much better when I got home.

Chloe was a bit fretful that evening, probably overtired. Once I finally got her settled, I wrote a few notes about Lesley's visit and tried to watch something relaxing and entertaining on television. I found I could not concentrate, so I decided on a shower and early bed, but as soon as I closed my eyes the images and sounds came flooding back. Thomas, looking at me with those sad eyes, surrounded by beeping and flashing machines. His plain wicker coffin. The tiny, cold funeral. Why had I not been able to cry then, when I couldn't stop now? Painful shuddering sobs were coming thick and fast, and I felt close to hysteria.

I tried to distract myself with my phone, knowing that it would not help me to sleep, but needing to shut out the traumatic pictures in my head. Suddenly, Facebook showed me a memory from three years ago. A picture of me and Thomas together on a beach in France. Such a happy photo. Such a happy holiday. I got up and went to look at it on my laptop, drinking it all in, the bright sunshine, the teasing glint in his eyes, the laughing mouth, his loving arm round my shoulders. I needed to remember Thomas like that, not sick in hospital, alone and afraid. Even though it was three o'clock in the morning, I decided to print the photo out. Typically, the printer cartridges needed changing, but I persevered, in spite of my exhaustion and shaking hands, and finally managed a good print version.

I took it back into the bedroom and propped it up, where I could see it from the bed. I lay down, gazing into his face. This was what I had lost, but also what I had once had. We had a really close, contented marriage. I was lucky to have had that. Remembering the little things we had laughed at, the silly family jokes, the hugs, and the fun outings together, I eventually drifted off to sleep.

I woke up still tired, but feeling more peaceful, and the first thing I saw was the photo of Thomas. It did make me feel emotional, even a little tearful, but it felt less painful than the memories from yesterday. I could smile at our happy faces.

I had always wanted to avoid creating any kind of 'shrine', or collection of photos and objects relating to my dead husband, which had always seemed to me to be very unhealthy and sometimes obsessive. I had seen friends and relatives stuck in a cycle of constant mourning and loss, and I knew I could not afford to live in the past. Chloe needed me now, in the present. But a photo to remind me of the good times seemed different, a step on the road towards being able to remember Thomas with love and gratitude instead of pain and anguish. At the moment, that was a long way off, but hopefully it would come one day.

Chloe seemed much more herself that morning and chuntered away happily, while I packed up the things for our night away. I wanted to be all ready to go, before we went on our walk with Beth. It would be the first time we had stayed away from home together since Chloe was born, and I needed to make sure that I took all the right things. I did not want to forget something in a last minute rush.

The sun was bright that morning, but it was not too hot. Chloe had her sunshade to protect her and I wore dark glasses and a hat, not just due to the sun, but because, after the emotions of yesterday, my face was showing signs of wear, which I had not been able to hide, even with more makeup than I usually wore. I did not want any questions from Beth, which might overset my fragile calm.

I was not sure how Beth would react to coming out again, but I was pleased to see that she was dressed and ready, when we rang the doorbell. She too was wearing a hat and sunglasses, disguising her face somewhat, although I could see that she was anxious because she was constantly biting her lips.

"Hi, Beth! Are you ready for our walk? It's a gorgeous day. Chloe, this is Beth. Do you remember her? Can you wave?"

Chloe did not wave, but she did smile engagingly at Beth. Right on cue. What a star.

"It's a lovely morning. Would you like to push Chloe again? Are you ready to go now?"

With plenty of inane questions and chat, I managed to urge Beth to come out, and to lock up behind her. She was hesitant and silent, but she came and pushed Chloe along the street. Like a blinkered horse, she stared straight in front of her to start with, while I kept up an unending flow of meaningless conversation, more for Beth than Chloe this time.

"Oooh, look, Chloe - it's a group of blackbirds. You don't often see them together like that."

Suddenly Beth spoke.

"That's because they are starlings, Sam. Not blackbirds."

I looked at her, surprised but relieved that she had spoken at last.

"Really? Oh yes, I can see their shiny feathers now and they walk differently, don't they? Thanks, Beth. I don't want to teach Chloe the wrong names."

Quietly at first, but with growing confidence, Beth began to talk about birds. She clearly loved them, and knew a great deal about their habits, as well as their appearance. Chloe was gurgling away, as if she understood, and I felt really pleased that Beth was coming out of her shell so soon today.

"Thanks for bringing me out, Sam." Beth said, when we reached the second corner. "I was terrified, and I nearly chickened out, but it has done me good. I couldn't do it on my own yet, but it is good to move properly, and see something other than the house and garden."

"You are very welcome," I responded. "I know that I needed Deb to push me into coming out of my cocoon. I couldn't have done it on my own."

"Cocoon. Mmm, that's quite a good name for it. I feel safe at home and so exposed away from it. But you and Chloe are somehow extending my safe place for me. Would you mind coming out with me on Tuesday again?"

I jumped at the chance, and suggested we might try going a little further, perhaps to the park. Beth looked uncertain about that.

"I don't know, Sam. We'll see. I just really don't want to meet anyone else yet, and it's always busier by the park. I can cope with you and the lovely Chloe, but just now, I don't think I can manage anyone else."

"That's no problem," I reassured her. "If you feel up to it, we can always extend our walk by an extra block in this direction."

Beth looked enormously relieved.

"That would be much easier, thanks, Sam. I'm sorry to be so useless and to waste so much of your time ..."

"Beth, I really don't want to hear you talking like that any more. Chloe and I are enjoying our walk, you are definitely not useless, and this is not a waste of time. It takes time to get your confidence back, I know that, and it is true that having Chloe helped me a lot in that. Hopefully being with us will help you too."

In an emotional voice, Beth said: "It already has. After a

while I forget that I am outside. Thank you so much, Sam. You are an angel."

I laughed at that.

"Far from it, I'm afraid. But we can do this together."

Once again, we did not go into the house with Beth, just waved and returned home in time for a quick lunch, so that Chloe could have a nap before we went over to Mum's house. I felt exhausted by the lack of sleep and the emotional strain of encouraging Beth out. Before I had time to think, I fell fast asleep on the sofa and was only woken by Chloe, calling out when she woke up. As usual, I felt horrible after sleeping in the day, and struggled to move and get her ready and into the car. The drive over seemed twice as long as usual and there was quite a lot of Sunday afternoon traffic, but in the end we got there and I handed Chloe over to Dad with relief, before carrying in all the equipment that I had decided was necessary for one night away.

"Goodness, Sam, what a lot of stuff! I thought you were only staying one night, not a week."

Mum teased me, but stopped when she saw my face. No sunglasses now.

"What's wrong darling? You look terrible. Has something happened?"

As often happened, when someone asked me that kind of question, I was suddenly overwhelmed with emotion and dissolved into tears, telling Mum haltingly, when I could get the words out, what had happened the previous night.

She gave me an enormous hug, sat me down and made me a cup of tea. She insisted on me eating some home-made sponge cake too. Then she sat with me and we talked for a while, mainly about Thomas, reminiscing about the good times we had, Christmas dinners together, the funny things he had said or done, the real Thomas, not the shell in the coffin or the sick man in the hospital. Gradually I grew calmer and more relaxed and was able to smile and laugh at the memories. It was so good to talk to someone who remembered him that way too.

"Thanks, Mum - that really helped."

"Any time, Sam, any time at all. You were lucky, you had a really wonderful husband and we loved him too, as if he was our own son. It probably made a difference that his parents had both already passed on, so he really wanted to be part of our family. We miss him terribly - especially as it felt, for a while, as if we had lost you too." Mum's voice broke. "But that's all over now and we have you back, and Chloe as well. She's such a blessing."

"I'm so sorry, Mum." I was trembling. How could I have been so selfish and ignored their hurt? It was true that Thomas had loved them very deeply, impressed from his first visit by the warmth and affection so evident in their home.

"Don't be, Sam. It was what you had to do at the time." Mum enveloped me in a bear hug, and stroked my hair as she used to when I was a small child and had hurt myself. It felt good, just for a moment, to let go of being an adult and a mother, and to be comforted instead.

We sat for a while, until Mum decided it was time for me to go and wash my face, and collect my notes ready to meet Daniyaal.

"You're so right, Mum. I really need to pull myself together. I've actually got a lot to tell him today …"

When I saw myself in the bathroom mirror, I realised why I needed to wash my face. It was streaked with tears and mascara and I looked a complete mess. I hastily tidied myself up, took some deep calming breaths and tried to think relaxing thoughts, without much success.

Downstairs, I looked through my notes, and that helped to focus me. There really was quite a lot to go through. Much more about Celia, Beth, and then Lesley. I was glad that I had kept notes, as it would have been easy to forget crucial details or mix people up. So much had happened that it felt like more than a couple of days since I had last reported in.

This time, Daniyaal asked if we could sit in the garden, so that he could take off his mask. He actually accepted a cup of tea and piece of cake, which helped to make the situation feel more normal. Mum and Dad took Chloe inside out of the sun and we started to go through my notes. Daniyaal had a lot of questions as I was talking, and probed my memory carefully for details, not just of what was said, but of expressions and tone of voice. At last we finished up, and he turned off the voice recorder.

"Let's sum up, then, Sam. We now know that Stephen knew Kate well and saw or spoke to her on a very regular basis, to the extent that his sister resented it. Since he also spent time with Charlotte, this may be important and I will follow it up."

"But I don't think he had anything to do with the killing," I said, rather anxiously. "He really seemed to like Kate."

"Let's just stick to what we know for now. You may well be right, but him spending time with Kate may have been a motive for someone else to kill her. Celia, for instance. She seems to be jealous of anyone her brother spends time with, and to be very fearful of him forming any close relationships. To the extent that she contacted the bishop in his last parish. That is definitely something I can chase up. It will be interesting to see what his last parish and the bishop think of him and of Celia."

I nodded in agreement. I could see that my information on Celia did open up some new avenues of investigation.

"Your friend Beth seems to be suffering from some mental health issues. We have talked about the murderer possibly being unstable, so although, from what you have reported, it seems unlikely, we need to take this into account. Could you possibly talk to her about Charlotte? We know how she reacted to Kate on that last morning, but I don't get a clear picture of her relationship with Charlotte at this point."

"OK, I'll talk to her on our next walk."

"Then we come to the most promising lead, at least on the surface: Lesley. She seemed to resent Kate and her success, wasn't aware of her illness, and displayed clearly racist attitudes. She has also expressed hostility to Charlotte, both now and previously. However, as you said to your friend Deb, it is not usual for a criminal, a murderer in particular, to be so open about negative attitudes towards their victims, so this may be a red herring. Still, we need to follow it up. I will interview Lesley again, and I think you said that Deb is going to meet up with her soon?"

"Yes, that's right. I have to be honest and say that I found her attitudes really upsetting and didn't feel I could cope, at the moment, with more of her bile. So Deb will meet up with her next week instead and I will talk to Emily. But if you need me to spend more time with Lesley, I will do my best to put up with it."

"Let's see how my interview and Deb's time with her go first. If you can see Annette and Emily and talk to Beth about Charlotte, that should work for us."

I was glad to feel that I knew exactly what he wanted me to do. And relieved not to have to see Lesley for a while.

"I really am very grateful to you, Sam, for what you are doing. I know it isn't easy, especially reporting back on friends like Beth, and on delicate matters like mental health issues. But you have definitely helped to focus our investigations and I feel that we are now starting to make genuine progress in this difficult case."

Daniyaal spoke quite formally, but his smile was genuine and I felt myself glowing with pride. Maybe it was exaggerated, but he seemed really pleased with what I had done, and I was glad to have made a difference, even in a small way.

"Thank you," I said, shyly.

We arranged to meet again on Wednesday evening, he put his mask back on, and I showed him out.

"Please thank your mother for the delicious cake. I really appreciate her kindness."

He had much nicer manners than I had expected, somehow, from a policeman. In fact, rather to my surprise, I liked him a lot. In other circumstances, he could have been a friend. But I was still a little wary of how he would use the information I had provided. I did not want my friends to know that I had been reporting back to the police.

It was so nice that evening to relax with my parents and be looked after. Chloe settled down early and we then sat together in the conservatory after dinner, sipping a glass of cold white wine and talking quietly, mainly about the case. Mum and Dad were both shocked about Lesley's opinions, although Dad said that he had heard racist views more often in recent times.

"Mainly among older people, who don't seem to care what others think and hark back to some kind of imaginary golden age. But from some young people too. I think Brexit, and the nasty campaign around it, allowed people to say things which would have been taboo a few years earlier. They probably always had those opinions, but now they think it is OK to express them. Sometimes loudly."

"Do you really think so, Dad? How depressing. I haven't had much contact with people recently, and I don't go on social media much, so I just hadn't come across it. None of my real friends think that way."

"There is certainly more of it among our generation," he said. "With some people, who were previously quite close friends of ours, we just can't talk about anything political, or controversial, as we actually find their views so objectionable. But of course we do have a few like-minded friends as well, thank goodness."

"It must be really hard to have to mind your tongue like that, though."

"It really is," said Mum. "One or two of my old school friends seem to read nothing but the *Daily Mail*, and are constantly ranting on about left-wing teachers and 'woke' culture. I just don't enjoy spending much time with them any more. Everything has become so divisive."

I was surprised. Mum had never been very interested in politics, although she did have very clear moral and ethical principles.

"We are a deeply divided nation at the moment, Rachel, you are right," agreed Dad, rather sententiously. "Some friends of ours have families who refuse to be vaccinated as well. It seems crazy to us, but even intelligent people are making very odd decisions just now. And conspiracy theories are really getting out of hand."

"Perhaps Lesley isn't as unusual as I thought, then. She certainly seemed to feel quite justified in her opinions, so I guess she must get support from somewhere. She was shocked when I called her out on the racism she was spouting. I'm pretty sure she has been vaccinated though - Deb told me everyone at the coffee morning had been jabbed and done a lateral flow."

"I certainly hope that is true, Sam. Otherwise it puts you all at greater risk."

I felt so grateful for having balanced, reasonable parents, and being able to discuss things like this openly with them. With special hugs all round that evening, we went off to bed and I slept like a log. I felt free from the weight of responsibility - for Chloe, the house, the investigation, everything - and just let it all go for once. No troubling dreams that I could remember, and I woke up feeling much more human, and ready to go back and meet Annette.

Mum and Dad were smiling as they waved me off as usual, but I had seen the anxiety in their faces at breakfast, when we talked about the 'suspects' I was going to meet that week. Both urged me to continue to be very careful, especially about accepting drinks from them. I understood that they were worried, but after such a good night's sleep, I felt strong enough to take on the world.

CHAPTER 16

Time with Annette and Emily

T ime was a little tight when I got back home, so I texted Annette to let her know I would be a bit late and then rushed out with the buggy to the park. I hardly recognised her out of her uniform. She was wearing makeup and looked younger and much more relaxed.

"You look great, Annette. What a lovely dress!"

Annette blushed, and looked pleased at the compliment.

"I don't often wear it, but I actually have two days off in a row, and it was such a treat to be coming out to meet you..."

I smiled at her.

"Let's go in and make our way over to the kiosk by the lake. It's so warm today, I feel like having an ice cream for once!"

Annette's eyes lit up.

"That's a great idea! I haven't done that for ages."

I was amused at her delight at the thought of such a simple amusement. It made me think that the rest of her life must be pretty tough.

We sat on the bench by the lake with our ice creams. I had insisted on paying for Annette's, which she only accepted on the understanding that she would pay next time. The babies were happily looking at the ducks and we were able to relax and eat in peace.

"Mmmm. So nice," she murmured, relishing every mouthful. "Thank you so much, Sam. That is a real treat."

"We must do it again soon. I had forgotten how much I like ice cream."

"That would be lovely. As long as I can fit it in around my shifts."

"What kind of pattern do you work?"

"The home where I work has three shifts and I usually do the evening, or sometimes the night one, although that means I don't really get any sleep at all. Normally I finish the evening shift at midnight and get home around one, so I can sleep until Simon wakes. But the night shift is a killer and as it ends at eight in the morning it is a real rush to get home before John leaves for work."

"What does he do?"

"He works shifts too, in a warehouse on the edge of town. We can usually match our shifts so that one of us is home with Simon, but sometimes it's difficult, and it's hard to get enough sleep. And we don't see very much of each other, as a rule."

"It sounds tough, especially as you are doing such a demanding job."

Annette smiled at me gratefully.

"You'd be amazed how many people think it is an easy unskilled job! Actually, with dementia sufferers, the early evening can be the worst - that's when they start to wander, and they often get anxious and upset. And it's frustrating that we are so short-staffed, so we can't spend the time we would like to with each resident. The practical tasks have to come first, like dealing with incontinence, and helping them to eat. We just don't have the time to give some of them the reassurance they need, which would actually calm down some of their dementia symptoms. I have thought about changing over to caring for people in their own homes, but you need a reliable car and mostly don't get paid for travel time, so we can't afford it."

This was the longest I had ever heard Annette speak, and I

listened with growing sympathy.

"Is it very badly paid?"

"Just over minimum wage, not enough to afford child care for Simon. We share a small car, but it's awkward when the shifts don't work out, and it takes both of us nearly an hour to walk to work if we have to. There are no buses when I come back either."

"Sounds really difficult."

"We just about manage most of the time, except when something unexpected happens like the car or the fridge breaking down. Then we're really stuck. Neither of us has family near enough to help with practical things and they have their own financial worries anyway. I can't help feeling that I live in a completely different world to most other people, especially the kind of people at the coffee morning. It's as if they can't see what is happening in our lives at all."

"I know what you mean," I responded. "I used to feel like that when I was teaching, and marking and preparation took up so much time, that I didn't seem to have any room for normal life. And even more so when Thomas died. It felt so wrong that other people's lives just went on as usual, when my world had turned upside down."

"He was a doctor, wasn't he? I think it feels the same for NHS staff as well. Like a self-contained bubble of a world that others just don't understand."

"You're right, Annette. We understood each other, but a lot of our friends just didn't get it."

"That's why I can't help feeling resentful when I hear Charlotte boasting about her lovely comfortable life. It's so hard, when I'm working all the hours I can and still can't get by properly."

"It must be so galling," I agreed. "I don't think she is very sensitive to others' feelings."

"She really isn't. Just now, you would think she would understand better, after what nearly happened to her, but she is back to being her old self, showing off about her fancy house and rich husband. I could shake her sometimes."

There was real anger in her voice.

"I haven't seen her for a while, so I didn't realise she was still behaving like that. Deb has been keeping an eye on her though. Lesley mentioned something about her seeing herself as a bit of a star somehow, having been the first 'victim'."

"Lesley! I don't know how she can criticise Charlotte. She is always going on about her problems now that her husband has left, but she is still in her nice house, paid for by him, she doesn't have to go out to work or struggle for money or anything…"

Annette's voice was rising with intense frustration.

"I must say, I find Lesley quite difficult too. She said something really racist about my friend Kate - I shouldn't tell you really, I don't like to gossip about people, but it made me so angry."

Annette turned to me in surprise.

"How could anyone be nasty about Kate? She was such a lovely person. I know it looked as if she had everything she could want, like Charlotte, but she didn't rub our noses in it. I could only envy her good fortune. She told me once that she came from a poor background, and didn't always even get enough to eat. She actually offered to lend me some money once, when I was struggling, but I couldn't do that, not borrow from someone I didn't know that well. We really try not to borrow from anyone."

"She wouldn't have minded. She had a truly generous heart."

"I could see that. She seemed to genuinely care about other people."

"Even when she was ill, she was more concerned about others than herself."

Annette looked puzzled.

"Was she ill then? I didn't know that, Sam. Someone said she had talked about being ill at the coffee morning, but I must have been out of earshot, I don't remember it at all."

I explained about Kate's cancer diagnosis, and the rough

treatment she was going through.

"I wish I had known," she responded. "I might have been able to help. My mother had cancer when I was still living at home, and I know some really useful tips on coping with the nausea and pain."

I found myself liking Annette more and more. Yes, she resented those who were better off than her, but that was understandable and her instinct was clearly to help and support. I felt frustrated that I could not help her financial situation, but hoped that if we got to know each other better, she might allow me to at least lend her some money at times.

I felt guilty that I was now so comfortably off. The tragedy of Thomas' death had brought me financial security in a way I had not expected. Life assurance had paid off the mortgage and his death in service benefit plus dependants' pension meant that I could look after Chloe at home without worrying about money. For now at least.

"Look, Annette, I'm not badly off now because of my husband's life assurance. If you are in difficulties, I could easily loan you something to tide you over. Don't let yourself get into debt over something I can help with."

I had to say it. Annette smiled at me gratefully, but there was pride and stubbornness in her voice as she shook her head and answered.

"That's very kind of you, Sam, and I do appreciate it, but John and I want to manage ourselves. We are working hard to make a better life for Simon and we will do it."

"I know you will, Annette. I respect that. But life can throw up unexpected problems. Just remember that I am here if you need me."

"I will. And thank you. Not many people have any awareness of how tough it can be on a low wage."

"I worked in a food packing plant during one of my university holidays," I said. "I was working twelve hour shifts, really tough work, but not earning enough to live on. Luckily I was able to live at home, so the money was all profit for me, but it certainly opened my eyes. I don't think many people realise how hard those on minimum wage jobs often have to work."

"You're right. Same with you teachers though! My sister-in-law is a teacher and I can't believe how many extra hours she has to work... And all people see is 'long holidays'."

We talked for some time, increasingly comfortable with each other, while we took the babies for a long walk. It felt as if Annette was already a friend, even though I hardly knew her, and we agreed to meet up again soon, shifts permitting. I was sure that she could not be the killer. It just was not in her nature, despite her resentment of Charlotte.

I suddenly realised that this investigation was pushing me into making more social contacts, and that it was actually doing me good. The terrible loneliness of the first few months after Thomas died was easing, and not just because I was back in proper touch with Deb and my family. I thought with pleasure of the interesting new people I had met: Annette, Sophy, Stephen, even Daniyaal, although he could not be counted as a friend. Life was certainly much more varied and interesting and yes, enjoyable. I felt rather guilty that the death of my lovely friend Kate had brought about this change, but I also had a warm feeling inside. I was not alone any more.

That evening, Deb rang.

"I have arranged for you to meet with Emily at her house tomorrow just after lunch, Sam. I know it's not the best time for Chloe, but she is really tied up with her business and that's the only time she could fit you in. Will that be OK?"

"As you say, it's not ideal, but I could probably leave Chloe napping and get Mum to come over and sit with her while I go. And if not, it won't do her any harm for once to miss her nap. Thanks, Deb, I appreciate it. How did you get on with Charlotte?"

"That's the main reason I'm ringing. Honestly, that bloody woman is driving me mad!"

"What has she done now?"

"Ever since Kate's death, she seems to have an inflated idea of her own importance. She wants to be at the centre of everything. She has now decided that we need to have a kind of memorial for Kate, at her house. She's somehow persuaded the vicar to say a few words and offer a prayer and now she's inviting everyone from the coffee morning. This Thursday, would you believe! Definitely not enough time to organise things properly."

Deb was talking faster and faster, a sure sign that she was upset.

"Honestly, Sam, I don't know what she's thinking of. We can't have a proper funeral or memorial for Kate for some time due to the situation with the police, and Martin and the rest of the family don't want this at all. They are just not ready. But Charlotte is pig-headed and determined and - and she will just go ahead with it willy-nilly. She asked me to make sure that you were there. And I have been 'given' a number of other people to ring and invite as well."

She did not sound at all like her normal composed self. Deb liked everything to be properly organised, not rushed through like this, with no thought of others.

"I don't think I really want to..."

"I know, Sam, I know. I don't either. But please come. I can't cope with this on my own. I just couldn't deflect her and she already has the vicar involved. And poor Celia is meant to be making cakes."

"But apart from our feelings, the likelihood is that someone there will be a murderer."

"I know. I said that to her. But she has a sense of impunity and immunity now, as the first attempt on her life failed. At least I have insisted that everyone must bring their own drinks. And no one has to eat cake if they don't want to."

I was flabbergasted. This seemed like a crazy plan. Deb wouldn't normally allow herself to be bulldozed into this, but she had clearly been knocked off balance by the suggestion and did not know how to refuse. I did not want to be involved, but I could not abandon her, not after all she had done for me, especially in the last few difficult weeks.

"Will everyone be there from the coffee mornings?" I asked.

"That's the point," said Deb, crossly. "She feels we all need to 'come together' and share our feelings of sadness. I don't know what's got into her but I can't see it being anything other than an embarrassing unmitigated disaster."

"Oh, I see. Oh dear. Definitely not something I will look forward to. Not so much a 'Memorial Coffee Morning' as a 'Memorial No Coffee Morning'! I don't like coffee mornings and I'm terrible at funerals anyway, and an MNCM really isn't my sort of thing at all," I said, trying to lighten the atmosphere.

Deb laughed half-heartedly but we agreed that we could not see a way around going to it. Feeling quite depressed at the prospect, I wrote down Emily's details and said goodbye.

I could not imagine that Daniyaal would think this would be a good idea. It seemed very risky to me. But maybe it would help to bring things to a head and we would be able to positively identify the likely killer. Maybe.

Having arranged for my parents to come and sit with Chloe while I visited Emily, I went to bed early. The good mood engendered by my night away and the pleasant chat with Annette had evaporated. Anxious dreams troubled my sleep and I woke up the next morning with a vague feeling of unfocused dread.

Our walk with Beth that morning went much more smoothly, however, and she seemed more relaxed and comfortable with being out of the house. We went a little further than usual and she coped well, until I mentioned the MNMC. Charlotte had rung her and begged her to come and she hadn't felt able to refuse.

"But I don't think I am really up to it, Sam. Not going to someone else's house. And it seems such a strange thing to do."

I reassured her that I was going too and that she would be able to cope. I offered to walk over with her and she grasped at that like a lifeline.

"If you would do that, Sam, I would be so grateful. It won't feel so scary if I am with you. Are you taking Chloe too?"

"Apparently all the babies are coming, as well as Lesley's Jackie. It should help to ease the tension."

"You are so right, Sam. I think having the little ones there too should make it much easier, at least for me. Chloe and I are good friends now, aren't we Chloe?"

Chloe twisted round in the buggy to smile at Beth. She really did seem to recognise and respond to her now. But as I walked home, I could not help feeling miserably apprehensive about Thursday morning.

Mum gave me a pep talk about the MNMC, when she came over to sit with Chloe.

"It'll be OK, Sam, don't stress about it. Think of it as part of your investigation and you will be able to keep hold of your emotions, I know you. It's a job, nothing more."

I knew she was right. Anyway, for now, I needed to focus on my meeting with Emily. She lived some way away, but I had decided to walk, thinking that the exercise would be good for me. Once again, the steady motion of walking seemed to cool my head and let the anxiety melt away. By the time I arrived at Emily's house, I felt much more normal.

As Emily came to open the door, two lively smallish dogs came running out to meet me.

"Merry! Pippin! Inside now. And don't jump up at Samantha." Emily definitely had the voice of command, and the dogs obediently calmed down and went back inside, tails wagging in welcome. Remembering that I was supposed to be asking for advice on owning a dog, I made a fuss of them both as I went in.

"Please call me Sam. Samantha just doesn't sound like me at all. The dogs are so cute! What lovely names - I've never heard them before."

"We called them after the hobbits in The Lord of the Rings. We both loved the film and they seemed like good, but original names. You have to think carefully when you choose a dog's name. Will you feel comfortable shouting it across a field? Some names just sound incredibly silly when you are out and about."

I laughed.

"That's so true! It could be very embarrassing. But Merry and Pippin sound good as names."

Emily invited me into the sitting room and offered me a drink. I countered with my tale of trying to lose weight - I had my own water bottle with me anyway. Emily smiled at me, with a shrewd look in her eye.

"Very sensible. I'm being careful about taking drinks from anyone just now too."

I flushed a bit. Was I that transparent?

"Anyway, sit down and tell me what you would like to know."

I had prepared some questions about whether it was better to wait until Chloe was older, or go for getting a dog now, and what type of breed was best for a house with a young child. Emily asked me initially why I wanted to get a dog in the first place.

"It's not just the pandemic, my life has changed so much, with Thomas dying, and giving up work for now. I think it will be good company for me, and also for Chloe. I didn't want her to be an only child, but now - well, maybe a pet might be just the right thing for her."

Emily talked me through the possibilities, but said that, in her opinion, it would be better to wait until Chloe was older.

"Dogs need a lot of attention and training in the early stages and so do toddlers! I understand that a dog could be a good companion for Chloe later, but just now it would only add to your burdens and I don't think you would see much benefit. Either the dog or Chloe might be jealous and that can be a recipe for disaster. Even if you took on an older rescue dog, you still need time to establish the hierarchy within the home and that can be very tricky with an unpredictable baby or toddler in the family."

"I hadn't thought of that," I admitted. Of course, I had not really been thinking of getting a dog at all, although the idea had been growing on me in the last couple of days.

"People don't tend to think things through properly before taking on a dog. It's a very big long-term commitment and shouldn't be taken lightly," said Emily, with a touch of severity. "Have you thought about getting a cat? Much easier to look after, but the right one might give you the company you are looking for."

I looked at her in surprise.

"I thought you were a dog person! I'm surprised to hear you recommending a cat."

Emily laughed.

"You don't have to be one or the other, you know. I have dogs now, but we had a cat previously, when the children were smaller. I am an animal lover, rather than just a dog lover."

"I suppose I just thought - well, don't you have a dog grooming business?"

"I do, but I have always loved animals in general. When I was at school, I was quite academic, and everyone assumed that I would want to be a vet or veterinary nurse. But I don't want to work with sick animals all day, and definitely don't want to have to put them down. I much prefer working with healthy, happy dogs and their owners."

I had never thought about it that way before. I suppose I had always assumed that if you loved being with animals you would go down the vet line. But it made sense really. I looked at Emily with new respect. She certainly knew her own mind.

"I guess the pandemic must have been difficult for you."

"Well, lockdown was tricky, as you will imagine. No money coming in at all. But luckily my husband was furloughed, so we coped, and since things have opened up, business has been booming. Lots of new people bought or adopted dogs and some of them need a great deal of help and advice, not just about grooming, but also about looking after their new pets. I have a waiting list at the moment and could be working all day, every day. But I want to fit my work around the family as much as possible."

Emily sounded such a grounded, sensible person. Someone who really had her life sorted. Not killer material, I would have thought, but you never know. I had promised to probe.

"Did you hear that Charlotte wants to do some kind of memorial meeting for Kate on Thursday? Deb and I are calling it the

MNMC - Memorial no coffee morning! What do you think about the idea?" I asked, rather tentatively.

"Oh dear, yes," she responded, with a grimace. "Not my sort of thing at all, and I didn't even know Kate very well. But Charlotte made me promise that I would go. She put me on the spot and I couldn't think of a good enough excuse."

"Is she a close friend of yours?" I asked.

"Well, that's difficult to say. She seems to like to talk to me and our children are similar in age so we're sometimes thrown together. She can be very kind and generous, but she does live in her own little world, and has a tendency to be rather self-centred. I know I could ask her for help if I needed it, but she would never notice that I was in difficulties. I find her ambition for her children a bit hard to take, if you really want to know. She seems to expect me to feel the same and I just don't. I think Asians have a reputation for being pushy parents, so she just assumes I will be like that too."

"Do you have to put up with much racism around here? I was really shocked at something Lesley said to me the other day, and it sounds as if Charlotte tends to follow stereotypes too."

"Oh, Charlotte type-casts everyone, but she isn't racist, at least not consciously. She would be just as likely to assume she knew what motivated you, because you were a teacher! She isn't really interested in what people think, so she just assumes that she knows. I'm sorry, that sounds really mean and judgemental. But I have spent a lot of time with her and I know how she ticks. Lesley, though - that's different. I think she does have racist tendencies, even though she would absolutely deny that they were racist. When we first met, she asked me what my other name was, my Asian name!"

"She didn't! How rude."

"I know. I had to explain that my mother just really admired Emily Pankhurst and the suffragettes and chose this name because she liked it, no other reason. She grew up in Manchester and had a real obsession with women's rights and education. But fortunately she decided that Emmeline would be going too far! I don't know if I could have coped with that."

"That was a narrow escape for you," I agreed.

"I don't think Lesley liked your friend Kate much, either," said Emily, more seriously. "She made some snide remarks about her. But that wasn't unique to Kate. She tends to judge people very easily."

"I got that impression too. She really dislikes Charlotte. I wonder if she will be there on Thursday."

"Oh, I should think she will go. She's a great one for gossip and she wouldn't want to feel that she was missing out. I'm really sorry, Sam, but I will have to go now. I have an appointment in fifteen minutes."

"Of course, Emily. Thank you so much for seeing me and spending so much time explaining things to me. I'm pretty sure you are right that a dog wouldn't fit into my life just now, but I will think about a cat instead."

"If you do decide to go ahead, I suggest an older rescue cat rather than a kitten. They really need adopting and the right kind of cat will fit easily into your routine."

While we were still talking, we went to the door, I thanked her again and left. It had been an interesting hour. Emily seemed to be a very perceptive woman, with a very clear-sighted view of the people she interacted with. Her observations, especially about Charlotte and Lesley, were helpful and tended to confirm my own impressions. I suppose we all tend to think that people who agree with us show good judgement!

CHAPTER 17

The dreaded MNCM

O n my way back home, I ran - almost literally - into Celia. She was going in the opposite direction, but her whole focus was on her phone and she very nearly walked into me. At the last minute, she looked up and saw me.

"Sorry, Mrs - Sam. I should have been looking where I was going."

"You look very stressed. Is there anything I can do?"

Celia looked surprised that I had noticed. She took a deep breath, before beginning to air her grievances.

"I do feel rather stressed, yes, you're right. I do expect to be asked before being told - yes, told! - that I am making cakes for Charlotte's ridiculous 'memorial' morning. I suppose Stephen either offered or agreed on my behalf, because he never thinks about all the work he is making for me, but even so, it would have been normal politeness for Charlotte to have rung and asked me. As it is, she has had the cheek to send me a list of the cakes she wants me to bake and how many people each one should serve! I'm so annoyed with her, and with Stephen too."

"Oh dear, that sounds really unfair. Would you like me to make one of the cakes?"

"You? Do you bake at all?" Celia's obvious surprise at my

offer could have been insulting, if I had chosen to take it that way.

"Not on your level, Celia - I'm no expert. But I can follow a recipe and if you give me a simple one, I'm sure I can manage something edible."

"I'm sorry, Sam, that was very rude of me, especially when you are being so kind. I know you are probably busy too, but I would really appreciate it if you could make one for me - maybe the coffee and walnut traybake? Would that be OK?"

I smiled. "I'm sure I can do that. And coffee cake is one of my favourites. Shall I get Deb to make one too? She makes a mean carrot cake, if that's on the list."

"Would you? That one can be quite time-consuming and I have to help at the toddler group this afternoon."

"No problem, Celia. Glad to help and I'm sure Deb will be too. It's all very last minute, isn't it?"

Celia's face darkened with renewed annoyance.

"It certainly is. I don't know what she's thinking, suddenly arranging something like this. Typical Charlotte, not thinking of all the work she is making for other people ..."

"I have to say that I am not looking forward to it at all. Do you know what she has planned?"

But Celia knew no more than me. She thanked me again for helping out, still seeming surprised that I would. She obviously had a very low opinion of me.

By the time I got home, Chloe was up and about, and playing happily on her mat in the living room. When I told Mum that I had offered to make a cake for Celia, she immediately said that she would make the carrot cake so that I would not need to bother Deb.

"If you're sure, Mum, that would be brilliant. Deb seemed very stressed about this whole stupid no coffee morning when she told me about it and I would rather not add to her burdens. I can pick it up tomorrow evening when I come and report to Daniyaal."

That afternoon, Chloe and I went to the shop for ingredients and I made the coffee cake. I took my time over it, as it was a couple of years since I had made a cake from scratch. Chloe sat in her high chair watching and laughing as the flour went everywhere and the icing sugar made a cloud. I could imagine us baking together in the future and was determined to get back into making cakes and biscuits more regularly. In the end, I was quite pleased with how the traybake came out, with the decoration neat and regular and pieces marked out on the icing.

"I know it's not *Bake Off* standard, but I think that's not too bad, Chloe," I said when it was done.

When I saw Mum's carrot cake on the following day, I was not quite so proud of myself. It was beautiful, decorated with tiny orange carrots with little green leaves.

"You don't need to thank me, Sam - I enjoyed it. I love baking, as you know, but your Dad and I shouldn't eat too much cake, so I don't get to do it as often as I would like."

"I'd forgotten how good you were at cakes. That lemon drizzle you made last time I was here was amazing, Daniyaal loved it. Can you pass me some of your favourite recipes, so that I can bake with Chloe?"

Mum was delighted at the idea and went off to search out her file of tried and tested recipes. When Daniyaal arrived, on time as usual, I filled him in on what I had found out from Annette and Emily and told him about Charlotte's plans.

"I have to agree with you that it is a very risky thing to arrange at this point in the investigation, Sam. The murderer will be there and we can't know how they will react. But it is also a great opportunity for us to see all the suspects interacting. If I can fit it in, I will try to pop in for half an hour or so. I might even try to drag the inspector along, although it is not at all her sort of thing."

"But surely then people will know that someone has been talking to you. I thought you wanted to keep that secret."

"Oh, I won't let on that I expected you all to be there," he reassured me, with an easy confident smile. "I'll just say that I wanted to talk to Charlotte in more detail about what happened to her. I do, in fact, so I can kill two birds with one stone."

I had to be satisfied with that, but I was a bit worried that I might give myself away to the others by saying something stupid. I had become quite comfortable with him, and was unsure how to cover that up when the others were around. Yet another thing to be anxious about.

It was cloudy and cool on Thursday morning, so I put an extra layer of clothes on Chloe and wore a bright red cardigan myself. No one had said whether there was any kind of dress code, but I was definitely not going to wear black. Kate would certainly not have wanted that. In fact, it did not feel to me as if the event really had anything to do with Kate. It was all about Charlotte. I put my carefully boxed cakes under the buggy and set off to collect Beth.

She looked awful. I was feeling anxious myself, but I could see that Beth was much worse. I took her hand and led her to the buggy.

"It'll be OK, Beth, I promise. I'll be there too and you can sit with me and Chloe."

"That's the only reason I'm going. I feel so sick," said Beth, in a low unsteady voice.

"Just try to breathe slowly, Beth. Out for longer than in. I'll do it too!"

So we walked along, breathing together, and it was true, it really did help. When we arrived at Charlotte's house, the garden gate was open, so we went in that way. Beth stayed with Chloe, while I took my cakes over to the table on the patio, where Celia was setting hers out. She had those special net cloche covers to put over them, to keep insects away.

"These look great, Sam," she said. "Did Deb really make this carrot cake? It's beautiful. I had no idea she was so good at decoration."

"My Mum made it, actually. She offered and I didn't want to put any more pressure on Deb. She already seemed a bit stressed about what was going to happen this morning."

"I'm not surprised at all. The whole thing is a ridiculous

farce." Celia spoke snappily as she put covers over my cakes as well.

Charlotte came to the patio door and clapped her hands imperiously. She still looked pale and drawn, with yellowish shadows under her eyes, but you could see that she was relishing being the centre of attention. She looked slowly around the garden at everyone, as if she was counting us, and made sure that we were all listening to her.

"Can you all please come inside now? Feel free to wear a mask if you want to, but I assume everyone has done a test today anyway, so you don't have to, if you would rather not."

She led the way into the large sitting room. She had set out chairs in a large, widely spaced circle, with herself in an armchair at the top end. I put my arm round Beth and we found a place near the door. Beth sat on a chair and I settled myself and Chloe on the carpet by her feet. Annette and Sophy were also both on the floor with their babies, but Lesley chose a comfortable wicker chair to sit on with Charlie. I waved Jackie over and whispered: "You can sit with me and Chloe if you like." The little girl sat very close to me, looking nervous as usual. Most of us had masks on, but Lesley hadn't bothered and looked down on us with pitying superiority. I was very glad of my mask. It should disguise any emotions I struggled with.

Stephen was standing in the corner, looking irritated, rather apprehensive and uncomfortable. I gave him a smile, forgetting that he would not be able to see it properly. But he seemed to know and gave me a tentative smile back. He had a mask in his hands and was twisting it nervously.

"I've asked the vicar to start us off in prayer," said Charlotte, self-importantly. "Please, Stephen, do start."

I saw Emily look round at Stephen, startled. She had obviously not been warned that there would be a religious section. Lesley's lips tightened, and she shot Stephen a look of contempt. I whispered to Jackie to close her eyes as the prayer began.

"Heavenly Father, we thank you for Kate's life and the blessing she has been to her family and friends. Thank you that she now has no more pain or distress and that she is safe with you. We ask you to comfort her family, especially Martin and the children, at this time of mourning and sadness. We ask you to be with all of her friends as they grieve, particularly Deb and Sam who were so close to her. Grant them your peace at this troubled time. In Jesus' name, Amen."

I looked up at Stephen with gratitude. Such a perfect prayer. I had tears in my eyes, but the emotion was manageable.

"But - Vicar, is that all? Aren't you going to pray for Kate's soul? I was going to light this candle," Charlotte said in a very disappointed voice. "I thought it would make a really moving ceremony. Isn't there a proper prayer, one from the Prayer Book, for situations like this?"

For once, Stephen responded firmly.

"No, Charlotte, I don't believe in praying for the dead, just for those left behind. Kate is safe with the Lord now, and does not need our prayers. If you want to light a candle, that is fine, but I won't pray for her soul now."

"But our old vicar used to do a lovely service, with prayers for the rest of departed souls, and candles and everything!"

"I know some Anglicans like to do that, but it isn't my way. I'm sorry, Charlotte, but that is my final word on the matter."

Charlotte looked very cross. She had set her heart on a ritual and expected 'her' vicar to deliver what she wanted. I was so glad that Stephen had the courage to stand up to her. She put down her candle next to a whole box of them.

"I thought everyone would come up and light a candle, all of you, one by one. But never mind. I suppose this will be easier to manage."

She looked around the room with satisfaction. At least we had all come together and she had us where she wanted us. Then came the bombshell, delivered in a saccharine sweet and slightly triumphant voice.

"So, what we will all do now is this: everyone will say a few words in turn about what Kate meant to them and how they miss her or what they are feeling sad about. You don't need to have anything prepared - just speak from the heart. You can stand up or come to the front if you like, or just speak from where you are sitting. It will be lovely to hear your heartfelt tributes - I am so looking forward to this."

There was a collective gasp of shock. I could hear Beth behind me murmuring "No, oh no, please no" and feel her legs starting to shake. I knew that under the mask my mouth had dropped open. I could not believe what I was hearing. She could not possibly be intending to do this.

I have never been so grateful to hear Deb's crisp confident voice.

"No, Charlotte, we are certainly not going to do that. Some of us here didn't even know Kate well, and those of us who did - well, this is neither the time nor the place." Her voice shook slightly, but she swallowed hard and got it back under control.

"But I thought -" wailed Charlotte, totally shocked that anyone could reject her beautiful suggestion.

"That's the trouble, Charlotte - you didn't think. You didn't ask any of us what we wanted to do. You just thought of yourself. And because you've been unwell, and I felt sorry for you, I went along with it. But I am definitely not going to take part in any kind of emotional striptease, for you or anyone else. If people want to talk about Kate over a nice piece of cake, well that's fine, it's up to them. But sitting here parading our emotions in front of everyone else - no way. There's no point in crying, I'm not going to listen to you. Come on Sam, let's get out of here."

Deb strode across the room to the patio doors. Someone - Lesley probably - sniggered and then turned it into a cough, but everyone else was stunned into silence. I scrambled to my feet, picked up Chloe, helped Beth up and stumbled outside with her. The emotional tension gave way suddenly and I began to sob angrily, but silently, behind my mask. Chloe was starting to cry too, affected by the storm of emotions fizzing in the air. Beth collapsed into a garden chair and stared into space, slowly rocking backwards and forwards.

"Let me have Chloe for a bit, Sam," said Sophy quietly. "Annette and I will look after her. You need a bit of peace."

Unresisting, I let her take the baby from me and nodded mutely. Chloe calmed down immediately as soon as I let her go. I walked over to a green bench under a shady tree and slumped down onto it. My mask was now soaked with tears and my nose was running profusely. Angrily I pulled it off and stuffed it into my pocket, before burying my face in a large tissue. 'How could she, how could she, how could she think of doing that' was running round in my head. I was crying, but the emotion I felt most strongly was fury.

Suddenly I felt a tentative hand just touch my shoulder and someone sat down on the bench beside me. With a deep breath, I looked up. It was Stephen.

"I'm so very sorry, Sam. I had no idea what Charlotte was planning to do. I would have stopped her, or at least warned you not to come. I'm sorry."

"It's not your fault," I managed to say. "I suppose she means well, but..."

With unaccustomed firmness, he denied that.

"No, I'm sorry to have to say it, but your friend Deb was right. Charlotte did not think of anyone but herself. I am afraid that she can be a very selfish woman. Anyway, it was completely inappropriate. Now, I am going to walk you home. You have had enough."

I protested that I did not need anyone to walk me home, but he insisted.

"We will take Beth back on the way. Sophy is putting Chloe in the buggy for you and Annette is telling Deb what we are doing."

"Oh, Deb - is she all right? I've never known her to speak out like that. She's been so good with Charlotte, so patient. But I was so thankful that she put a stop to it all."

I looked round and could see Deb sitting on the patio with Emily and Celia.

"She was magnificent," said Stephen. "But I think the reaction is setting in now and she too will be off home very soon. Everyone will, I think. Come on, now, Sam."

We scooped up poor Beth, who was still rocking herself, arms tightly wrapped around her body. Stephen spoke quietly and calmly to her and I could see the tension starting to leave her body. When we got to the buggy, she automatically took the handle as usual and we left by the garden gate, after thanking Sophy and Annette for their help. Charlotte was nowhere to be seen, thank goodness.

Walking slowly to let the emotions calm down gradually, we finally reached Beth's house. She tried to smile as she said goodbye, but I could see how shaken she was. I knew this had set her back, but insisted on arranging to go for another walk with her on Saturday. She did not have the strength to argue and went wearily inside, shutting the door immediately.

Stephen and I walked on in silence. Chloe had dropped off to sleep in her buggy and it was very quiet. Eventually we arrived home.

"Thank you so much, Stephen," I said quietly. "You deserve a hug for doing that, but I guess it would not be wise. I - I appreciated your prayer as well, you know."

Stephen took my hand, very gently, and held it between his two hands. Somehow it felt like a hug.

"Please look after yourself, Sam," he said. "This has been a very difficult morning and you need some time to recover. Get your Mum to come over if you can, to look after Chloe. And let me know if there is anything, anything at all, that I can do to help."

I couldn't look at him, because I knew the tears would come again. I squeezed his hand and turned to go into the house.

CHAPTER 18

Fallout

I was not at all surprised to receive a call from Deb that evening. I knew she would need to talk through what had happened.

"How are you now, Sam? I hope you are feeling a bit better. I was so grateful to Stephen for getting you and Beth out of the place so quickly."

"I'm OK, thanks, Deb. You are right - Stephen was a big help. I don't know who told him to do it, but - "

"No one did. He just decided. I have to say, I saw a different side of him this morning and I have a lot more respect for him now."

"I told you he was nice."

"I know you did, but there is a difference between 'nice' and 'decisive'. He really took charge. I could see that Celia was pretty shocked at how firm he was. She was about to protest about him taking you home, when he shut her up with a really fierce glare. I've never seen him look like that before."

I was surprised too. That did not sound like the Stephen I thought I knew.

"Anyway, I'm glad you were out of it, but you missed all the excitement!"

"Excitement? What do you mean? Surely there wasn't any more drama to come?"

"There really was. Just after you left, the doorbell rang and Sophy trotted off to see who it was. The rest of us were just sitting like zombies in the garden, eating cake (by the way, your coffee cake was delicious) and wondering how soon we could leave. I could hear Charlotte muttering and sobbing in the living room. No one paid her any attention until Lesley, of all people, went in to talk to her and calm her down."

Deb did not sound like herself at all. Her mind did not usually flit around like this. She was always clear when she described things.

"Deb, calm down. What is it? Who was at the door?"

I heard her take a breath.

"You're right. I'm going to sit down. Too much emotion today. OK. It was the police at the door, that good-looking Sergeant Evans, you know - the one you saw a couple of times."

"Oh, him," was all I could think of to say. I needed to be careful now. "What was he doing there?"

"Apparently he had come to interview Charlotte in more depth about what had happened to her. He didn't expect a houseful - or rather a 'gardenful'. He was obviously shocked."

"What did he say?"

"He brought Charlotte and Lesley outside, got everyone sitting down, and then took his mask off and spoke to all of us at once. You could see he was quite angry. He told us that we were stupid to take the risk of meeting like this in a large group, not because of Covid or anything, but because of the murder. He kept using the words 'murderer' and 'killer' as if he wanted to shock us. And it did. It was like a slap in the face."

"I can imagine it was," I murmured.

"He said the killer was there (he didn't seem to notice that Beth and Stephen had left), among us, and we couldn't be sure how they would behave. We shouldn't meet up as a whole group again until the murderer was caught. And they were close to making an arrest, so it would not be long."

"What! He said that?"

I had not expected that at all. Daniyaal had not given me any hint that they were closing in on a suspect. Rather the opposite.

"I know. Who can it be? He looked round at everyone when he said it, there was no hint at who he meant. But it sounds as if they must be making progress."

"I suppose they must. Well, that is a good thing, if it is true. The whole thing is hanging over us and it's oppressive, having to be careful all the time, and to suspect everyone. And Kate's killer needs to be caught."

"You're dead right, Sam. This can't go on much longer. Anyway, he sent us all off with a flea in our ear and stayed there to talk to Charlotte. Lesley actually offered to stay with her, but she refused. She looked rather subdued, as well she might. It was her fault that we were all there, after all, apart from the way she upset everyone."

"I see what you mean about excitement. A shock for all of you. Did you pick up anything which might show who the killer is? I'm afraid I was worse than useless. Sorry for letting it upset me so much."

"Don't apologise - it is Charlotte who should say sorry, not you! I was much the same, I'm afraid, just too wound up to think straight. But I will try to go over it all in my mind later and see if anything comes to the surface."

"Me, too - I will try, anyway."

"I feel better for talking to you, Sam. It helps. Jack is working late tonight and doesn't really understand why I'm getting involved in all this and I can't talk to the kids about it."

"It helps me to be able to talk to someone openly too," I agreed, still feeling guilty that I had not told her about Daniyaal.

"I suddenly feel really exhausted. I guess all the adrenaline is gone. Time for bed, I think."

We agreed to talk again on Saturday and hung up. Deb obviously felt relieved to have talked it out, but she had given me some new things to think about and they kept whirling round in my head. Did Daniyaal really have a chief suspect? Who could it be? Had he been keeping their actual progress from me in case I let something slip? We had agreed to meet on Friday evening to talk about what had happened at the memorial morning, so I would not have too long to wait to find out.

CHAPTER 19

Another death

In fact, Daniyaal called on Friday afternoon. His voice sounded different, very cool and professional. Immediately I knew something was wrong.

"What is it, Daniyaal? Do you need to rearrange our meeting?"

"It's not that, although, yes, we will need to rearrange to Saturday, if that is OK with you. I will be busy all night, I think. I have some bad news for you."

I started to tremble and held my breath. Not more bad news. Not another friend gone.

"I'm afraid Charlotte has been found dead. In her home."

A guilty feeling of relief surged through me. At least it was not someone I was close to. If I was honest, not someone I really cared about.

"Oh no, what happened? Another murder?" I tried to keep the relief out of my voice.

"I can't give you much detail right now, we're still investigating, as you will imagine. But yes, it looks like another murder. We'll talk tomorrow, but I am partly ringing to ask you to be extremely careful. Whoever this killer is, they are determined and ruthless. Don't take any risks just now and don't push any difficult questions. You've been really helpful to me, but you won't be any help if you are the next victim."

I gasped.

"Do you really think I could be in that much danger now?"

"Not just you, any of your group, but yes, you in particular, if it comes out that you have been helping us. I will say more tomorrow, but for now, would you please think of going to stay with your family for a few days? I would be happier knowing that you are not alone in that house."

His voice sounded warmer now, but it was frightening how worried he seemed.

"I - I'll ring my parents now and see if I can go. Thank you for looking out for me."

"I don't want to feel that I have put you in serious danger, Sam. OK, I must go now. A lot of things to process, as you can imagine. See you tomorrow at around half past six."

The phone dropped out of my hand onto the sofa. It must be serious, if he was so urgent about me leaving the house. I was surprised to find that my legs were shaking and I felt weak and wobbly inside. I looked over at Chloe and felt an icy rush of fear for her. Immediately I picked up the phone and called Mum. She was surprised to hear from me, but very happy to put us up for a few days. I did not begin to try to explain why. That would wait until I got there.

I wandered rather aimlessly around the house picking up things I thought we might need, then suddenly sensed the urgency afresh and bundled Chloe, the luggage and buggy into the car. Afterwards, I could not remember the drive at all, just the moment when I arrived and fell into Dad's arms, sobbing with relief.

Once we had everything inside and Chloe was settled, my parents wanted to know what had happened. I was not able to be very coherent, and they needed to ask questions to find their way through the maze of my confusing observations, as I mixed up what had happened at the memorial and Charlotte's death, but in the end they had it clear. Dad sat back in his chair and looked at me solemnly.

"Your Daniyaal is right, Sam. This is a very serious situation and you are definitely at risk, although you have at least kept the fact that you are working with the police quiet. Even without that, it must be obvious to most of them that you and Deb are asking questions and that means that you could have unknowingly upset someone, who is clearly ready to kill."

"He's not 'my' Daniyaal, Dad. But I suppose you are right - and so is he. I ought to warn Deb to be careful too."

He agreed and went to make a cup of tea for me while I tried ringing her. Unfortunately she was already on the phone, so I sent her a message to ring me as soon as possible and to be careful.

As I sipped my tea, I could feel the tension slowly melting away. At least Chloe was safe here and it was good to be right away from everyone. I had not often stayed overnight at my old home since marrying Thomas, since we did not live far enough away to make it necessary, but now, on my own again, it felt like a sanctuary. My own house, which had been my place of safety during the pandemic, suddenly felt exposed to much more risk. But I knew that I would be eager to go back soon, once I had my confidence back.

The phone rang, jarringly, bringing me back to the present. It was Deb.

"Have you heard, Sam? The news?"

I suddenly realised that I only knew because Daniyaal had told me and I could not say that to Deb.

"Yes - it's dreadful, isn't it? Scary."

"I've just been talking to Michael. He and the kids are in a terrible state. The house is a crime scene and I offered them the chance to come and stay with us, but they are going to his parents in Oxfordshire. After this, I don't know if they will ever come back."

"You are so good to be thinking of them. I just hadn't thought about how it would affect them. I'm afraid I was just bound up in feeling shocked, and anxious too, but mainly shocked. I just can't fathom it."

"I know what you mean, Sam. She was, at times, a very irritating woman and her behaviour on Thursday was pretty unforgivable, but she didn't deserve to die for it. And if she could be killed like that, it could be any of us."

"Do you know what happened or what the police are doing?"

"No, Michael had no idea. He just collected the minimum of things for him and the children and had to leave. I guess we will find out soon, when they arrest someone. They said they were close to an arrest before, so hopefully…"

"I really hope you are right. We can't go on like this. I'm staying with Mum and Dad for a few days just to be with someone, and Dad says that you and I must be much more careful and avoid asking too many questions. He thinks we might really be at risk."

It was good to be able to report my father's concern, since I could not mention Daniyaal.

"I suppose he might have something there. Let's think about it over the weekend and see what happens. I just can't think straight at the moment. But now that you mention it, Jack was very worried when I told him on the phone, and he insisted that I stay home and not meet up with any of the group. So I guess he has the same concerns. Oh, I don't know, part of me feels that it can't be real, but there is a bit of a knot in my stomach."

"Me too, Deb, me too. Let's just take a step back for now."

We agreed to have a quiet weekend with family and leave the police to do their work. I messaged Beth to cancel our planned outing and did my best to put it all out of my mind.

Saturday passed peacefully with a family walk in the woods in the morning, and quiet time in the garden after Chloe's nap. The murders felt distant, somehow unreal, in the warm summer sunshine. They occasionally came up in conversation, but felt more like a puzzle than a direct threat. I refused to think about the warnings from Daniyaal and my father. That was another world.

We had an early dinner together with Chloe and she settled quickly, tired after so much fresh air and attention. I almost dozed myself, sitting quietly with Mum and Dad, but was jerked out of the pleasant feeling by the doorbell. Daniyaal was here.

Dad insisted that we all sit in the conservatory with the doors open, so that Daniyaal could take off his mask, since Chloe was in bed. He was determined that he and Mum would hear what was going on and take part in any discussions.

"I'm very concerned about this recent development, Sergeant Evans. I feel that my daughter, and even my granddaughter, are now definitely at risk. And I would like to know what you are going to do about it."

Mum nodded her agreement. She was looking anxious and strained. I had not realised what an impact it was having on her.

"I completely understand, Mr Hambledon. I have also reassessed the risk to Sam and that is why I asked her to come and stay here for a while. I don't see a direct threat at the moment, but with this killer, you just can't tell and I can't expose her to more danger."

Daniyaal spoke in a quiet and very professional voice, but there was genuine concern in his eyes.

"But Daniyaal, Deb said you told everyone on Thursday that you were close to making an arrest. Surely if you know who it is, you can pick them up now."

Daniyaal looked slightly guilty. Not a look I was used to seeing on his face.

"I'm afraid that was a lie, Sam. The inspector suggested that we needed to shake things up, make the killer nervous so that they would be more likely to make a mistake and reveal themselves. We thought if we pretended to have made more progress than we have, it would have the desired effect. Unfortunately it seems to have done more than that - it could be why the murderer attacked Charlotte again."

"But I thought you interviewed her after everyone had gone."

"She wasn't in a fit state to answer questions sensibly, so I actually arranged to see her on Friday afternoon."

I looked at him in horror.

"You mean someone killed her on Friday to prevent her talking to you! But what could she have had to say that would help? Deb talked to her a lot and didn't get anything useful."

"Well, she might not have realised that something was important. Probably Charlotte didn't either. Just something around the coffee she drank that first morning, perhaps. Or there may have been nothing at all. The killer may just have been afraid that there was something she could tell us and decided not to take the risk."

"But surely killing her that way must have been really risky too. It's not as if we were all there at the time, so the pool of suspects must be smaller. Don't you have any idea who did it? And how did she die anyway?"

Carefully, methodically, Daniyaal went through what they knew. Charlotte died from an overdose of soluble paracetamol and codeine. Since she already had liver damage, it killed her much more quickly and the dose probably wouldn't have been fatal for someone in good health. It appeared to have been mixed with very strong orange squash - there was residue left in a glass.

"Surely Charlotte wouldn't have voluntarily taken something like that. Are you certain it wasn't suicide? She did have a very difficult morning on Thursday, I suppose."

"It was designed to look like suicide, we think, as with the first attempt on her life. Several empty packets of the stuff had been left conspicuously by the glass in the kitchen. However, they had absolutely no fingerprints on them, so we think they were planted afterwards, once Charlotte began to feel woozy and lay down in the sitting room."

"Can't you find out who bought them? You have to ask at the pharmacy counter for drugs like that don't you?"

Mum was nodding - she had bought similar things for my aunt when she had terrible back pain.

"We'll try, of course, but no record is kept of who buys it and there are so many pharmacies it could have been bought from. We might get lucky - someone might remember a face, but we can't count on it."

"I still don't understand why Charlotte would have taken something like that. It would taste foul."

"We don't know for sure, but apparently she had told her husband that several friends were coming round that morning and one had a suggestion for a tonic to help with her liver damage symptoms. She didn't say who, unfortunately, and Michael was in a rush so he didn't really take it in. She mentioned that the vicar was going round at lunchtime 'to make peace'. We don't know if he is the friend with the tonic that she meant or if that was a separate person."

"I presume you have spoken to him already though. I am sure he wouldn't have anything to do with it."

Apparently Stephen admitted to having gone round at midday, but said that Charlotte would not let him in. She said that she was not feeling well and needed to lie down, but would see him on Saturday if he came over then. He thought she looked pale and sounded shaky, so he agreed to come back the next day.

"Obviously, he has to be a suspect, I'm afraid, Sam. By his own account, he must have been the last person to see her alive and he admitted that they had not parted on good terms on Thursday."

"I guess that is true, but I know he wouldn't kill her. He's not like that. And it sounds as if other people went to see Charlotte that morning anyway."

"We just don't know if that's true. He's the only one to admit to going. We did house to house enquiries as normal, but you know what it is like round there. All those big houses with large gardens, hedges and driveways. Nobody saw a thing, not even the vicar on his bike and he isn't exactly inconspicuous. So we can't know if anyone else went there, although we're obviously starting to question everyone who was at the coffee morning on Thursday. But if they know there has been another murder, even an innocent person might not be truthful about it."

"Do you want me to try to find out?"

My parents both said 'no' together and Daniyaal frowned at me.

"Did you not listen to me when I said I couldn't risk you any more? Of course not. We will do routine interviews and see what comes out, if anything."

I understood what he was saying, and was relieved in a way, but still felt I had to be involved.

"Can you get a good idea of exactly when she was poisoned? I remember you said it was quite clear last time that Kate had drunk the poison at the coffee morning."

"It's not as clear-cut this time, I'm afraid, due to the bad state of Charlotte's liver. We rushed through a post-mortem last night, as we are now dealing with an urgent situation, a possible serial killer, but it only showed that she had ingested the drug some time during the morning. So we're back to looking at motivation, alibis if anyone has them, and putting pressure on the possible suspects."

The words 'serial killer' were shocking. Somehow I had associated them with overt violence, sadistic murders, not the poisoning of two ordinary women in our quiet little town.

"I would like you, therefore, to tell me everything you can remember about what happened on Thursday morning. It could be very important, Sam."

Daniyaal always sounded so professional and measured when he spoke. I did not know why, but I found his slightly over-formal way of expressing himself reassuring somehow.

Having put my thoughts in order when going through the events with my parents, my account was rather more fluent this time. I tried to focus on how people reacted to Charlotte, but it was difficult, as I had been so busy reacting myself. Closing my eyes helped me to visualise the scene more clearly, but I was not sure that anything I said helped at all. I knew how upset Beth had been, and how angry Celia was about the whole thing, but that was about all.

"I'm sorry I haven't been much help," I apologised, when

Daniyaal had finished recording and questioning me.

"It all helps to position people and give us an idea of how relationships were strained that day," he answered. "It sounds as if most of the group was angry with Charlotte for her insensitivity, but the people who really turned on her, unexpectedly, were your friend Deb and the vicar. Not high on the suspect list before now, and obviously a clever killer avoids showing open hostility, but we have to look at them more closely at this point."

I shook my head emphatically.

"I'm positive that Stephen would never do anything like that, and I can assure you that Deb is definitely not the killer. She and I have been investigating the murder together. And she loved Kate so much. It's just not possible."

Daniyaal looked doubtful but allowed himself to appear to be persuaded.

"You may well be right. I really could do with getting her detailed account of what happened too, as she was still there when I arrived, and she will have seen how the others reacted. But I won't get much opinion or detail from her in a formal interview."

"I could arrange for her to come here if you like. I actually wanted to ask if I could tell her that I have been reporting back to you. It's been very uncomfortable keeping secrets from my best friend."

Daniyaal smiled sympathetically.

"I know it has been tough for you, Sam. I suppose it won't make much difference at this point. Everyone knows the two of you have been asking questions, as your father pointed out. I agree that she is not a likely murderer, but she could be a very valuable witness."

I nodded vigorously.

"And she spent a lot of time with Charlotte after the apparent 'suicide attempt', so she may be able to help you there."

"Very well. If it is acceptable to Mr and Mrs Hambledon, could you arrange for her to come over tomorrow morning? I would like to talk to her as soon as possible."

Mum and Dad agreed and we left it that I would call Deb to set it up. With repeated serious warnings to me to take care if I went back to town, Daniyaal left and walked out quietly to his anonymous grey car.

CHAPTER 20

Deb

I chose to ring Deb as soon as possible after Daniyaal left, so that I would not have time to worry about confessing my deception to her. My heart was in my mouth, however, as she picked up. I did not want to spoil our friendship. It was so important to me.

"I have to tell you something, Deb, and I don't know if you will be angry with me about it. Please understand, if you can, that I didn't want to leave you out." I took a deep, slightly shaky breath.

"Ever since Kate's murder came out, I've been reporting regularly to Da - to Sergeant Evans on what you and I have found out. He came to me because I had only been at the first coffee morning with Charlotte, so I couldn't be a suspect. I told him that there was no way you were a suspect either, and he half accepted that, but still felt that it would be easier for you not to know. It worked out so well that you were keen to investigate too - I was able to pass on much more information. But I really wanted to tell you that the police were involved too. Just wasn't allowed to. Only my parents know, because we've been meeting at their house."

Deb was silent for a while as if she was waiting for more. I held my breath, palms sweating and stomach churning. Finally she spoke.

"Is that all, Sam? I thought you were going to tell me something awful. I'm getting to expect that now, with everything that is going on. Of course, it's fine that you were consulting with the police and I understand that you couldn't tell me. How come you can tell me now?"

Feeling almost faint with relief, I explained the situation and asked if she would come over on the following morning to talk to Daniyaal.

"No problem at all, Sam - Jack and the kids are going to a rugby match, so I would have been on my own anyway. It will be lovely to see your parents again after so long. I spent so many happy hours at your house when we were teenagers ..."

"I know they will enjoy catching up with you too. Thank you so much for being so understanding. I was afraid you might be really upset with me."

"Not at all, Sam. I'm actually glad that the police have been taking such proactive measures to try to solve these cases. If we had found anything conclusive or really suggestive, we would have had to take it to them anyway, so this way is much easier. I'll try to think through what happened on Thursday, especially after you had left, so that I am ready for tomorrow."

"See you soon, then, Deb - ten o'clock tomorrow morning, if that's OK." I messaged Daniyaal straight away to let him know that the meeting was all set up and went back in to reassure my parents that Deb was not angry with me.

"I never thought she would be, Sam," said Mum. "Deb is so sensible and straightforward. All she wants, like the rest of us, is for this situation to end as soon as possible, and for Kate's killer to be caught."

I knew she was right, but it had been a constant anxiety in the back of my mind, keeping things from Deb, when she had done so much to help me after Kate's death. I still felt guilty about it, but at least everything was out in the open now.

We both had masks on when she arrived the following

morning, so we decided to risk a hug. It felt so good and I could feel my residual anxiety melting away. Deb was so wholehearted and open - I could be sure now that I had not damaged our relationship. Mum insisted on giving her a hug too.

"I did a lateral flow before I came over, Sam," Deb reassured me. "It should be safe and hugging is allowed now, if we are careful."

"I know. It feels strange though. We've gone so long without touching each other that it's hard to go back to it, somehow. But I am enjoying all the new social contact now, I have to admit. I hadn't realised how isolated and lonely I had become. If you hadn't pushed me to come out of my shell, I don't know if I would have done it for a few months yet."

Deb smiled.

"I knew you were at the stage where you needed me to be firm with you. You know me, bossy as always! But it was the right thing to do."

"You are very right, Deb," agreed Mum. "I'm so grateful to have my daughter back and to be able to get to know my gorgeous granddaughter."

"I love babies at her age. So responsive and engaging, but they can't move and cause havoc yet! Any time you need a babysitter, Sam, I'm happy to oblige. Chloe is just gorgeous and she seems so placid and easygoing as well."

Like any mother, I loved listening to praise of my child, but just then Daniyaal arrived. As it was another beautiful day, he, Deb, and I went out into the garden and he got out his voice recorder and explained to Deb what he was doing.

"I would prefer it, actually," she responded. "It means you have a record of what I really said rather than your notes or memories. Do you get it typed up later as well?"

"Usually, yes. Thank you for your cooperation. May I call you Deb? Mrs Smithson sounds so formal and I am used to hearing a lot about you from Sam. It wasn't appropriate in our formal interviews, but here I really want to hear your opinions and impressions, not just the facts, and I find it helps if we are more informal with each other."

"No problem. What should I call you, Sergeant?"

Daniyaal smiled at me.

"I can tell that Sam did a good job of keeping her meetings with me secret. She calls me Daniyaal, and that is fine with me."

"Interesting. She managed to remember to refer to you as Sergeant Evans whenever we mentioned you." Deb looked at me with new respect.

Then we began. Daniyaal wanted Deb to start from the moment she arrived at Charlotte's house, not only after I had left. He asked plenty of questions and elicited quite a different viewpoint, since Deb had been on the other side of the room. She had been able to see Beth's obvious distress at Charlotte's insensitive suggestion, Emily's annoyance at the idea of a communal prayer and, of course, my own reaction. But she had also noticed that Celia was absolutely furious with Charlotte.

"Her eyes were blazing, she had bright red spots of colour on her cheekbones and her mouth was tight with anger. I thought she was going to explode when Charlotte dared to criticise Stephen's prayer. She had already opened her mouth to have a go at her, when Stephen stepped in. Then she was even angrier at the idea of us all sharing our individual feelings about Kate. It's one of the reasons I felt I just had to intervene, apart from my own anger and how Sam and Beth were feeling."

"That's interesting, Deb. I didn't notice Celia at all at that point."

"Can you tell me how Lesley reacted, Deb?" asked Daniyaal. "Sam thought she might have sniggered after your outburst, but wasn't sure."

"I was actually surprised at how she looked. I didn't take it in at the time, but when I was thinking back last night, it came back to me. She obviously found the whole idea of Stephen's prayer funny and wasn't at all interested in lighting candles. But she did look disappointed when I said we wouldn't be doing what Charlotte wanted. I think she really wanted to do it. But I don't know whether she wanted to share her feelings or hear what other people had to say."

"Mmmm, from my experience of her, she loves gossip and takes an unhealthy interest in finding out all the gory details. I think she would have loved me to tell her all about - about Thomas and how he died. So she probably wanted to listen to everyone else. But maybe she would also have taken a perverse pleasure in passing on her unpleasant opinions about Kate and seeing how we reacted."

"You really don't like her, do you, Sam?" said Deb. "It's unusual for you to take such a strong dislike to someone. But I have to say that you may well be right. I just don't know."

Daniyaal continued asking his gentle questions, drawing out every detail of Deb's conversations with the others, after she stormed out of the living room. Then we reached the part I had not been able to help with at all - the reaction to Daniyaal's arrival.

"Well, most of us were a bit shell-shocked anyway by what had happened and then the extra surprise of the police turning up. I was sitting with Celia and Emily. Celia had calmed down a bit by then, partly, I think, because she was trying to help me to bring my emotions under control. She looked very surprised when you said you hoped to make an arrest soon and I think a bit anxious, but I wasn't at my best, so I can't be sure about the anxiety. Emily was much less emotional than the rest of us and just looked thoughtful. She looked round searchingly at everyone else, so it might be worth asking her what she noticed, although she might not say. She's very careful about anything which might seem like gossip, our Emily. I guess she has to be careful with confidentiality in her line of business. She's very self-possessed and you often can't tell what she is thinking."

"We did actually interview Emily yesterday, as we hoped she might have an alibi. She was helpful on facts, but you are right, she refused to make any judgements or pass on any opinions."

"Did she have an alibi?" I asked. It would be good to start reducing the list of possible suspects.

"Not quite. It would have been difficult for her to go to Charlotte's, but not impossible and there are no CCTV cameras on the roads nearby that we can check for her van. But she's certainly less likely to have managed it."

"That's something, I suppose," said Deb. "I noticed Sophy and Annette, who seem to be becoming good friends, looked at each other when you were speaking about your progress and both of them looked pleased rather than anything else. But who knows? Annette definitely doesn't get on with Charlotte and was furious with her for upsetting you, Sam. She was so pleased that the vicar insisted on taking you home."

"I know I don't have any evidence for it, but I can't believe it was Annette, or Sophy either. But really, it doesn't seem possible that it was anyone. I don't like Lesley, I'll admit, but she's just rather unpleasant, not someone I could imagine being a murderer."

The more I got to know the people involved, the more surreal the situation seemed. Yes, there were resentments and tensions, and some people I did not get on with, but nothing seemed major enough to bring about a murder, let alone two.

"How about Lesley and Charlotte? Any obvious reaction there?" Daniyaal brought us back to the subject in hand.

"Well, Charlotte was pretty distraught at the time but, to be quite honest with you, I was feeling pretty unsympathetic and not wanting to look at her. Lesley was close to her, actually trying to comfort her, which surprised me, as I know she isn't Charlotte's biggest fan. I couldn't see her face, but I did see her whisper something to Charlotte as you finished speaking, and, as you know, she offered to stay with her while you interviewed her. She looked rather annoyed when you sent her away with the rest of us, and was muttering something about officious policemen as we walked out. I think she likes being at the centre of things, especially if there's any drama going on."

"Charlotte mentioned to her husband that several friends might pop in on Friday as well as the vicar. Would you think that Lesley might have been one of them?" asked Daniyaal.

"They haven't been very close in the past, but I guess it is possible. She would certainly want to know what was going on."

After a few more questions, Daniyaal switched off his recorder.

"Thank you both, that has been really helpful."

"Have you found out any more? Is there any forensic evidence this time?" I asked.

"Lots of fingerprints and DNA, but that's not much help, given that all of you were there the previous day. It's very frustrating. And the decoy packets of soluble painkiller were completely free of fingerprints and DNA, so the murderer must have worn gloves. It's not uncommon, since the pandemic, for people to have thin gloves available, I suppose. And only Charlotte's prints on the glass itself. No sign of the orange squash used to mask the taste, so the killer must have taken that away with them. And no witnesses in the area to anyone going to the house, not even for the vicar, who we know did go there. The inspector is really fed up with this case. She's getting a lot of pressure from her superiors now that a second murder has taken place, but we really aren't much further forward."

"So what is your next move? Or can't you tell us that?"

"We'll obviously re-interview everyone, might talk to family members as well to see if anyone has changed their behaviour. The inspector is quite keen to narrow the field a bit, so that we can then try to put some real pressure on the main suspects, interview them down at the station under caution, that sort of thing. As I told you, Sam, she is a great interrogator and she might be able to crack this, although the suspects here certainly aren't the kind of people she normally has success with. The trouble is, once we make any arrests, we won't be able to keep it out of the media. So far, we've been really lucky with the type of deaths and that no one has gone to the papers with it, but it can't last. Not now that there is a possibility of a serial killer around."

Deb and I looked at each other, shocked. It had not occurred to either of us that the media might be interested in what was happening in our small town, but now that Daniyaal mentioned it, we realised that we had been very fortunate not to see our lives plastered all over the papers.

"We were glad that there was so much attention on 'Freedom Day' and 'Eat out to help out'. No one was paying attention to our small investigation here, but I think you need to be prepared for some press attention in the next few days."

Daniyaal spoke sympathetically, and followed it up with some sound advice on how to handle the media, especially how to respond to phone calls if they came.

"Lesley will love this," I said. "She was really excited about a murder in our boring little town. She'll be so happy if we make the television news."

"Oh Sam, I'm afraid you're right. She will be in her element. I can just see her trying to sell a human interest story to the papers, too."

"I don't think there's any way to stop her," I said, depressed at the thought. I remembered only too well my own brush with the media and their insatiable search for emotional stories to sell.

"Right, well, ladies, I'm afraid I must make a move. We have some more forensic work to finish up and a more detailed search of the garden to conduct. I don't think it will reveal much, but you never know. Routine can bring up unexpected finds sometimes. I know you will keep your eyes open, but please don't actively try to investigate any more. It is just too risky. However, if either of you sees or remembers something useful or indicative, please do get in touch and I will arrange to meet with you again. You have my number."

With that, he was gone. It felt quite strange not to be going to see him again in a couple of days. I had grown used to our regular meetings and would miss them. It made me feel that I knew what was going on. I would miss him too. He felt like a friend now.

"What do you think, Sam? Should we keep asking questions, or back away for now?"

Deb looked uncertain and I felt the same.

"I don't know. I feel that we have a chance to talk to these people when they are off guard and that is a big advantage. But Daniyaal's right. It is risky and we might stir up a hornet's nest. I suppose what I think is that we should try to behave normally with them, and keep a note of anything that comes up rather than going out deliberately to find it."

Deb looked relieved.

"I agree. We'll keep our eyes and ears open, but we won't try to ask awkward questions any more. When are you coming home?"

"I think I will come home tomorrow and arrange to walk with Beth on Tuesday. She needs support more than ever and I can't believe she could possibly be a murderer."

"You're right. I'll call you on Monday evening to make sure you are OK. Maybe we could meet for a coffee on Tuesday afternoon? Just a normal chat for once."

I agreed. It would be good to have some social time with no agenda. It was time to try to get back to normal, if that was possible, and leave the police to do their job.

CHAPTER 21

Home again

Mum and Dad were reluctant to let me and Chloe go, but they could see that the situation might go on for weeks, or even longer, and I had to go home at some point. They insisted on arranging to check in by phone once a day and we agreed that we would meet up again soon. But Chloe needed her own things - I had not managed to bring a very sensible selection of clothes or toys when I left in such a hurry. And I needed some privacy and time to think things through on my own. I reassured them that I was done with investigating the suspects, and we set off for home with a full cake tin and some fresh runner beans from the garden.

I really had left the house in a mess. Once Chloe was safely napping, I went round tidying things away and decided to take my holiday photo with Thomas downstairs to the mantelpiece. It made the room feel lighter and friendlier. The kitchen needed a good clean and by the time Chloe woke up I was ready to sit down, with a sense of achievement. I read Chloe her favourite book and decided to order some more for her online. She loved being read to and would even turn the pages on her board and soft touch texture books, although she did spend a lot of time chewing the corners too.

Deb rang that evening as promised and I told her that I felt much better, much more relaxed and ready to see Beth the following morning. She had agreed to another walk, which seemed to me to be a good sign. Deb had heard again from Michael, Charlotte's husband.

"He said the police have nearly finished with the house now. He is planning to come back midweek to collect more things, but they won't be moving back in, for now at least. The girls are very shaken, and are clinging to him and his parents, and they just don't want to come back here. I can understand that - it must hold very difficult memories, especially for Clemency. "

"Poor Michael, it must be awful," I said. "It was hard enough for me losing Thomas, without having to comfort children as well, not to mention explaining to them about a murder. He must even be feeling guilty for not believing Charlotte when she said she hadn't been attempting suicide."

"He's absolutely dreading it coming out in the media as well, so it will be much easier for them to handle, being so far away. He said they might come back one day, when the murder is solved and the kids are more able to deal with it, but in fact I don't know if they will ever return. Sad really - I was always closer to him than to Charlotte and he was one of Jack's best friends. Still, we will keep in touch and I suppose we can visit."

I had not known that the two families had been so close. Thomas and I had such busy working lives that we hadn't had much time for socialising or seeing friends regularly. As Annette had said, working in teaching or the NHS was like living in a different world. I was very aware of how my life was now changing.

I was pleased to see that Beth was not only ready, when we turned up for our walk, she was smartly dressed and not even wearing protective sunglasses. She looked much more confident and came straight out to push Chloe along, chatting away happily to the baby all the time about the birds and flowers we could see.

"Wow, Beth, you seem so much better. You look great!"

She looked over and smiled at me.

"I feel much more normal. Thursday was a horrible experience in many ways, but once I got home and calmed down, I realised that, if I could cope with that, I could manage most things. It wasn't pleasant, but I didn't actually have a meltdown or a panic attack - thanks to you and the vicar - and it was not as bad as I feared. Nobody was staring at me or laughing. Sometimes imagining something is worse than the real thing."

"You are so right, Beth. It was an awful morning, but it's over and we both got through it."

"It actually helped me to see that you, and even Deb, were really upset too. It made me feel less inadequate. I tend to assume that everyone else is coping fine, and I am the only one struggling, but I could see that wasn't true."

"You're not inadequate at all, Beth. You are making real strides and I was amazed at how well you managed. And I'm so pleased that you feel better today. I was afraid that the murder, on top of the stress of Thursday, would set you back."

"Well, it is a bit scary, knowing there is a murderer around, but I can't pretend that I feel sad about Charlotte. I feel a bit guilty about that, but there it is. She was so very selfish and insensitive. If one of us had to die, better that it was her. I'm not unhappy that she's gone."

I was shocked to hear that from gentle Beth. There was a hard edge to her voice and a hint of ruthlessness in what she said. But then she carried on chatting away as normal to Chloe, as if nothing had happened.

"Do you think we might manage the park next time, Beth?" I asked.

"Oh, I think that would be a lovely idea, Sam," she surprised me by saying. "I would love to feed the ducks with Chloe. We can take some bird seed from home. That's supposed to be better for them than bread."

"What do you think about meeting Deb there? I know she would love to see you. She is always asking me how you are."

Beth hesitated for a moment, looking slightly doubtful, but

then she nodded firmly.

"Yes, it would be nice to see her. We can do that."

Soon we were back at Beth's house. We arranged to meet up later that week and this time Beth actually stood on the doorstep and waved us off. I was stunned by her progress in such a short time. It was actually as if the second murder had helped her recovery. I did not want to think about why that might be.

On the way home, we ran into Stephen. He was walking rather slowly and heavily, not in his normal rush to be somewhere. He did not notice us at all until I spoke to him.

"Hello Stephen. Is everything OK? You don't seem to be your normal self."

"Oh, Sam - sorry, I didn't see you. And Chloe too. Nice to see you."

His voice trailed off. He did not sound as if he thought it was nice to see us.

"What is the matter? You can tell me. Look, let's sit on this wall quietly and you can tell me what is wrong. I can see that something is."

Unresisting, he allowed himself to be guided to a low stone wall and sat slumped on it, looking at the ground.

"Is it the murder? I know you were the last person to see Charlotte alive. Is that what is eating you?"

Slowly, hesitantly, with a return to some of his previous social anxiety, Stephen began to tell me what had happened. On Thursday evening, Charlotte had rung him, distraught, and begged him to come over on Friday. She said she was sorry for everything, needed to 'confess' to him (although that was not part of his approach to the ministry - and his voice was firmer when he explained his reasoning to me), and receive his forgiveness. She insisted that she also had something important to tell him and needed his advice on whether to talk to the police about it.

Reluctantly, in fact very reluctantly, he agreed to go over for a short visit at lunchtime. He was not looking forward to the orgy of emotional outpourings he was expecting, but felt that it was his duty as her pastor to try to calm her down and bring her to a better understanding of what she had done wrong.

But when he arrived and rang the bell, she took a long time to answer and then hardly opened the door. She looked terrible and sounded exhausted. He was concerned, but she insisted on sending him away so that she could go back and lie down. She just pushed the door shut and he was left there, wondering if he should ring her husband and let him know she was unwell.

"But I didn't. I should never have left her like that. I - I might have been able to save her. At least I could have prayed with her, for her. Instead, part of me was thankful that I would not have to spend more time with her. I have let her down, but also let down my ministry, I have let God down. I still held resentment in my heart and had not forgiven her for - for hurting you, and of course Beth and the others. I have prayed and prayed, but I still feel the weight of the guilt for it on me. I don't know how to cope with it."

Poor Stephen. His delicate conscience was torturing him, but he really had not done anything wrong.

"Look, she sent you away. If she had wanted you with her at that point, you know very well that she would have let you in. The fact that you visited at all will have told her that you forgave her, and that would be a comfort. I don't think you going in or calling Michael would possibly have made any difference to whether she survived or not."

He drew in a shuddering breath.

"No, you're right actually, Sam. M - Michael assured me I could not have saved her. Her liver was already so damaged that she could not have survived at that point. But I should have tried. And the police - I think the police think I might have caused it, that I might be lying. They think I might be the - the killer."

I looked at him with concern. It was true that Daniyaal had said he had to be a suspect, as he was the only one who admitted to going to the house and was the last person to see her alive, but I did not think that they actively suspected him.

"That inspector, she kept on and on, asking me the same questions. Had I actually gone into the house? How did I really feel about Charlotte? Was I worried that she would tell the police I had tried to kill her before? Had I thought she would be better off dead? What was my motive for killing her? I don't know what I said in the end, I was so battered and confused."

"But they must have realised it wasn't true. They didn't arrest you, did they? I guess they have to push, to try to get you off balance in case you had killed her. But we know you didn't, so it will all be OK."

I was not very coherent. I was worried for him. He looked so haunted and desperate.

"The trouble is, although I may not have given her poison, I feel as if I did kill her by not reacting better. So I am guilty in a way. And if I hadn't been so cross with her on Thursday -"

"That would not have made any difference, you know that. She wanted to see you, so she wasn't angry with you. And whoever did kill her, did it for their own reasons, not because of you."

"I suppose that may be true. Thank you, Sam - you are such a wonderfully kind person, taking the trouble to make me feel better, when you have enough on your plate."

His face was so painfully full of mixed emotions that I couldn't look at it any more. It was too naked and vulnerable. I felt a tightness in my throat and chest that I could not explain.

"Come on, Stephen, when did you last eat? Did you have any breakfast today? No, I thought not. Let's go and have a toasted sandwich and coffee in the park. You will feel better when you have eaten something and it would make a nice change for me to have lunch out for once. I have a rusk in my bag for Chloe, which will keep her going until we get home."

Urging and cajoling, I got Stephen to his feet and we walked on to the park. He sat with Chloe while I collected the food and I could see that she was cheering him up, smiling at him and pointing at the ducks on the pond. When the sandwiches came, he wolfed his portion down immediately and then looked at me in surprise.

"I didn't realise how hungry I was! Thank you so much, Sam. I really needed that. Ow, I think I've burnt my mouth, but never mind. This coffee is really hot too."

I laughed at him.

"Melted cheese is always hot! I have hardly started mine. Have an extra quarter - you look as if you need it."

He protested but allowed himself to be persuaded and ate the extra piece with more caution, sipping the coffee as if it was delicious instead of rather over-brewed and tasteless. The colour had come back into his face and his eyes no longer had that dull look of despair.

We sat together for a while, enjoying Chloe's pleasure at her favourite ducks, and then I needed to go to get her lunch.

"Please look after yourself, Stephen. It is not as bad as you think. I am sure the police don't really suspect you and you have nothing to beat yourself up about. God forgives everything when you're truly sorry doesn't he? You would be saying that to me if our positions were reversed. So let it go."

Stephen's face had darkened a little as my words brought his worries back to mind, but he nodded more positively and was able to say goodbye, thanking me again and again.

"Don't be silly, Stephen - you would do the same for me. In fact, you did when Kate died. And we're friends now. I must go, but I really want you to put all those negative thoughts out of your mind."

His eyes were warm with appreciation.

"Bye, Sam. See you soon. You're a good friend."

As I walked home quickly, I reflected that we really did have a strong friendship already, even though I had only known him for a short time. Shared adversity makes strong bonds. There was something very endearing about his honesty and openness. I hoped Celia would look after him properly. He certainly did need taking care of at the moment.

CHAPTER 22

Pingdemic hiatus

E arly that afternoon, I unexpectedly received a call from Daniyaal.

"Sorry, Sam - I have some bad news for you."

Not more bad news, I thought. I did not know if I could take any more. I held my breath.

"I'm afraid I have tested positive for Covid. No symptoms as yet, but the inspector has also tested positive and is beginning to feel unwell. You'll be getting a ping on your Covid app in the next few minutes I think. And your parents too."

"Oh no, that is such a pain. I guess I have to get a PCR test." But it was a relief in a way. No more deaths.

"Yes, that's right. The drive-in centre at the sports ground is the quickest. Your friend Deb will also have to isolate. Anyone we have spent time with in the last three days, so that includes Emily, I think, and definitely Lesley, as we interviewed her yesterday. Lesley is furious - I rang her first as I knew she would be difficult about it. She intends to make a complaint, although I don't know what about."

"But it's not your fault. I know how careful you always are with masking and distancing. There's just so much of it about. I saw Stephen today. Will he have to isolate as well? It sounds as if he had quite a tough interview with the inspector."

"No, we saw him on Friday, so he should be OK. I know the inspector was a bit hard on him, but he was the obvious suspect, the only one we knew had definitely been there, so it was legitimate for her to push him a bit."

"I understand that, but he was very down about it. It seems to me that the inspector might have gone a bit too far with this. He feels guilty enough about not insisting on going in with Charlotte or ringing Michael. He thinks it's partly his fault that she died, and then the hostile tone of the questioning on top was just too much."

"Oh, I understand. Poor chap, OK. I will try to contact him and reassure him that he could not have saved Charlotte. The surgeon who did the autopsy was quite clear about that. Once she had taken it, nothing could be done. Anyway, I must go - lots more calls to make, I'm afraid."

"Thank you for letting me know. It helps that it isn't just an anonymous ping. If you like, I can ring Deb and my parents for you. Save you a bit of time."

"That would be a big help," he answered, gratefully. "Obviously I won't be around for a while, but do let me know if anything strikes you. If you use my email or message me, I will ring you back. Another DS will be carrying on with our interviews, but I think it would be better for you to speak to me directly if you have anything to pass on."

"I won't see anyone for a few days either, but I will get in touch if anything arises."

"Bye, then." He was gone. I looked at my phone, and he was right, I had the notification already. I rang my parents and Deb quickly to explain what had happened and then went online to set up a PCR test. I was lucky enough to get one for later that afternoon at the drive through centre.

I did not think that I had Covid - Daniyaal was always careful to meet masked, or outside in a ventilated place and it did not sound as if he was symptomatic - but whatever the result, I would need to self-isolate for ten whole days. I was surprised how much that upset me, given that only a few weeks ago I had been voluntarily self-isolating for most of the time. Somehow, my new-found freedom, and meeting up with friends, had become natural, and going back to a life with only Chloe for company seemed harder than before.

The test centre was very efficient and I was soon driving home with Chloe. Hoping for a negative result, of course, but also dreading the next ten days. I decided that I had better warn Beth about the 'ping' - she would not have to isolate for now, but it would be better if she knew that there was a possibility that I might be infected. Stephen too.

Beth was fine about it, although she was disappointed that we would not be able to continue our walks. As Deb had been pinged too, there was no one else she felt comfortable enough with for now. I suggested she try little things, like walking to the shop rather than relying on online deliveries for all her food, and she said she would think about it. We arranged to meet on Zoom midweek - I thought I would really need some adult contact by then.

"You'll be OK when you readjust to it, Sam," she said. "You really just have to relax into a different routine and find some little treats to keep you going. Do you need any shopping?"

"Thanks, Beth - I'm OK for now. I managed to book an online order while I was waiting to go out for my PCR test."

"Well, don't hesitate to ask. It would be a good incentive for me to go to the shops!"

Unfortunately Stephen's phone was off and he was out when I rang the rectory, so I had to leave a message with Celia. She was not in a good mood at all.

"Well, I really hope you haven't passed it on to him, that's all I can say," she said, crossly. "He's had a terrible time since Charlotte's death and having to isolate would be the last straw. I suppose we should be glad that the inspector and that sergeant came here on Friday, otherwise we would be isolating too, but honestly, she was so horrible to him. I wasn't allowed to be in the room with him, but I could hear her shouting and shouting at him, and he was in a dreadful state when they finally left."

"It's really unfair. Just because he admitted he had gone to visit her, they seem to have treated him like the chief suspect. I am very glad that he has someone as sensitive and supportive as you to look after him, Celia." I hoped that a bit of mild flattery might help.

"Oh, well, I - I will do my best. But you know how he is. He's really bad at standing up for himself. I keep telling him to put it out of his mind and pull himself together, but it doesn't seem to make any difference."

I took a breath and counted to ten before I responded.

"Sometimes, when you are really down, it isn't that easy, Celia. You know that," I said, trying to be diplomatic. "But at least he has your amazing baking and cooking to keep him eating well."

There was a bit of a silence at the other end of the phone.

"Mmm, I haven't actually - er - been making any meals for him for the last few days. He said he was not really hungry and - and I have been too busy and wound up to bother."

"Oh dear, I know eating well is really important in trying to recover from a shock like the one he has suffered. I think carbs can actually act as a natural tranquilliser. So maybe he could do with one of your amazing cakes..."

"Oh, OK, Sam," she snapped. "You don't have to rub it in. I will make sure he is eating properly."

"I know you will, Celia. I know he can rely on you for the support he needs."

She snorted and said goodbye abruptly, but I hoped my words had had the desired effect. I was really worried about Stephen and now, unable to go and see him, I had to do my best to ensure that Celia took good care of him. I thought she would, now that I had helped her to see him as wronged and vulnerable rather than just irritatingly weak. But I made a mental note to ring him or try to call him on Zoom later in the week to make sure he was doing better.

That evening, once Chloe was in bed, I looked on Netflix for a box set to watch. I had not binged on box sets earlier in the pandemic, finding most television too gritty or sentimental in my fragile state, so there was plenty of choice. But having something to look forward to each evening should help to pass the time.

Now that she was seven months old, Chloe was trying out all types of solid food, so mealtimes were messy but interesting affairs. She seemed to really like pureed cauliflower, but also enjoyed all kinds of finger food. It was lovely to see her growing up and responding more and more to her surroundings at home as well as outside. I decided to try some new recipes this week, as I was forced to stay at home, and took the time to add some extra ingredients to my online shop, which was due the following day.

"So, Chloe, just me and you now for the next few days. Shall we do some fun things together?"

She gurgled engagingly and waved her carrot at me. This wouldn't be so bad. It would be good to focus on her for a time, although I knew we would both miss our walks. The new books I had ordered for her were coming that afternoon. And at least her strict routine would help the days to pass.

While she was napping after lunch, the doorbell rang. I had put a note on the door explaining my Covid status, so it should not be a problem. I put on a mask and went to open the door, expecting it to be the book delivery, but in fact there was a two pint bottle of milk and a loaf of crusty bread from the bakery on the doorstep. I looked up and saw Stephen standing further down the garden path.

"Celia told me you had been pinged," he said. "She hadn't remembered to ask if you needed anything, so I thought I would just bring you some milk and bread anyway. I'll bring you some cake tomorrow - she's baking this afternoon."

"That's very kind of you both," I said. "You didn't have to do that, but I'm very grateful. I love crusty bread and that's something I miss with online shopping." I smiled at him, knowing he would see it in my eyes despite my mask.

"Anything you need, just let me know. It's helping me a

lot to focus on other people's needs, instead of my situation. I gather Deb and Lesley have also been pinged, so I am putting together a small group of volunteers to help with collecting prescriptions and getting shopping in."

He did sound less desperate and his eyes looked brighter.

"That's a really good idea. Thank you for thinking of us. It was a bit of a shock to get pinged like that, but I'm pretty sure I don't have it, so you and Beth should be OK."

Just then, my phone started to ring inside the house, so I had to say goodbye quickly and go in. Stephen stood and waved before turning to go. What a lovely man he was. So thoughtful. I hoped he was eating properly now.

The phone call was Deb. She had her test result through and it was negative, which was a relief to her. I checked my phone while we were talking and I had a negative result too.

"I hope Mum and Dad are clear too. That was my main worry, that they might have picked it up. Dad's a bit vulnerable with his high blood pressure and obviously they are both older. They decided to go for the PCR at home, so they won't get a result for a couple of days."

"If you are clear, Sam, I'm sure they will be too. You were much closer to Daniyaal, and spent longer with him."

"Are you keeping away from Jack and the kids or just staying home? I should think it would be difficult to keep separate from them inside the house."

"You're right, but I am trying as far as I can. We want to go away on holiday at the start of August and I don't want to risk jeopardising that. But now that I have the negative test, I think I can take a few more risks and spend time at home with them. It's just so frustrating not to be able to go out though."

I agreed. The lack of exercise was already getting on my nerves and I thought I would need to do some kind of Zoom class during Chloe's naps to keep myself going.

"That's a great idea, Sam. Maybe we can join the same online class? It wouldn't be like seeing you in person, but it would be better than nothing."

Deb said that she would find a group we could join at a suitable time and rang off, sounding much happier. She loved to have something or someone to organise. I rang Mum quickly before Chloe woke up to let her know about my negative test and just to check up on the two of them.

"The main problem will be missing you and Chloe," she said. "Our neighbour has been really kind and brought us some shopping and my friend Jo is going to pick up your Dad's prescriptions tomorrow. Neither of us has any symptoms and we have plenty of work to do in the garden, so we'll be fine. I just hope you won't be too lonely, though."

I told her about Stephen bringing me the milk and bread, and the exercise class I was going to do with Deb.

"That's good, Sam. Try to keep busy and the time will fly by. I'll speak to you tomorrow. Maybe we could do a WhatsApp video call when Chloe is up and about, so that I can see her too?"

I was impressed. This was quite something from my rather technophobic mother. But it was definitely a good idea. Chloe had only just got to know her grandparents properly and I wanted to keep that relationship going as well as we could during this period of isolation.

By the next day, I had video calls arranged throughout the week with various people, which really helped me with the feeling of being shut in. I had a short chat with Stephen when he brought round the cake from Celia and he seemed busy and much calmer. The exercise classes were fun and Chloe seemed to be at a point in her development where she was learning new things every day. I felt frustrated at times, but also safe, which was a definite bonus. I tried not to think of the murder, but it kept coming back into my mind at quiet moments.

In the end, I rang Deb to talk about it.

"I just don't believe it was Stephen. I feel so sorry for him, he looked awful on Tuesday, not himself at all."

Deb audibly hesitated.

"You know, that could be because he is feeling guilty about it. If it was him. I know you really like him, but he was there,

160

and the police obviously suspect him. According to Sophy, the gossip around town is that maybe he really is the 'crazy vicar' you get in all the television programmes."

"That's terrible! He must be so distressed by it."

"I don't suppose anyone says it directly to him. But he is probably getting a lot of sideways looks and people avoiding him. Celia has definitely picked up on it - I hear she is looking more and more strained, but also constantly furious. She bites your head off if you dare to speak to her, according to Sophy."

"Do you think she might be a realistic suspect? She was very angry with Charlotte and she's very possessive and protective of Stephen. Thursday morning might have been the last straw."

"But what about Kate's murder? She didn't have a motive for that, did she?"

"Not exactly, but if you remember, Debs, she did resent Stephen spending time with her, and even he said she was jealous of Kate's looks, and she thought their friendship might cause gossip. That was important enough in the past for her to go to the bishop with it. So it is possible."

Deb seemed doubtful.

"I don't know, Sam, it doesn't seem like a very good reason. There is a big difference between going to the bishop and murdering someone."

"Yes, but no one has a really strong motive, as far as we can see. That's what makes this so difficult."

"You felt it might be Lesley previously. Have you changed your mind?"

"Not really, but she seemed to be quite sympathetic to Charlotte on Thursday. She certainly didn't seem to be angry with her like the rest of us, and I can't think why she would choose to kill her now."

"Oh, it's impossible, Sam. I just don't know. I get a kind of feeling for who it can't be, but I find it really hard to assess who might actually be guilty."

"I know. I even found myself worrying that it might be

Beth, because she was so cross with Charlotte and so happy that she had died rather than anyone else."

"Hmmm. I can see why that might disturb you. It's not like her and it is just a bit suspicious, I suppose. Have you told Daniyaal?"

"No. It can't be her. You know it can't. And what would I say to him? That she seemed glad that Charlotte had died? If I am honest, I would also be glad that it was her and not most of the others. I can't go to him with something as vague as that. Can I? It's not evidence of any kind."

"I don't know, Sam. I think you probably ought to tell him and trust him not to overreact."

"If it was just him, I might, but the way the inspector treated Stephen has knocked my confidence in the police a bit. I'll think about it. Anyway, everything is on hold at the moment with the Covid issue."

"Not entirely. There's a new sergeant who has been doing the rounds. I know he has spoken to Annette and Sophy and probably other people too. But I understand that you might want to wait until you can see Daniyaal in person. It is delicate."

We discussed it further for a few more minutes and then ended the call, but I continued to feel anxious about it. The sensation of being powerless to do anything made it worse. I decided that I would try to speak to Daniyaal in the next couple of days, and see if I could just mention my concern in passing.

That night my sleep was troubled with frightening dreams. In the one I could remember most clearly, Beth and Stephen were both cowering on the ground, in the middle of a crowd of people, who were throwing things at them and taunting them, and Daniyaal was standing by them with a strange blue light in his brown eyes and a cold look on his face, not doing anything to protect them. I couldn't make my way through the crowds to do anything about it. I woke up with a crushing feeling of anxiety and apprehension.

I took the opportunity to talk to Mum about it during our video call. She was very calm and reassuring.

"I think you can trust Daniyaal to respect your confidence and to treat your mixed feelings about Beth with caution. Dad and I really like him, and I certainly would feel that I could go to him with that kind of vague information. Besides, I don't actually think her response is that suspicious, given what happened on Thursday."

"I know, that's why I'm reluctant to share it, but it is bothering me all the same. You're right, I'll speak to Daniyaal about it tomorrow."

"Try to do it this afternoon and get it over with, love," said Mum, sensibly. "Hopefully you will be able to sleep better then. Although I gather bad dreams are quite common during lockdowns and self isolation."

"I think I'm really missing my walks. Somehow they allow me to get things into proportion. Oh well, we're more than halfway through now, not long to go."

Mum agreed and we arranged another call on Tuesday. She sounded well and relaxed, but she and Dad were obviously missing Chloe, and could not wait to see her again.

When Chloe was upstairs for her rest, I forced myself to message Daniyaal and ask if I could give him a quick call. His response came back really fast, so I rang immediately, before I could chicken out.

"Hello, Sam - how are you and Chloe? Was your test clear? You have no symptoms?" His voice sounded warm and friendly, which put me at my ease, but I could hear that he was unwell.

"We're both fine, thank you, and so are Deb and my parents, you will be pleased to know. How about you? You don't sound too good."

"I've been better," he admitted. "This Covid has hit me harder than I expected, having had two doses of vaccine. Very glad I am not unvaccinated. I'm more myself today but it has really knocked me out. Unfortunately the inspector is even worse and has had to go into hospital for a few days. Not critical, but needing more oxygen support. I don't think she has any underlying conditions, but we were both pretty tired and run

163

down when it hit us."

"Oh dear, I had hoped it would be a mild illness for both of you. Do look after yourself and don't go back to work too soon. I know how that works - I did it several times at school and ended up much sicker. Everyone says this takes quite a long time to get over."

Daniyaal murmured something vague in agreement, but I knew that he would be under a lot of pressure to return soon, especially if the inspector was off.

"Anyway, Sam, what's up? Why did you want to call?"

"Well, obviously I wanted to know how you were, but I just needed - er, needed to run something past you. I'm a bit nervous about it, as I know it's probably nothing and I definitely don't want to - to get people into trouble unnecessarily. I don't want to cause another heavy-handed interrogation."

"Look, Sam, if you're saying and thinking that because of what happened with Stephen, I promise I won't go in boots and all. I can't undermine my inspector, and she has more experience than I do, as you will understand, but I would have handled the questioning rather differently and I hope you know that. You can trust me not to overreact."

"That's what Mum said, and Deb told me I ought to let you know. But it's difficult now that it comes to it, especially over the phone." I took a deep breath. "Here goes. I was a bit disturbed by how my friend Beth responded to Charlotte's murder. She didn't sound like herself at all. She is normally really gentle and forgiving, but she looks better and happier since Charlotte died, and she seems to be still angry with Charlotte and - and she said that if someone had to die, it was better that it was Charlotte."

There was a short pause, as if Daniyaal was waiting for something more. He took his time in answering and seemed to choose his words carefully.

"I think, under the circumstances, that's probably a reasonable thing to say, you know, Sam. She wouldn't have wanted to lose a close friend. The surprise is that she actually said it to you. A lot of you are probably secretly thinking it, but she was the one to put it into words."

"You are right, Daniyaal - I have been pushing that thought out of my head, whereas she accepted it. Maybe that is healthier, I don't know."

"I understand why you are concerned, but on its own, this isn't anything to worry about. I will interview Beth again when I am back at work, but I won't send DS Botts, as he doesn't know her or the background, and with her mental health issues we owe her a duty of care. But try not to worry about it. I don't think, myself, that Beth is our perpetrator, but if she is, she needs proper mental health care. I know she is your friend, but you can't condone murder, and she would then have also been the person to kill Kate."

"I know. I think that is why, in the end, I felt I had to tell you, to get it off my chest. I do trust you to treat her sensitively. Thank you."

"No need to thank me, Sam - that's my job."

"I suppose there haven't been any further advances in the case?"

"Not really. DS Botts has interviewed a few more people, but none of them has a watertight alibi for the Friday morning, although Annette and Emily look unlikely suspects, due to work commitments. We've had some feedback from the vicar's last parish too. I can't go into details, obviously, but he seems to have come out with a fairly clean bill of health and was much missed, unlike his sister. Celia made herself very unpopular there and seems to have a reputation for having a very short temper and for bearing grudges."

"I'm afraid she is prone to getting very angry, even furious. But that doesn't mean that she would poison someone, does it?"

"No," he said carefully. "But the particular type of poisoning we are dealing with suggests planning but also an impulsive nature, so you never know. I will talk to her again next week, assuming I can get out and do it."

"I might be able to chat to her a little. I asked her to look after Stephen, so that might give me an excuse to contact her.

We're not exactly the closest of friends. I suppose I could ring Lesley too, just to see how she is during isolation."

"Please continue to be careful, Sam. I know you feel safe because you are stuck at home, but that won't last, so you need to watch what you say to people really carefully. I don't want you to be the next victim."

"Neither do I, don't worry. I'll be very careful and won't ask difficult questions. Anyway, I'd better go, as your voice is giving out and you need to be resting. Get well soon, Daniyaal. And thanks again."

"Thank you for calling, Sam. Feel free to ring again if you are worried about something. Bye."

CHAPTER 23

The media spotlight

hile we were stuck at home, I had taken to watching the local early evening news, which was on just after Chloe had her tea. That evening, there was a shock waiting for me. I never read local papers, so I had no idea if the murder had received any coverage, but that evening, it was the main story on the local programme. There was a reporter in Charlotte's street, talking about the murder and then they showed some old photographs of Charlotte and her children. So far, they did not appear to have made the connection with Kate's death, but that was only a matter of time. I was just feeling thankful for the Covid restrictions keeping me out of it, when they moved on to a Zoom interview with Lesley, of all people.

Introduced as 'a close friend of the victim', she talked about how sad it was for Charlotte's family and friends, with an obviously fake dab at her eyes with a tissue. I was fuming. They asked her about the police investigation - as if she would have known anything about that - and she mentioned the Covid problem and then threw in: "Of course, the vicar was the last person to see her alive. I understand that he has been helping them with their enquiries."

The interviewer cut her off, not wanting to encourage her

to develop her opinions publicly, but the damage had been done. I felt like throwing something at the television. How could she throw Stephen to the lions like that? I wanted to give her a piece of my mind.

Suddenly the phone rang. It was Deb.

"Did you see her?"

I could barely speak, I was so angry. If Chloe had not been there, I would definitely have been swearing.

"That woman! How could she?"

"I couldn't believe it, Sam. Talking as if she had been Charlotte's best friend, as if she knew and cared about Michael and the girls, when I don't think they've ever even met! Pretending to be inconsolable. She was just enjoying the attention."

"And then to mention Stephen, Deb. He will be really in for it now. They'll be camped out on his lawn and attending all his services. 'Helping them with their enquiries' - it makes it sound as if he is a criminal, as if he did it. I'm so cross with her."

"I know, it's just dreadful. What can we do? What do we say if the media contact us? I'm afraid they will soon make the connection with Kate's death and then - it could go national. You know how excited they get about a serial killer of any kind."

"I know, I know. I'm so glad Michael and the girls are not here. At least we're still in isolation for a few more days - and Lesley is too. That may help. Shall I ring Daniyaal and get his advice?"

"That's a really good plan. I'll message Celia and offer her and Stephen our support. She will be spitting feathers."

"I'll ring Stephen once I've spoken to Daniyaal. He needs to know how to handle things too." We hung up quickly to get started, both feeling marginally better for getting the fury off our chests and having something positive to do. I put Chloe to bed quickly, so that I could concentrate, and fortunately she settled very quickly.

Daniyaal was surprised to hear from me again so soon, but offered some really useful advice for me and Deb as well as Stephen.

"If you say nothing and try to avoid them, they will just keep on and on, and you will have no peace. I suggest that you prepare a simple statement and stick to it, don't take any questions afterwards. For Stephen, the best thing is to focus on the grief in the community and the church's desire to offer comfort to everyone affected. Yes, he was the last to see Charlotte, on a pastoral visit, and he has been able to give some helpful evidence to the police on her appearance at that point."

"Can you slow down a bit, Daniyaal? I'm writing this down. It's good."

"Finish with thoughts and prayers being with the victim's family and friends. He could mention that prayers will be offered in the Sunday service. That should do - focus on the church's public role at a time like this. Nothing there for the media to get their claws into. I would try to ensure that Celia isn't around - her obvious anger and emotion would be a distraction."

"Great idea. Anything for the rest of us?"

"Well, if it's about Charlotte, you can also focus on how shocked and saddened you all were to hear of her death when you had seen her so recently. Mention sympathy for the family and leave it at that."

"And if they connect it to Kate's murder?"

"I'm afraid they are bound to, at this point. DS Botts will make a minimal statement and say we are investigating and can't give any further details at this point. He'll say that there will be an additional police presence to reassure the community - not that it would be of any use in these circumstances, but it is standard procedure. Kate's family should go away for a time if they possibly can. Can you contact them and suggest it? If they find out that you and Deb were very close to Kate, and that is very likely, stick to simple statements about your sadness at the loss of a wonderful friend and your sympathy for the family. "

"That's so helpful, Daniyaal. I'll get on to it straight away and make sure that we all have a statement prepared and are 'singing from the same hymn sheet' as far as possible. If I can face it, I will even ring Lesley and suggest what she needs to do, although it will be very hard not to scream at her."

"It would be worth it, if you can get her to back off from talking to the media though. You could suggest that she might be in trouble if she reveals elements of a police investigation. That might work."

"Mmm - that's a good idea. I'll give it a try."

Deb was delighted with all the suggestions and we shared out our friends between us, so that we could pass on the advice we had been given. She said she would speak to Martin, Kate's husband, for me - I didn't feel up to that.

The first person I rang was Stephen. He was almost incoherent, clearly overwhelmed with anxiety, but he gradually calmed down as we spoke. He wrote down Daniyaal's advice and I got him to practise reading his prepared statement, calmly and clearly.

"Treat it like one of your online services, Stephen. You are great at those. Talk to the camera, not the people. And I suggest that you wear a smart dark suit, tidy yourself up as much as possible and make it as formal as you can."

"But I don't know when they will come!"

"I know, so just make sure that you are ready. Have the statement in your pocket and make sure you are smartly dressed before you leave the house. And I think Daniyaal is right to suggest keeping Celia away from the cameras and the microphones."

"No problem there - she is so angry that she is refusing to speak to them at all, ever."

"This time, I really don't blame her, Stephen. I'm so cross with Lesley as well."

"I know it wasn't helpful, but I don't suppose she meant to cause any trouble, Sam," he replied. "I expect she just got carried away."

I decided that now was not the right time to correct him on that. I had too many other people to call.

"I have to go now, Stephen. Please don't worry. We're all with you. You can do this."

"Thank you so much, Sam. I really am very grateful. And please thank Sergeant Evans if you speak to him."

I contacted Beth and Annette and they were both delighted to be given such clear advice and said they would prepare a statement straight away, just in case. Deb was doing the others. Then there was Lesley. The one I was dreading.

In the end, I treated the call with her as if she were a reporter and prepared what I was going to say really carefully. A bit of judicious flattery, then I would pass on Daniyaal's advice, and then the veiled threat of consequences if she interfered with the police investigation.

"Hi Lesley - I saw you on television this evening - you handled them really well, I thought, and you looked amazing. That colour really suited you."

"Why, thank you, Sam," she said, obviously surprised. She was about to go on, but I interrupted shamelessly.

"Sorry Lesley, I'm in a bit of a rush this evening. We've had some advice from the police on handling the media. Now that the news of the murder, or rather the two murders is out, there is bound to be some press attention. They suggest that we all prepare a simple statement, emphasising our shock and sadness and sympathy for the family - just as you did this evening - and then leave it at that. Don't answer any questions at all, as that can get you into difficulties. If we reveal something that is important to the police investigation, we could be in real trouble. So we have to be exceptionally careful in what we say and not imply anything or give the press any additional information. OK?"

Lesley sounded a little anxious.

"Really? I didn't know we could be in trouble for that. OK, Sam, I will do my best. Jackie, for goodness sake, go and see why Charlie is crying! Don't just stand there like a lemon. You can see I'm on an important phone call."

"Don't worry, Lesley - I have to go now anyway. I have lots of other people to ring. Well done again for coping so well with the media. I wouldn't have been able to do it."

I hung up as quickly as possible. Hopefully it had worked. If Lesley could be persuaded to be more cautious and to keep things confidential, we had a chance of escaping the full battery of media attention. Working out exactly what to say in advance had certainly helped, so I went straight to the computer and typed up my own statement, printed it out, and put it in my pocket so that I would be ready.

By the next evening, things had certainly stepped up a gear. The murders - now both were mentioned - were on the main national news. There was still a reporter outside Charlotte's house, but this time they included short interviews with people in her street, all saying how shocked they were that this could have happened in such a quiet, safe place. A short clip of Lesley's interview from the previous day was played and then they cut to a shot of Stephen, looking very smart, outside the church. He looked rather pale, but very composed and he spoke directly to the camera as I had suggested. Not a trace of his usual hesitancy. His statement was word for word what we had practised and came over very well. I sighed with relief and realised that I had been holding my breath.

Deb messaged me to say how well he had done and my father rang later to say that he had seen it on the news.

"I thought the vicar came over very well, Sam. Your coaching obviously worked."

"He's very good at recorded services, so I suggested he treated it like one of those. I had a student once who could perform really well on stage, but was very hesitant in the classroom. Stephen seems to be a bit like that."

"Anyway, I think it worked to deflect attention and there wasn't much of Lesley at all. I have to say that I did not warm to her. Her display of emotion seemed very unnatural."

"You're such a good judge of character, Dad. She really didn't like Charlotte at all and I still don't know why she was so sympathetic to her on that Thursday."

I messaged Stephen to congratulate him on his television appearance and said that I would ring him on the following day.

Feeling a little less anxious and oppressed, I went to bed early and slept more peacefully than I had for days.

Next morning I received the call on the landline, which I had been dreading.

"Mrs Elsdon? Sonya Hart from the *Sun* newspaper here. We wondered if you had any comment on the murders in your town, especially since the first victim was a close friend of yours."

I took a deep breath and unfolded my written statement, silently thanking Daniyaal for his advice.

"I won't answer any questions, but I do have a statement for you. Here it is: like everyone in our community, I am shocked and saddened by the recent murders of two local women. My thoughts and prayers are with their families and loved ones. As a close friend of the first victim, Kate Rigby, I am mourning the loss of a wonderful friend and amazing person, and will not be making any further statements."

"Can I ask you to tell me more about Kate Rigby and -"

"No further statements. Goodbye."

I put the phone down, shaking a little, but feeling that I had done my job. If only I had had Daniyaal's advice when Thomas had died. It had been so difficult dealing with intrusive media people during that chaotic time.

I had three further phone calls to deal with that day, but I had to stay at home anyway, so I could not be approached in the street, and there would not be any photographers around. I kept the front curtains closed all day, just in case. I knew some of their tricks. One of my neighbours rang to tell me that they had been questioned by a journalist, but had said very little. Hopefully none of this would be interesting enough to find its way into the television news or the papers. I began to hope that I might have got away with it.

But the next morning someone 'kindly' pushed two newspapers through my door. The *Sun* and the *Daily Mail*, my least favourite papers. Immediately, I could see that I was on the front page of both. An old picture from when Thomas died and I was looking grief-stricken and lost. In one headline, I was 'brave

Samantha', in the other it was 'tragic Sam', both saying that I was distraught at the loss of my best friend only a few months after the loss of my husband to Covid. One of their favourite human interest type stories.

I felt sick. The worst thing was feeling so powerless. I could do nothing to stop it. I wanted to scream and tear up the papers, but Chloe was there, and it would frighten her, so I swallowed hard and smiled brightly at her despite the angry tears pouring down my face. How dare they make a mockery of my life, my feelings like this? But no good would come of thinking like that. I put both papers straight in the recycling bin and washed my hands immediately. I felt contaminated by them.

I have never been so frustrated at not being able to go out for a walk. Chloe and I spent the morning trying to keep busy, so that I did not have to think about anything. She was in a very grizzly mood for once, teething again, and needed all my attention, which helped a bit. I put my phone on silent so that I could ignore any messages and had already taken the home phone off the hook. I was not ready to speak to anyone yet.

When Chloe finally went for her rest, I rang my parents. They never touched the *Sun* or the *Daily Mail*, but a friend had told them about the articles and they were very angry on my behalf. But soothing too.

"Look, Sam, I know it's awful, and so embarrassing for you, but it will blow over quickly. They don't have anything new, not even a fresh photograph, so it will surely be a one day wonder and they will move on tomorrow."

They had me on speakerphone, so that they could both join in the conversation.

"Your father's right, Sam. It will soon be forgotten. At least you won't be out and about in the town, where it would be much worse. By the time we are out of isolation in a few days, most people will have forgotten about it. And your friends don't read that type of paper anyway."

They were right. If it had to happen, this period of isolation was definitely the best time for it. I knew everyone would see and share the picture and the article, but it would surely not hold their interest for long.

Later that afternoon, I spoke to Deb and to Sophy, who both felt the same way. I just needed to ride it out. It would pass.

I hardly dared to look at the news that evening. Unfortunately, they had clearly picked up on the story in the papers, but had nothing to put on screen other than the old photograph and my statement to the press. So not too bad.

Soon after the news had finished, when I had just put Chloe down to sleep, I had a call from Lesley. I had forgotten to leave the landline off the hook. I could hear that she was angry and in a spiteful mood as soon as I heard her sharp nasal voice.

"So, little miss goody two-shoes. You told me not to talk to the press and then you go and get yourself onto the front pages! And even on the television news. You are such a pathetic hypocrite! I thought you were genuinely giving me good advice, but you obviously just wanted the limelight for yourself."

The vicious invective went on for a while before I could speak at all. She was almost spitting at me down the phone. I felt dirty and humiliated. I had not thought anyone would take it like this.

"Look, Lesley, you don't understand," I managed to say, eventually when she paused for breath, in a very shaky voice.

"Oh, I understand fine, thank you, Sam. You couldn't stand someone else being the centre of attention, could you?"

I gulped and tried to explain.

"I literally gave them a statement like the one I suggested for you. On the phone. You may notice they don't have a photo and I didn't go on Zoom or answer any questions."

"So where did they get all that guff about 'tragic Sam's tears welling up in her eyes' from then? Mars? It sounds just like you - you're always crying about something."

"I'm afraid they just made it up. They do that. They put my statement together with me as the bereaved widow from January and made up a story."

"I don't believe you. They can't get away with telling lies

and making things up, so you must have given it to them. You're an attention-seeking bitch, a -"

"I'm sorry, Lesley, I can't take any more of this," I said and put the phone down. Then I carefully took the receiver off so that she could not ring back. I checked that my phone was on silent and curled into a ball on the sofa, feeling numb and completely drained. I had never faced a personal attack quite like that before and I felt as bruised as if she had hit me physically. The sick feeling I had felt when I first saw the papers had returned and I was shaking violently.

Eventually the reaction wore off and I was able to uncurl myself slowly. The house was in darkness by now. My head felt muzzy and vague. I did not even have the spirit left to feel angry with Lesley. Moving automatically, I went to the kitchen and made tea, sat at the kitchen table and drank it, and then went up to bed, still without any conscious thought. I do not remember getting undressed or into bed.

CHAPTER 24

The comfort of friends

The next two days, the last of my isolation, went past slowly but inevitably. I texted friends and my parents to say that I was not answering calls or messages for now and completely ignored the outside world. Luckily we had plenty of food in the house, and the weather was pleasant enough for us to be in the garden for some of the time. There were a number of rings at the doorbell and loud knocks on the door but I ignored them. They were not for me. I watched some nature documentaries on Netflix but avoided the news. Chloe was real life. Everything else was just noise.

Slowly, by the evening of the second day, I began to come to life again. Perhaps I would manage a walk on the next day, although the thought of going out at all made me shudder painfully. I would wait and see how I felt.

My personal freedom day dawned and I woke up earlier than usual. The sun was bright behind the curtains and it already felt warm. Chloe was in a really sunny mood and her smiles melted away the stiffness of my frozen face. I started to feel more human. Suddenly I smiled at her.

"Hey Chloe, do you want to feed the ducks today?" I said brightly. She giggled and waved her hands. I took that as a yes. We got ready and I put her in the buggy. I kicked away the post and what looked like hand-written notes which had accumulated under the letterbox by the front door and unlocked it. Opening the door, the sun fell on our faces and it felt as if we were emerging from a long dark tunnel, as we went down the garden path to the pavement.

We turned left towards the park. Chloe seemed excited and was chatting away in her own special language. It was so good to walk. I did not really think about anything, just strolled on, feeling the morning breeze on my face, smelling the scent of summer flowers, enjoying the sudden shade under the trees. Even the diesel fumes, from a van chugging past, seemed new and fresh. It was early in the day, the school holidays had just begun, and there was no one about. We had the world to ourselves.

It could not last, of course. Once we reached the park, it was full of dog walkers and joggers, making the most of the cool of the early morning. It was going to be a hot day. Suddenly I heard a voice and someone ran up behind me.

"Sam! We've all been so worried about you. Are you OK?"

It was Emily, looking anxious, but smiling warmly at me. I felt myself smiling back automatically.

"Hello, Emily. And Merry and Pippin! Look Chloe - two cute dogs. Aren't they sweet?"

I bent down to stroke the excited dogs.

"Is this your first trip out too, Emily? I heard you had to quarantine as well."

"No, actually I never got pinged. Don't quite know why, but I was very relieved - and so were my clients, I can tell you. Some of them could not have coped with a further delay. I think maybe I fell just outside the time limit, as I was interviewed early on Saturday morning and the inspector and sergeant didn't test positive until Tuesday lunchtime. Anyway, it certainly made life easier. But how are you, Sam? We've been desperate to make contact but just couldn't find a way."

Emily really sounded concerned. I felt guilty for shutting everyone out.

"I'm so sorry if I worried anyone. Just had to be alone for a while."

"I do understand. That awful stuff in the papers must have been hard to take.."

I looked up at her.

"It wasn't really the articles. It was - well, Lesley rang me …"

I could feel the tears pricking in my eyes. I had not been able to cry at all for the last few days, but a few kind words were enough to release the emotion. Maybe I was as pathetically weepy as she had said.

"That woman! You don't mean she had the gall to contact you? We knew she had been saying horrible things about you on social media, and via messages to people around here, but not that she had said them to you. I'm so sorry, Sam. We did our best to stop her. Sophy, Annette and I went round to her house. I've never seen them so angry and Annette's language was something to be heard."

"You didn't need to do that, to defend me. I - I'm OK really."

"We didn't even know she had spoken to you in person, we were just furious with her for what she was posting. As Annette said, her husband would have gone round to sort Lesley out, if she had dared to say things like that about her, but you don't have anyone to do that for you. So we went. Stephen offered to go, but he's - well, I'm sorry, he's just too soft. He would not have said what needed to be said, and if she had started crying, and apologised, he would simply have forgiven her. I suppose he has to, in his job, but it wouldn't have been enough. Nowhere near enough."

I was astonished at the strong feeling in her voice. We had only known each other for such a short time, but she and the others had really wanted to stand up for me. It gave me a warm feeling inside and a lump in my throat.

"Celia would have come too, but we didn't think that was a good idea. She is so wound up at the moment, we couldn't be sure that she would stop at words. She walks round like an unexploded bomb at the moment. I don't think I would risk approaching her if I was one of those reporters wandering around the town looking for a story."

I never thought Celia would consider defending me, although I could certainly understand how angry she was on Stephen's behalf. That Emily thought she might even become violent was worrying though.

"So we rang the bell, and knocked on the door as well, and stood in the garden, waiting for her. She tried to pretend that she didn't know why we were there, but it was obvious that she did. When Sophy started in on her, she actually looked a bit frightened. And then Annette joined in. I had the dogs with me, and they were growling and barking, because they could feel the animosity. As I expected, she tried pretending to cry, and insisting that she hadn't meant any harm, she was just stressed out by quarantine, but we just would not accept that. In the end, she promised to take down the posts and never to put anything like that out there again."

"Wow, I'm amazed you managed to persuade her to do that."

"Well, it wasn't easy. She's a stubborn cow, I'm afraid. But she knew that we would not back down, and that if she didn't put it right, she would be completely ostracised in the whole area and blocked from all the local social media groups. She couldn't bear that. She has to have an audience."

Emily really was a very shrewd judge of character. Lesley definitely did need attention, all the time. That much was clear from her abusive phone call. But I was amazed that three people I barely knew would feel so strongly about an injustice to me. Emily could see that I was feeling very emotional and gave me a quick hug round the shoulders. It surprised me, because she did not seem like a very tactile person in general. She was normally very self-contained and business-like.

"We all care about you, Sam. You would stand up for us, and we were happy, really happy, to do the same for you."

I couldn't speak. The tears were suffocating me. I squeezed Emily's hand to try to express my thanks.

"We're all having a meeting at Deb's house this afternoon, at two o'clock, now that she is out of quarantine. Would you come along? Please do. It's a kind of council of war about how to deal with the media and the whole situation. We would all love to see you. We've been so worried about you. We've even been contacting your parents to see if they knew how you were."

I gulped, sniffed and nodded.

"I'll be there. Th-thank you."

With a last attempt at a smile, I turned away abruptly, and pushed Chloe back home. I was too emotional to go and see the ducks, but feeling a hundred percent better knowing that people had not listened to Lesley, that the others did not judge me as she had.

I had not even taken my phone with me on our walk, having become used to it being on silent, and therefore no longer essential. But as soon as I got home, I picked it up, ready to ring my parents. Meeting Emily had made me realise how hurtful my silence must have been and how anxious Mum and Dad would be. How could I have been so selfish? When I looked at my phone, I realised just how many unread messages and missed calls I had. No wonder people had been concerned.

"I'm so sorry, Mum. It was horrible of me to ghost you like that. I didn't mean ..." My voice trailed off into a sob. What was the use of trying to justify myself? It had been wrong. And I did not even know why I had done it.

"No apologies between us, darling," said Mum, her voice sounding emotional. "I know something must have happened to make you cut us off again. Just remember we always love you, no matter what, and we are always there for you."

Haltingly, I tried to explain about Lesley's phone call and the impact it had on me. Looking back, I could not explain such a powerful reaction, but at the time it had been overwhelming, and shutting myself in with Chloe had been my only way to get through it.

"I think, if I could have come to see you and Dad, I would have found a different way to cope and welcomed your comfort, but being in isolation I just - I don't know why I did it. I'm so sorry to have worried everyone."

Mum sniffed loudly, I could tell that she was crying and hated to hear it.

"It sounds as if your body and brain just went into auto-pilot, Sam. Went back to the old way of coping. It doesn't matter. I knew you would come back to us at some point. But, that horrible Lesley - I'm so angry with her I could burst. How dare she speak to you like that? Your father will be furious. Can we come over today as we're all out of isolation? I'm dying to give you and Chloe a hug."

I explained that I had agreed to go to Deb's that afternoon.

"That's perfect, then. We'll come over after lunch and stay with Chloe while you are out. Maybe we can have a takeaway that evening? It would make a nice change."

"Oh, Mum, that's a great idea. I would love to do that. I can't wait to see you."

Once off the phone, I looked around the room to see if I needed to do any cleaning or tidying. Irrationally, I always wanted things to be pristine before my parents came. But actually everything was extremely clean and almost too tidy. I remembered that I had spent hours doing mindless cleaning during the last couple of evenings, once Chloe was in bed and I had no other distractions.

I hugged Chloe and sat down to play with her until lunch. When my parents arrived, I could not speak, just held out my arms to them. I suddenly felt as if the world was back in the right place. I was so lucky to have a family like this one.

Walking over to Deb's house felt strange - no buggy to push. The weather was hot and sultry and I was glad of the shade of the trees on the street she lived on. I sipped at my water before going up to the door. Dad had been very insistent that I must still not accept any drinks offered to me while I was there. I had needed the reminder. After the Covid ping, media issues and conflict with Lesley, the murders had seemed less important, but the risks were still there, however much I might want to feel that none of my friends, old or new, could be the guilty one.

I felt rather nervous as I rang the doorbell. How would people react? I need not have worried. Deb came straight out of the front door and gave me an enormous hug.

"I'm so glad you're here, Sam. Missed you so much. Come on through - we're in the garden. I know we don't actually have to be, now, but it just feels better, somehow. I see you have your own water. That's good. Emily meant to tell you that we all have our own drinks. I can't believe we need to worry about it now, but the murders are still hanging over us and we have to be safe."

She was talking very fast, eyes bright, holding my hand as she led me through the house.

"I really missed social contact, Sam, in isolation. Obviously I have Jack and the kids, but it's not the same and they are out most of the day. In fact, the kids went off on a summer camp with the scouts the day before yesterday and won't be back until just before we go on holiday - hopefully. No more pings, please!"

Finally she stopped gabbling as we arrived in the back garden. After so long on my own with Chloe, the place seemed intimidatingly full of people, but they were all smiling invitingly. Sophy and Annette were sitting together with their babies on their knees, and waved me over to an empty chair next to them.

"So nice to see you again, Sam," said Sophy, Annette put her hand out and just touched my knee, a kindly gesture which almost overset my fragile composure. I smiled waveringly at both of them.

"So many people," I murmured.

"Not everyone's here, in fact. Beth has been great, collecting prescriptions and delivering bits of shopping for Stephen's volunteer group (which has taken on a lot more clients), but she just didn't feel ready for this kind of gathering. And Celia couldn't make it. To be quite honest with you, she's really not herself at the moment and is avoiding people as much as she can. I know she can be annoying, but I really feel sorry for her at the moment. There are horrible rumours flying around all over the place, but nothing tangible that you can deal with. It's very frustrating."

I saw that Stephen was there, and noticed him looking over at me rather anxiously. I smiled reassuringly at him.

"Are people still saying that Stephen might be the murderer?"

"I think that's still one of the common theories among people who don't know him personally, but there are plenty of others. We're all under suspicion really - each one of us has been whispered about or discussed on social media at some point. Now that it is all out in the press, the whole thing has become the hottest topic of conversation all over town and there are plenty of amateur sleuths who think they know who the murderer is. So we're tending to stick together and go around in pairs at least, when we can, as it's less intimidating if people start whispering or pointing."

I had not realised that things had become as fraught as that. Shut away in isolation and then off social media for my own reasons, I had been insulated from it.

"Oh dear, that must be hard for you all. Is that what this meeting is all about?"

"Well, partly. We feel we can't go on with this situation. We have to find out who the murderer is so that we can get back to normal life. But it was also because we were so worried about you. We hoped Deb would be able to get through to you, once she was out of isolation."

"Emily told me that you both went to confront Lesley. I can't thank you enough for defending me. I really appreciate it."

They both brushed away my thanks and insisted that they had positively enjoyed being able to express their feelings so clearly for once.

"We would have said a bit more, I can tell you, if we had known that she had actually rung you and verbally abused you. How she dared! But hopefully she knows, now, that she can't get away with that sort of thing any more."

I had never heard Annette sound so assertive. She was in her carer's uniform as usual, ready to go on shift later, but she looked much more confident and less downtrodden. She told me that, on Sophy's advice, she had asked for a more regular shift pattern at the care home.

"I was amazed. They let me have exactly what I wanted and even offered me a small pay rise, for loyalty, they said. Sophy said they would not want to lose me just now, with such a shortage of care workers and so many vacancies, and she was right. It's so good to feel wanted and to have a bit more control of my life." She smiled gratefully at Sophy. "I would never have had the guts to ask without her pushing me to do it. I'm going to get John to ask for better shifts too. He's a key worker too, and his firm needs people with experience like him."

"If you let them get away with it, they will just exploit you," said Sophy, firmly. "We need people like you more than ever just now, and you deserve to be recognised for the hard work you do."

Just then, Deb stood up and was obviously ready to speak. We all quietened down obediently. Somehow, you could not avoid doing what she wanted you to. She really had the voice and manner of someone you wanted to obey, without being bossy in any way.

"Thank you all so much for coming. I know we are all glad to have Sam back," she said, to murmurs of agreement and smiles all round. "And it's great to finally be out of isolation - it seemed like an eternity. However, we need to talk about how we are going to move the situation forward now, especially with regard to the murders and the media attention. Any ideas?"

After a fairly long pause, several people started to talk at once. Deb began to act as chairperson so that everyone could be heard. There were plenty of problems aired and a few pretty impractical suggestions made, but in the end no one had found a solution. But then Deb pulled things together.

"So, we are agreed on a few things: one, no one will talk to the media on their own. We use our basic statements and back each other up. We avoid answering questions if we possibly can. Two, if we see or hear anything suspicious, even from a close friend, we pass it on to Sam. She is the only one who is not a suspect and she can evaluate it and decide if it needs to go to the police. Three, we will try to stick together, and protect each other from any nasty gossip or difficult scenes, when we are out and about. And four, Sophy and Emily will keep an eye on social media, so that we can report any nasty posts and get them taken down as soon as possible."

We all looked at her in admiration. How had she managed to make a concrete plan out of our vague ideas and comments? No wonder her previous career, as PA to a senior international businessman, had been so successful.

After some more general chat, we dispersed, feeling much more positive. I hugged Deb and thanked her and then walked out, finding myself beside Stephen. He too was looking much stronger and less fearful.

"I do think Deb is amazing," he said as we set off down the street. "I need to get her involved in the church somehow. She would really knock the rotas and committees into shape, that's for sure."

I agreed. And Deb actually enjoyed organising things, and especially people.

"She's coming to Chloe's blessing next month, so you can try to grab her then. I can see that she would be a real boon to the church, and I think she would be in her element. But would Celia mind? She does such a lot at the moment."

Stephen's face darkened a little and he frowned.

"I'm really worried about Celia. I've never known her to be so unstable and emotional and she is even forgetting her own appointments, and not reminding me about meetings. She burst into tears last night, when she was watching the local news and the murders were mentioned again, even though it was just a brief sentence or two, nothing controversial. I have never seen her cry before, not when she had to give up her studies, not even when our parents died, never. It's just not like her."

"Poor Celia. It sounds as if things have really got to her, and I can totally understand that. Would you like me to try to meet up with her sometime? I know we're not close, but we have talked a bit. I would certainly like to try and help if I can."

Stephen's eyes rested on me for a while, full of warmth and appreciation.

"Would you do that, Sam? In a few days, perhaps, when you are fully recovered. I know you have had a terrible few days. I so wanted to help, but all I could do was pray for you."

Slightly embarrassed, I looked away.

"That's very kind of you, Stephen. I really appreciate it. You've been very good to me."

"Well, I - I - you're my friend, Sam. It's not just a vicar thing. I want to be a good friend to you."

He sounded so sincere, that I could not help reaching my hand out and giving his hand a quick squeeze.

"You have been a fantastic friend, Stephen, and I know I can rely on you. I must go and see to Chloe now, but I'm sure we will meet up again soon. You are welcome to come for a walk with us one day if you would like to."

"I would love that, Sam. See you soon."

That evening, with my parents, I talked through Deb's plan, while we enjoyed our takeaway. It felt like a very relaxed meal and both of them seemed happy and less concerned, about me and about the situation.

"Your Daniyaal will be back on the case soon, I'm sure, Sam, and I trust him to make some progress on finding the killer."

"I keep telling you, Dad, he's not my Daniyaal," I said, blushing a little. "We had to meet regularly for the case, you know that. I like him a lot, but we can't really be friends in the current situation."

"I know, I know, I'm only teasing. I just hope he can get this whole thing sorted so that we can relax and you can enjoy time with your new friends. It's so good that you have been able to meet such nice people. It's the one compensation for this awful situation."

I agreed. I had made some lovely new friends, but at the moment, there was always the edge of suspicion or uncertainty when I was with them, and I wanted it gone.

CHAPTER 25

Real danger

Over the next few days, life seemed to return to a more normal pattern. Chloe was still teething, but loved to spend time with my parents, and was becoming ever more communicative. I managed to meet up with Beth and Deb for a walk and picnic in the park, although we all brought our own food and drink, just to be safe. Now that people were allowed to meet indoors and go on holiday again, the park was a little less crowded, although it was noticeable how many more dogs were walked there every day. I loved to see all the different shapes and sizes, and so did Chloe, but I was glad that I had spoken to Emily about it before taking the plunge myself. I saw some people really struggling with controlling their dogs, and those with small children as well clearly had a lot on their hands. Maybe I would get a cat in the autumn, but I was not sure yet.

Beth seemed to be continuing to make progress and enjoyed chatting to us both. She would not talk about the murders at all, but was eager to discuss her volunteering. She had enjoyed helping Stephen so much that she had gone on a council list now, to support people who could not get out. She was still avoiding meeting people inside or in large groups, but the absolute fear and avoidance of social interaction had dissipated. The grateful thanks of the people she helped was a real boost to her self-esteem and gave her a feeling of purpose.

I arranged to help Celia with the next old people's coffee morning, thinking that would be a good time to chat to her. She sounded listless and strained on the phone. Her voice had none of its normal sharpness and intensity. I could understand why Stephen was worried about her. I thought she sounded really depressed.

The media attention had drifted away, as other more exciting stories appeared, and the town gossip mill also seemed to have lost interest in the murder case, since nothing appeared to be happening. Daniyaal was now back at work, conducting interviews, but apparently the inspector was too unwell to return yet, and was only recovering slowly. He still had DS Botts helping him and I saw them occasionally from a distance. I had the feeling, somehow, that they did not get on very well. There was nothing comfortable or familiar about the way they walked together. Daniyaal would wave back if he spotted me, but DS Botts had a singularly disapproving way of staring at me. I was glad Daniyaal was back. I would not feel comfortable reporting anything to the other sergeant.

I had not heard anything from Lesley and was glad of it, but out of the blue I received a message from her. I almost did not look at it, afraid that it might just be more abuse, but in fact it was an apology and a plea. She said that she was terribly sorry, had only now realised how offensive what she said had been, and just wanted to see me, to make it right face to face.

I took several hours to reply. I did not really want to see Lesley at all. But I had never been one to bear a grudge and I hated the thought of having an enemy in the town. Bitterness poisons everything and, much as I dreaded it, I knew I had to face up to her and let go of my resentment and anger. For my sake, and Chloe's, not for Lesley's. So I agreed, reluctantly, that she could come round for half an hour, on the following morning. I did not tell anyone that she was coming. I knew that they would probably try to dissuade me from seeing her at all, and that they would be right in many ways. But I felt I had to do this. If she became abusive again I would ring someone straight away and I knew that they would come and rescue me.

For this reason I had my phone in my pocket when she came to the side gate and knocked. Chloe was happily sitting on her blanket, surrounded by cushions, playing with a board book about trains, which she particularly loved. Lesley had brought a sleeping Charlie in the buggy and Jackie, wide-eyed and anxious as ever, who trotted straight over to Chloe.

"Do you want a drink, Lesley?" My voice sounded cold and hard, although I tried to look welcoming.

"Oh, yes please, Sam, it's so hot today. Just a glass of something cold will be fine. Thank you." She was obviously determined to be conciliatory. I stalked inside to pour a drink for her and get some juice and biscuits for Jackie. This was going to be difficult.

I was still getting things onto a tray, when Jackie crept in and came over to me. She tugged at my skirt and mumbled: "Chloe".

"Oh dear, is Chloe upset? Don't worry, she's teething and that makes her cry more often. I will be there in a sec."

But the little girl looked up at me with really scared eyes and said: "Mum", pointing out to the garden.

I do not know why, and it certainly was not a reasoned reaction, but somehow I knew something was wrong. I was about to run outside to see what was happening, when I remembered my phone and swiped it on quickly. No time to think, I just went to recent calls and clicked on the first one I saw.

Suddenly I heard Lesley's voice from outside, calling my name with urgency in her voice. I thrust my phone into my skirt pocket and rushed outside holding the tray precariously, so that some of the drink spilled. Jackie was still clutching my skirt and came out with me, but she slowed me down and I almost tripped over the doorstep.

"What is it, Lesley? Is something wrong?"

As I emerged onto the patio, my heart stopped, and I

dropped the whole tray with a loud crash. My brain simply would not take in what I was seeing. Lesley was sitting at the table, with Chloe wriggling restlessly on her lap, and she had a knife. A very sharp-looking, dangerous kitchen knife. She was holding it to the side of Chloe's neck, so that the baby could not see it. For a horrible moment, I thought I was actually going to faint as things began to go black and there was a roaring in my ears.

"Sit down, you stupid cow. You can't faint now," spat Lesley. The hostility in her voice upset Chloe, who began to whimper. I could not speak. The terror had completely gripped me like a hand squeezing the life out of my heart, but I did slip into the nearest chair, never taking my eyes off that knife.

A terrified prayer was running through my head - 'Oh God, please no, please don't let her do it. Please God, please.' Over and over again. I think my lips were even moving, but no sound was coming out.

"You're pathetic," she snarled. "You actually believed I was going to apologise. To you! Of all people. You have no idea at all. You're a stinking hypocrite and a foul cowardly little rat! That Sergeant Botts let it out when he came to interview me again. You've been talking to the police, to that stupid coloured sergeant, all the time. I don't know what you said about me, probably all lies anyway, but it was obviously enough to get them looking into me. They've been round to my house three times already. So when I'm finished here, I'm going to leave this boring little town and go somewhere a bit more exciting."

I was not really taking in what she was saying. Please ... Please, God, no.

"What's that you're saying? Please? You should be begging. I quite fancy making you go down on your knees before me. That would be a laugh. You think you're so superior, but you're going to have to beg for your life, for your child's life, from me."

Not stopping to think or even for her to force me, I did it, I slipped from the chair to the ground, to my knees, hands clasped in front of me. But not begging her, begging God to save Chloe.

She laughed triumphantly.

"If only your friends could see you now, down on your knees in front of me! They think you're so wonderful - but they don't know how weak and useless you really are."

Chloe cried out, but then sat more quietly, looking down at me. I tried to put all my love into my eyes. Stay still, my little one. Don't move, don't give her any excuse.

"Maybe you think I'm crazy, but I'm not. I'm just clever. I'm really good at this. None of you even suspected it was me all along, and the police - well, they had absolutely no idea, they were worse than useless. Even when I was just experimenting, trying things out, no one could work out that it was me. It was so funny to see smug little Charlotte, with her perfect life, begging people to believe that she hadn't tried to commit suicide. She needed to be brought down a peg or two, and I did that. She was desperate. It was so satisfying seeing her squirm, seeing her get more and more anxious and sicker every day."

She was enjoying her story, sneering at her victim, so much so that the knife dropped a bit. I was so focused on that knife. I had to distract her, keep her talking somehow. She loved an audience - she was bound to want to tell me how clever she had been, now that it was finally out in the open. I tried to moisten my lips and speak, but only a croak came out at first.

"But Lesley, why Kate?"

"I didn't intend it to be her when I went. I just thought about how successful I had been with Charlotte. OK, she wasn't dead, but it had hurt her more than killing her would have done. And her perfect family! So I was looking for someone else to pick on. I actually thought of Sophy - she's so cocky and sure of herself - or your friend Deb. I don't know why she has the cheek to think that she can organise everything. She's nothing special."

It was working, she was loving explaining her motivation to me. But to think I could have lost Deb - I could not face that thought.

"But then Kate turned up, looking all prim and proper. And everyone was hanging on her lips, making her, her, of all people, the centre of attention. No one wanted to know what I had been through. It was all about Kate. I wanted to slap her black face, make her shut up. But I had a better way to shut her up. I had decided to go with co-codamol this time as it was stronger and would have a greater effect. I used to work part-time in a pharmacy when I was a teenager, did you know that? I don't think the police even bothered to find out. So I know something about side effects and dosages."

She actually sounded less hostile towards me now that I was her audience, as if she wanted to make me admire her brilliance.

"I didn't actually think she would die - she shouldn't have done. Maybe it was to do with the cancer treatment. I didn't know she was ill. Or perhaps she was just weak, maybe she had bad genes or something."

Anger stirred again in my heart, but I pushed it down.

"She had a condition that affected how her body processed codeine. She could never take it," I managed to get out.

"Really? That's interesting. I didn't know that. Anyway, she died, but this time no one thought it was suicide, which was a bit disappointing. It made you all so sad, but it wasn't as satisfying as humiliating Charlotte. I wanted her to suffer, not die in her sleep."

I was shaking at the effort needed to keep my voice neutral, my words inoffensive.

"You probably could get away with it then, Lesley, with a good lawyer. You could say the dose wasn't high enough to kill her and the same with Charlotte."

"I could, couldn't I? But then I did kill Charlotte and that time I really meant it. I was so fed up with her whining and attention-seeking, her smugness and the way she looked down on me because I wasn't rich like her, because I don't have the perfect family any more. But in the end, I had to protect myself. She knew I had worked at a pharmacy and I couldn't risk her telling the police. So I sucked up to her, made her feel like I sympathised with everything she had been through. I said I would go round with a special tonic I knew about, which would make her feel much better. Ha! She was such a sucker. She was delighted to have someone on her side, when all the rest of you had turned against her."

"You took a big risk. She could have told Michael that you were going round - she nearly did."

"I would have found a way to manage it, don't you worry. Anyway, risks are what this is all about. The more the risk, the more exciting it is! I thought at first that she might have seen me tampering with her coffee, but now I don't think so. But she definitely needed to go. So I made up a really strong concentration of soluble paracetamol and codeine with orange squash and gave it to her. I told her it would make her very sleepy, but that she would wake up feeling much better. And she believed me - at least at first."

"It was clever of you to make her drink it herself."

Lesley suddenly looked a bit suspicious.

"Don't think you can get around me like that. I know what I did. But yes, it was clever. I knew she would be affected really quickly, with all her liver damage. She soon started feeling woozy. I reassured her, but she had a look of real fear in her eyes, as if she somehow knew what was happening, knew what I had done. I stuck with my role of helpful friend, but it was so good to see her looking frightened, suspecting what I had done but still not accepting it. I helped her to lie down on the sofa, assured her that she would feel better when she woke up. I was laughing inside. She would never wake up. Then I went and put the empty packets by the glass. I was using latex gloves all the time, you know, so only Charlotte's prints would be on the glass. It would have been such a bonus if everyone had thought she had killed herself. But I suppose that was too much to hope for."

"No fingerprints on the packets."

"Oh, is that how they knew so quickly? I should have thought about that. I could have pressed her fingers onto them, but I wanted to leave while she was still more or less conscious. That worked out so well. Making them all suspect that soppy vicar! As if he would have had the guts to do anything like that."

"I don't understand why you spoke to the press though. Didn't it draw attention to you?"

"Well, yes, but it was so much fun putting the suspicion onto him. He's such a slimy hypocrite. Pretending to be so caring, but only with the people he likes. He never gave me any real help or support. And I loved having everyone listen to me and not know what I had done. It was a delicious feeling - I loved the risk, it made me feel alive! I felt so powerful."

Her eyes were blazing with delight and the knife was waving around, not so near to Chloe.

"Until you, you took it all away. The media were much more interested in you and your 'tragedy' than in what I had to say. I started to really hate you then. Before that, you were just a nonentity. I even thought at one point we could be friends, as we had both lost our husbands, but you're so PC, so conventional, I knew we had nothing in common."

I had to stop myself from telling her that we could never have been friends, but I think she saw it in my eyes.

"I know what you are thinking. You think you are above me. So superior, always on the moral high ground. And you've got them all thinking you are so perfect. Even Annette - I couldn't believe it when she came round and shouted at me like that. Why would she want to defend you? She resented Charlotte as much as I did. I don't know what you did to get them all on your side. Somehow you wormed your way in and now they all love you!"

Her eyes slipped to Jackie, still standing as close as she could to me.

"Even my own daughter! She was always a daddy's girl, we never got on at all, but now she loves you so much. It's Sam this, Sam that, until I have to make her shut up."

Her voice was vicious. I did not like to think what she must have done to make Jackie be quiet.

"I want her to see you suffer, you know. I gave Charlie something to make him sleep, so that he wouldn't get in the way, but

I want Jackie to see that you are only human, that you are weak and useless, and that you can't protect her, or Chloe, or yourself."

Her voice was rising into a frenzy. I looked over at Charlie's buggy. I had been worrying about how quiet he was.

"Oh, don't worry - I know how to dose him. How do you think I get him to sleep so well? And it didn't do Jackie any harm did it?"

Chloe was starting to moan and whimper again, struggling against Lesley's strong hand. I dared not let this go on any longer. I looked up at my beautiful daughter and suddenly found the ability to speak more clearly.

"Look, Lesley - it's me you want to hurt. Take me instead of Chloe. Please. I'm begging you."

Lesley looked thoughtful.

"Well, I think probably the best way to really hurt you, would be to kill Chloe."

I screamed in terror, but only inside my head. I could not let her hear it. She must not know what I felt.

"But I suppose once she's dead, you could run off or come at me - I wouldn't have any hold over you any more." She sounded horribly rational and calculating.

"I guess it might be better to kill you, first."

That little word at the end dropped like ice into my heart. So she would still kill Chloe after me. Somehow I had to stop that happening, but make her think that I was still docile.

"How are we going to do this, though?" she mused. "I'm not putting Chloe down until I have you in my hands."

I thought quickly.

"We could get the buggy and you could put her in there once I get over to you."

Lesley's eyes narrowed, thinking it through.

"That could work. Where's the buggy?"

"It's in the hall by the front door. Jackie could get it, couldn't you, darling? You're such a brave little girl."

I looked down at the quiet child, with those over-intelligent eyes. She nodded determinedly.

"Oh well, go on then, Jackie. I don't know why you always want to please Sam, but I guess it's useful now. Go quickly and come straight back with the buggy."

The little girl hurried into the house. I looked at Chloe, praying, praying for her safety. Praying for her to be calm for now. It seemed like an eternity until Jackie came back with the pushchair.

"You certainly took your time," snapped Lesley. "Bring it here."

With some difficulty, Jackie manoeuvred the buggy round the table until it was next to her mother.

"Now, you, come here. And no tricks or your daughter dies." It sounded theatrical, but the threat was all too real.

She actually held the knife against Chloe's throat. I held my precious baby's eyes and made a long quiet 'ssssh' noise to try to keep her calm, while I struggled up from my knees and moved carefully round the table.

"Jackie, can you please wheel Chloe over toward the gate as soon as she is in the buggy? I don't want - I don't want her to see this." My voice shook at the end, but Jackie nodded. It was all I could do to protect her, to protect them.

Somehow Lesley managed to slide Chloe into the buggy, still holding the knife to her and then made me turn my back to her. I could now feel the knife pricking into my back through my thin summer dress.

"Go, Jackie, go please." My voice sounded strangled, but it was enough. She pushed the heavy buggy over the grass towards the side gate.

"Not too far, Jackie," insisted Lesley, but the little girl just kept on going as if she had not heard. I was so proud of her.

Now my knees began to shake. Could she really kill me in cold blood? If I didn't anger her, would I survive? But I could feel her trembling with suppressed excitement. This was what she wanted to do. I knew she wanted to make me suffer. She pressed the knife painfully against my back. It felt as if it had broken the skin and something warm and liquid began to run down my spine under the dress.

"I will still kill her, you know," she whispered into my ear with disgusting relish. "But first, I'm going to hurt you - really really badly."

I could not stop the shudder going through my body, but I was not going to beg for my life, or even for a quick death. I could beg for Chloe's life, but I would not give Lesley the satisfaction of grovelling to her to try to save myself. I closed my eyes and took a slow calming breath and held it, waiting for the pain to come.

Suddenly, just as I could feel Lesley reaching her other arm around my neck to pull me back into the knife, the whole garden exploded with noise. I felt a sharp blow on my back, but then strong arms came round me, pulling me away from Lesley, and I heard Daniyaal's voice in my ear:"Sam! You're OK, I've got you." My eyes flew open onto a scene of chaos I could not make sense of.

The garden seemed to be full of people, all moving with purpose, all shouting loudly, although I could not make out the words. Two burly men with police stab vests on were fighting with Lesley, trying to wrest the knife out of her hand while she struggled wildly, screaming and swearing. Both of them were already bleeding slightly from cuts to the hands and arms.

Daniyaal swung me gently round and let me down into a chair. He gave me a swift, searching look, nodded, and turned to help them, grabbing Lesley's wrist and squeezing it hard, saying "Drop it, drop it now" in a voice I hardly recognised, full of contained fury. In the end, she squealed in pain and let it fall. It landed on the edge of the table and lay there, with blood dripping slowly from the tip. I could not take my eyes off it. The overwhelming noise seemed to dim, as if it was coming from a long way away.

The three men managed to get Lesley onto the ground, still shouting obscenities at them and kicking out when she could. They eventually put handcuffs on her behind her back and suddenly she stopped fighting and went still. Immediately, they pulled her up to her feet. She was facing me and I could see the personal venom and hatred still in her eyes. Suddenly she spat right at me. I could not even flinch. None of it seemed real to me. But it fell short anyway. Daniyaal surged forward, but a tall woman officer in jeans and a stab vest, put her arm up to stop him, saying, "No, Sergeant - she's not worth it." He fell back obediently, and looked away.

As if she had shot her last bullet, Lesley became very passive. Her eyes were now just empty, black holes in a face still red with exertion. Some spittle was dribbling down her chin, but she seemed unaware of it. The officers turned her round and began to walk her towards the gate, which stood wide open. As they went, the female officer looked back at me, smiled warmly and mouthed: "Well done". I tried to make myself smile back, but my face would not work.

As reaction started to set in and I began to shake all over, I looked round for Chloe, but could not see her. I realised that she had been screaming in terror for the last few minutes.

"Chloe!" I tried to shout, but only a croak came out.

All at once, the crowd of unknown people between me and the gate parted and I saw Chloe in her buggy, struggling and wailing. Jackie was next to her, trying to hold her hand and comfort her, but to no avail. I began to try to struggle to my feet, but stopped as Daniyaal pushed the buggy up to me. As soon as she saw me, Chloe stopped crying and held out her little arms. I sobbed as Daniyaal passed her to me and I enveloped her in a hug, trying not to squeeze her too hard in the sudden rush of emotion. As I leaned forward, rocking with her tightly enclosed in my arms, Daniyaal suddenly exclaimed:

"Sam! You're hurt. You didn't say. You're bleeding. Did the knife get you after all?"

"It's nothing, just a scratch. I felt her hit my back, that's all."

He wanted to take Chloe off me in order to have a proper look, but I would not, could not let her go. He turned and told a constable to fetch the paramedics.

"They're just checking the prisoner over," he said.

Daniyaal's eyes blazed.

"This is urgent," he snapped. "We have a stab wound here. Go and get them straight away."

The constable hurried off. As he approached the gate, more people ran in. It was my parents and Deb, looking frantic. As they rushed up to me, I tried to tell them it was all OK, but the words stuck in my throat and suddenly the tears came, pouring down my face. Mum took one look at me, the knife, and my bloodstained dress and gently took Chloe from my grip, holding her gently, talking quietly to her, soothing her, and walking up and down the lawn, with my father in close attendance.

Deb, taking in the situation at a glance, took little Jackie by the hand and walked her over to the other buggy, where Charlie was now starting to murmur as the drug wore off. Daniyaal looked at me rather anxiously, muttered impatiently, and then rushed off to see where the paramedics were.

A very gentle hand touched my shoulder. I turned to see Stephen, his face pale with fright and lips bitten until they had bled. Celia was hovering in the background, looking very anxious and strangely uncertain.

"Stephen! How did you get here?" I asked through my tears.

"That can wait, I can see that you are hurt." He took out a spotless white handkerchief, made a ball of it and pressed it against my back. Suddenly I realised that it was actually hurting a lot and I winced at his touch.

"Sorry, I know it hurts, but I need to put pressure on it, you know. To stop the bleeding."

His hand held my shoulder as he put even pressure on my back. It was painful, but it seemed to bring me back to reality. I looked across the garden to where Deb was trying to comfort a crying Charlie with Jackie clinging to her legs.

"Celia, do you think you could help Deb? The children ..."

My voice failed as I remembered how brave Jackie had been. She saved Chloe. Celia looked at my face and did not wait for any more explanation, but hurried over to help.

All at once the paramedics were there, pushing Stephen out of the way and taking control of the situation. I just let it happen, with my eyes following my parents and Chloe. I breathed a prayer of thanks. She was safe. I could let go. I barely noticed the paramedics cutting open the back of my dress and dealing with the wound. They were trying to talk to me, using my full name, Samantha, but I just could not make myself respond.

"She needs a lot of stitches and I think they will keep her for observation," one of the medics said quietly to Daniyaal. "Looks like severe shock and she seems to have lost quite a lot of blood. We'll take her in the ambulance. I'll just go and get the cart."

"But I can walk," I tried to say through the fog, and attempted to pull myself up.

"No, you can't," said Stephen firmly. "Please just let them look after you."

Daniyaal brought my mother and Chloe over to me.

"You definitely need to go and get your treatment," she said firmly. "Chloe is fine now, and you know she will be happy and safe with me and your father. We'll stay here tonight. I think you'll need to stay in hospital. You can trust us to keep her safe and well."

I looked at Chloe, so content in Mum's arms, and nodded dumbly. Just let it happen. Then I remembered Jackie and Charlie.

"What about those poor children? What will happen to them now?"

"A WPC has already contacted their father and he is coming to pick them up from the station. It'll probably take a couple of hours, but they will be fine."

"Please, please can you let them stay here, with people they know, until he comes? Jackie -" my voice broke again. "Jackie saved Chloe, she was so brave. And I think Lesley has been abusing her. And she drugged poor little Charlie." I stumbled over the words, the tears coming again, as the events of the morning started to come back.

"Of course, if you are happy for them to stay here, their father can come here. I'm sure Deb and Celia will look after them. I'd better get a doctor to check them over anyway, from what you say. But I think that it can wait until he arrives. There's been enough trauma for them already."

I tried to brush away the tears and thank Daniyaal, but the words wouldn't come. Stephen quietly took my hand and held it gently, until the cart arrived and I was wheeled away, trying to hold back the sobs which seemed to come up from my feet and shake my whole body. I turned my head away, so that people wouldn't see. But Daniyaal was walking by my side.

"Don't try to hold it in, Sam. Better not. They'll give you something to calm you down when you get to the hospital, I expect. But this is a normal reaction, shock and trauma. I'll come and visit you tomorrow morning and see how you're doing. I'll have to get your statement, but it can all wait for now."

He pressed my hand as he said goodbye while I was loaded into the ambulance. The paramedics chatted soothingly to me and I closed my eyes, my body still shaking with painful sobs.

CHAPTER 26

Reaction

After a night's heavy medication-induced sleep, I woke up in a hospital bed, with a stabbing pain in my back as I rolled over. There seemed to be a thick bandage on my wound, and I struggled to push myself up into a more comfortable position. I was glad to be in a small room on my own. I felt desperately thirsty and reached painfully for the jug of water by the bed. It was warm and tasted slightly stale, but it was what I needed. I sank back and the discomfort eased a little. My brain would not work, it had just shut down. I could not think about what had happened or what was coming. Gradually I drifted into an uneasy doze, until a nurse came in. She did her observations gently and quietly, and then asked if I was hungry. I shook my head. Not at all. In fact I felt a bit nauseous.

"Are you in any pain?"

This time I had to nod. Yes, it was increasingly sore and painful.

"I'll bring you something to take. Just rest if you can. I'll make sure you aren't disturbed for now."

She smiled down at me and I tried to smile my thanks. When I had taken the meds, I drifted off to sleep again, welcoming the oblivion, letting the darkness ooze up and take me.

Later, I was woken by someone bringing in lunch for me. It was not very appetising, but she said I should try to eat, so I forced some of it down. It did give me a little strength and I began to come to myself, although I still could not think clearly.

After another doze, I awoke to see Daniyaal sitting in the chair by my bed, mask on as usual, looking down at his phone, as if he was reading something. It took me several tries to get a word out, but in the end I managed to say hello.

He looked up quickly, smiling, but with concern in his bright eyes.

"Sam, it's good to see you awake at last. I'm so sorry that we didn't treat your injury properly yesterday. It meant you lost a lot more blood than you should have done. Apparently you will have to stay in for another night, just until your blood pressure comes up and you are stable."

"Is that why I feel so weak and sleepy?"

I felt my voice coming a bit more clearly now.

"Never mind, Daniyaal, you were rather busy! And you got me help as soon as you knew I was hurt. To be honest, I didn't realise, myself, that I had been stabbed. I just felt a blow between my shoulders, never thought it was that hideous knife. And holding onto Chloe did me far more good than anything else, anyway."

"I know, but I have experience of stab wounds and I should have checked. I should have noticed all the blood. At least the vicar put some pressure on the wound for you. I was quite surprised that he acted so quickly. I've always thought he was a bit scatty and vague."

"He can be, but he's really good in a crisis."

I smiled at him rather uncertainly.

"Have you come to take my statement?"

He shook his head.

"I've spoken to your doctor and he says you are not up to that yet. I just wanted to see for myself that you are OK."

"That is very kind of you. Now that I am starting to feel human again, I have a lot of questions about what happened, how you all got there in time. I can't understand how it all worked out."

"Well, the doctor wants you to rest, so I'll tell you everything and then you don't need to ask questions. OK?"

I nodded. The more I thought about it, the less I understood how he had arrived in the nick of time. I did not know if it was just that my brain still was not working properly, but it was a real puzzle.

"Where should I start? Well, DS Botts and I were at the other end of town, talking to one of Emily's clients to see if we could get a better alibi for her, when a call was passed through from one of your neighbours, old Mrs Pereira from the house behind yours. She had heard a crash and then loud angry voices from your garden and went upstairs to see what was going on. She couldn't see much, but she saw enough to be really worried about you and to ring us. I had just put the phone down and we were getting into the car to come over and investigate, when I had another call. This time it was from Celia. She was very agitated, but managed to explain that you had called Stephen and not said anything, but left the line open. He could hear what was going on and made her ring me straight away. Luckily I had given him my card."

"I completely forgot that I had left the phone on! It was in my pocket. It just went out of my head as soon as I saw - saw Chloe, and that knife."

I gulped hard. That image would live with me for a long time. I did not think I would ever quite get over it.

Daniyaal smiled reassuringly and patted my hand.

"It's OK, Sam, you know she's safe now and Lesley won't harm anyone else again - ever, hopefully."

I drew in a shuddering breath and nodded, asking him to go on. So many people to thank for saving me and Chloe.

"Botts and I don't always see eye to eye, but he's very good at tech stuff. He said that there was a way for us to be able to hear what was coming through on Stephen's phone as well - we would try a low-tech way which would be quicker, but there was a hi-tech approach which would also be possible. I think, in fact, they just used Celia's phone with Stephen's on speakerphone, but I don't know for sure. I was focused on driving as fast as I safely could – we couldn't risk putting on the lights or siren, as that would spook Lesley, so it wasn't easy. I called the station on the radio and they got plenty of back up over to your house, as well as - well, as well as an ambulance. We knew you and Chloe were in terrible danger."

His voice roughened a little as he said that. The echo of those moments of real fear showed in his face. He swallowed hard and carried on.

"Soon we could hear what was happening in the garden too. Obviously you know what was said, you were there, but it was awful listening to that woman threatening you and Chloe. I could hear little gasps and groans from the vicar too, so I can only imagine what he was thinking. He had got Celia to drive him over to your house, and was sitting in the car waiting for us when we arrived."

"I wondered how he and Celia got there."

"He utterly refused to stay at the rectory. Insisted on coming. And, as it happened, he was useful. Surprisingly so."

"I told you he was good in a crisis." I smiled. People always judged Stephen by his manner and were put off by his social anxiety, but he definitely had hidden depths.

"I suppose you're right. Well, we were in a quandary. We couldn't storm the house or garden, not while Lesley had Chloe as a hostage. No one had a key, so we couldn't get in quietly. We decided to be as silent as possible and try to choose the best moment to intervene. By this time the inspector had arrived."

"I thought she was still off sick."

"She was, but she heard what was happening and insisted on coming over to help. She was amazingly impressed at your calmness and quick thinking, you know, Sam. And she really isn't easy to impress."

"I wasn't calm at all, not really. Not inside. But I had to keep her talking for as long as possible, to keep Chloe alive." My hands trembled again at the thought of what could have happened. I shook my head to chase away the terrible thought and asked him to go on.

"Well, it was you offering to take Chloe's place that really helped, Sam. I honestly don't know how we would have approached it otherwise. We heard Lesley agreeing to it and sending Jackie in for the buggy. The inspector thought we might be able to get her to open the door for us. But obviously she doesn't know our voices or anything. So Stephen insisted that he could do it. He knew that Jackie would recognise his voice, and hopefully trust him as a friend of yours."

I looked at him in complete surprise.

"You mean she did open the door? I suppose she might just have been able to reach up to the handle, but I - I would never have thought she would or could do something like that."

"She's a really special little girl, Sam. Stephen was whispering to her through the letterbox, but we didn't really know if it would work. She never said anything, but suddenly the door opened up. We knew we couldn't just come in and rescue you, with Chloe still in Lesley's hands, but we moved quietly up through to the living room and waited by the patio doors for an opportunity. The inspector had the backup team by the side gate ready to go at the same time."

"I can't believe all this. It's like something out of a film. How on earth did you manage to stop Jackie from letting on to her mother when she came back?"

"Stephen talked to her very seriously about how much danger you were in, and she just nodded. She doesn't talk much, but she's so intelligent. Anyway, we just had to trust her. I had more trouble persuading Stephen and Celia not to come with us when we went in to grab Lesley! But they did understand that it was very risky and that they could inadvertently put you or Chloe in more danger. I made them stay in the kitchen, so that they weren't tempted to run out after us."

"It must have been hard for them to wait like that. How did my parents and Deb arrive? I was so thankful to see them."

"The inspector contacted them as soon as she arrived at the scene. She thought they might be needed or might have a front door key. That's also when we first contacted Lesley's husband. We hoped he might be able to talk Lesley down, if it turned into a traditional hostage situation."

"I don't think that would have worked. She was - she was enjoying herself. I don't think I've ever seen her look so happy and excited."

"Mmmm. I don't think that she is insane in the legal sense, although her lawyer will probably try to say that she is, but the inspector, who knows a lot about psychology, was using words like 'narcissistic psychopath' and 'personality disorder', so you're probably right. She certainly has sadistic tendencies, that was obvious listening to her talk. Getting away, literally, with murder twice just encouraged her down that path, let her follow her innate instincts. I think your vicar friend might say that she was just evil."

"I don't know, Stephen doesn't seem to think that way, but the pleasure she took in hurting me, even in hurting her own daughter - there has to be something very wrong with her."

I shuddered again at the thought.

"I really want to get home and see Chloe."

He looked at me with pity in his eyes. I could see that he understood something of the pain caused by the flashes of memory which kept coming, now that I was more awake.

"I think they will let you home tomorrow. I know that your friends would all, all of them, love to come and visit you, but the media are lined up outside and are desperate for some dramatic pictures, so we all decided that it would be better not to do that. And all those cameras and that shouting would be far too traumatic for Chloe. They'll be at home waiting for you in the morning. I'm going to make a short statement about the case when I leave and hopefully that will pacify them for a while. But I think you may need to speak to them very briefly tomorrow when you leave the hospital. I am going to try to make sure that they leave you alone at home, on the understanding that you will say something here. Is that OK with you? I know you would love to get away from them completely, but if you avoid them, the paparazzi will keep trying to sneak a photograph of you, and you will all be pestered at home non-stop."

After everything that had happened the last time I was in the papers and on television, I really did not want to give them anything to work with, but I could see the sense in what he was saying. Better to get it over with.

"Can you make sure someone brings me a comb then, please? I can't go out there with my hair all matted like this."

"It looks fine to me, but of course. They'll have to bring clothes and things for you anyway. You can't go home in that hospital gown."

I laughed and winced. Laughing was definitely painful.

"What about her children, Jackie and Charlie? How are they?"

Daniyaal looked concerned.

"Well, you were right about Charlie being drugged. He was given a small dose of some narcotic to make him sleep. And it seems that she had used that drug on him before. It may cause him a few problems going forward getting used to being without it, but hopefully he will get over it soon. As for Jackie, the doctor did find some serious bruising, burn scars, and even evidence of healed broken ribs. All in places where they would not be seen. Definite signs of serious physical abuse - and that is without the evidence of emotional abuse we have from what we heard Lesley saying."

I felt sick. Such a lovely little girl, brutalised like that.

"I hope so much that she will begin to recover now. She deserves to be happy. She saved Chloe's life."

"I know, Sam. Her father and grandparents are taking good care of her and she will get counselling, which should help. I think, when things have settled down, she would really like to see you. She kept asking us where you were, how you were. Deb and Celia looked after her very well, but she just wanted you. I think your kindness made a really powerful impression on a child who had not experienced much affection in her life recently."

I felt such love for that brave girl. If I could, I would help to make things better for her.

"I would really like to see her again soon. Please send her my love, if that is possible. I will never ever forget what she did. And I hope that I can stay in touch with her."

Daniyaal looked at me with understanding in his eyes.

"I think her father would like that. I understand that it is important, to you and to her."

"Thank you so much for coming and taking the time to talk me through it all, Daniyaal. I really appreciate it."

"You deserve to hear what happened, Sam. Actually the inspector said that, when she gave me permission to come. We're - we're all extremely happy and relieved that you are alive and safe, and so is Chloe, and that this very unpleasant case is finally solved, thanks to you."

"Not really thanks to me, but yes, it feels good that I no longer have to suspect any of my friends. You've been very kind to me. I - I'll miss our talks." I was a bit embarrassed to say it, but felt that I needed to.

"Me too," he said, warmly. "Maybe, when the court case is over and done with, we could meet for a coffee?"

"I would like that."

After he had gone, I felt utterly exhausted. I still had no strength or stamina. I was quite glad to have another night's rest in prospect before facing the media, even though I desperately needed to see Chloe, and my family and friends. I slept restlessly for most of the evening and then much better all night, feeling more comfortable once they had given me some more strong painkillers.

Next morning, Deb appeared quite early, soon after breakfast. The doctor had been round and discharged me, but said I needed to rest and to keep an eye out for any signs of infection in my wound. I was to be very careful indeed when picking up my baby, he said, as I had a lot of stitches in my back and they needed to heal.

"I wondered who would come to pick me up," I commented. "I'm glad it's you, Deb."

"I don't want to hurt your back, but I would love to give you the biggest hug. Have a virtual one, anyway."

We smiled lovingly at each other. Having Deb there was like having a sister with me. Then Deb helped me to get dressed, putting my arms into the sleeves so carefully, to avoid hurting me. She had brought a comb, wipes and make-up, and a mask for me to wear. She made me sit still and quiet as she got me ready, touching me as gently as possible while she made me more presentable.

"We can't have you looking a mess on television," she teased, before continuing, more seriously. "Stephen is here, and he will wheel you out. You know they won't let you walk! Celia has the car ready to bring up to the door when we've finished. Your father wanted to come, but your mum thought that pushing the wheelchair wouldn't do his blood pressure any good. And they've both been working so hard, tidying up the house and garden for you. It was left in quite a mess when the crime scene people were finished. Are you going to be OK going back there? I know it will be full of – well, of very traumatic memories."

Deb sounded hesitant, worried.

"I did think about that last night. It won't be easy to go back there, after everything that has happened. But Thomas and I made that garden together and I won't let that - that woman ruin it for me. The longer I put it off, the harder it will be, so I would much rather go straight home."

"I think you're right," responded Deb, thoughtfully. "You have so many good memories of that place. And you will be making more, with Chloe, your parents and all your friends."

Soon I was ready, or as ready as I would ever be. I had jotted down a few words to say on the previous evening, remembering Daniyaal's previous good advice. I popped the piece of paper into my pocket and put my mask on, while Deb went to fetch Stephen and the chair.

He still looked pale and a bit haggard and there were deep shadows under his eyes, but he was smiling brightly, I could see his eyes glistening above the mask.

"So glad to see you looking better, Sam. Can you get into the chair yourself, or do I need to help you?"

I smiled at him gratefully.

"I'm much better now, thanks, Stephen. I can manage. I just need to move slowly and carefully to avoid jarring it."

In spite of what I said, he took my arm and guided me carefully into my seat. I looked up at him over my shoulder.

"I will say more when there is time, Stephen, but I just want to thank you, and Celia, for everything you did yesterday. You saved me, and Chloe."

He reddened.

"Not really. Anyone would have done the same. Just glad it was my number you rang and I happened to be free and at home to pick it up. But - in spite of hearing all those terrible things she was saying - I held on to hope and just prayed all the way to your house. Non-stop. I knew - I trusted - hoped that God would protect you both from her. Deliver them from evil, that's what kept going through my mind. And He did."

I reached up to touch his hand.

"Just accept the thanks, Stephen. Please."

He nodded silently, his eyes bright with unshed tears, and we moved out of the side room, through the end of the ward and down the corridor. Deb was waiting at the end of the corridor.

"Ready?" she asked. I took a deep breath and nodded. Then it was out into the blazing glare of television lights and flashing cameras, with constant shouts of 'Sam, look this way, Sam!'. It was intimidating. It was all I could do not to flinch away and cover my eyes.

Slowly I took out my small piece of paper and took off my mask, as we were now outside. The noise gradually quietened down. Microphones and mobile phones were thrust towards me. I tried to focus only on the words on the paper.

"I - I would like to thank everyone involved in my rescue yesterday - they saved my life and that of my baby daughter." A pause, while I gulped back the emotion which tried to seep out. "I would especially like to thank the police involved in this case, particularly Sergeant Evans and Inspector Morton, who have given me exemplary support, and took such swift action yesterday when things came to a head. Thank you also to the paramedics and hospital staff who treated me and made me comfortable. Now that it is all over, I am hoping to go home and get back to some kind of normality. Thank you. That's all I have."

I folded the paper and hoped that would be it. I really did not want to answer any questions, but they started to fly in, everyone speaking at once. Then one relatively quiet but very assertive male voice came through the muddle:

"How did you feel when your baby was being threatened by the killer?"

I felt angry that anyone could ask such a question.

"How do you think I felt? I felt as if my life was ending, as if my heart would explode - but I could not let it happen. I had to do everything I could to save her."

I could not see who had asked the question, but I glared fiercely in the direction of the voice, anger helping me to control my emotions.

Deb stepped confidently forward and held up her hand.

"No more questions," she said firmly, and Stephen quickly wheeled me round the corner to the car where Celia was waiting.

"Well done, Sam. I'm sorry about that question, but you answered it brilliantly. You really sounded strong and fierce, not as if you were just a victim. You're amazing. And it's done with now." Deb gave my arm a squeeze as we sat together in the back of the car. I tried to breathe slowly and calmly. All over. And soon I would be home.

As we pulled up outside the house, I felt a strange mixture of excitement and apprehension. I could hardly wait to see Chloe, but I was not sure how my body and mind would react to seeing the garden again. I did not know if I would be able to control my instinctive reaction. Deb looked at me, and could see that I needed a moment.

"Just give her a minute, Stephen, before you come and help her out. She just needs to get her breath."

I squeezed her hand gratefully. You never had to explain things to Deb.

"OK, come on then. It's time." I tried to speak calmly, but my voice was shaking.

"You'll be fine, Sam. You are equal to anything. You are such a strong person." Amazingly, it was Celia reassuring me. Not something I would have expected to hear from her.

"Thank you so much, Celia," I said quietly. "That means a lot." I realised that I had tears in my eyes, but that it did not matter. I was home and it was time to go in.

Deb gave Stephen a signal and he came round to open the car door. Carefully, he helped me to get out and took my arm to support me up to the front door. Before we could ring the bell, the door opened and Dad was there, looking happy but very emotional, more so than I ever remembered seeing him. He insisted on taking over from Stephen and leading me through the house. The others went round to the side gate, to give us some privacy, and time to take it all in. The house smelt strange, an odour of bleach and other cleaning products overwhelming everything, even the scent of the huge bunches of flowers I could see on every table and window sill.

"So many people have brought flowers for you. Even more after seeing your Daniyaal on the television news last night. He talked about your amazing heroism, and how you had saved Chloe's life by taking her place," Dad said, when he saw me looking at them.

"But - he shouldn't have said that. I - I was so frightened. I was screaming inside. I wasn't brave or heroic at all. I feel like a fraud. I was literally on my knees in front of her at one point, praying for Chloe not to be killed, I was so scared." Another shudder ran through me at that terrible memory.

Dad felt it and turned me round to face him.

"Look, Sam, of course you were terrified. Anyone would have been. But the point is that you didn't give up. You did everything you could to save her and - and you risked your own life for her sake. And you so nearly lost it."

Dad's voice was trembling with emotion and tears ran, unnoticed, down his tanned cheeks.

"I'm so very proud of you, Sam. I'm upset because we almost lost you. But I can't regret what you did, not one bit of it."

Gently, so as not to hurt my back, he put his arms around me and hugged me, whispering in my ear that he loved me. Then he stepped back, took my arm again and led me towards the patio doors.

"And he's not my Daniyaal, as I keep telling you," I said, laughing, to break the tension.

"I think he really is, now, as far as I'm concerned," Dad responded, half-seriously. "After all, he saved your life."

So many people to be grateful to. But yes, in the end, Daniyaal was the one who had pulled me away from Lesley and that wicked knife.

"I hope you won't mind, Sam, but it's rather busy in the garden. Everyone wanted to see you, all your friends, and in the end we decided it would be less tiring for you to see them all at once! So they're all there, waiting. And Chloe, of course."

I looked at him in surprise. This was definitely not what I had expected. Oh well, I thought, just go with the flow. I nodded to him and we finally stepped through the doors onto the patio.

There was a muted cheer. Dad took me straight over to a chair and Mum brought Chloe and passed her over to me. Not seeing anything or anyone else for the moment, I held her facing me and looked into her sweet smiling eyes, overwhelmed by a surge of love for her. She gurgled at me and I pulled her into my arms and hugged her, as if I would never let her go.

Eventually, I released the hug and held her safely on my knee, looking up now at the garden and the people crowded within it. There were Stephen, Celia and Deb over near the gate, next to a table covered with food and drink. Emily, Sophy and Annette were in a close little group, looking slightly anxiously at me, but smiling broadly. They even had a sign with them saying 'Welcome home, Sam'. Even Beth was there, sitting a little way from the others, but she had come. I felt so blessed to have such lovely friends.

The garden itself still had the design Thomas and I had created, but it had been transformed. The old garden furniture was gone, even the table, and the new set was positioned differently. No blood stains could be seen, although there were some new planted pots I did not remember dotted around the place. The lawn looked new - it did not look as if it had been trampled by so many feet only a couple of days ago.

I smiled and broke the nervous tension I could feel around me.

"It looks as if I have had a garden makeover! It's amazing. How on earth did you manage that in such a short time?"

"Everyone helped. It was a real community effort - even the local garden centre got involved," said Mum, happily, obviously relieved that I liked it.

Suddenly everyone was talking and laughing. Celia started handing round cake and Deb organised champagne, fizzing away in beautiful tall glasses I had never seen before. Friends popped over to chat to me one at a time and I felt the warmth of their affection, even if some flashes of memory brought tears and moments of the shakes at times.

Eventually Beth came over, rather hesitantly, and sat down beside me for a few minutes.

"I'm so happy that you are both safe, you and Chloe," she said, quietly. "I had to come today, just to see you both. You've done so much to help me."

"Don't be silly, Beth - we loved spending time with you. I'm looking forward to getting back to our walks, and maybe another picnic, where we can actually share the food. I am so proud of the progress you have made. I thought you would find something like this much too noisy and intimidating."

Beth smiled.

"So did I. I forced myself to come, dreading it, but actually it's fine. I'm enjoying seeing people and even managing to chat a bit. Hopefully I can start inviting people round again soon."

It was wonderful to see the transformation in her. The old Beth was back, not fully herself yet, but well on the way. She walked back more confidently and went over to Deb, to offer some help with refilling glasses.

Soon, they could all see that I was getting tired, and I knew Deb and Mum would clear them out quickly. I simply did not have the words to thank them all properly, so I went for something cheesy.

Projecting my voice a little, as I used to in the classroom, I called over to Deb.

"One thing you have to promise me, Deb."

"Whatever you want, Sam. What is it?" She looked over at me. They all listened in, wondering what I was going to say.

"No more coffee mornings, ever!"

Everyone laughed.

"Definitely not! You're right, they are banned from now on."

And that was that.

THE END

ABOUT THE AUTHOR

Rosie Neale

Rosie has always wanted to write, but a career as a languages teacher never left sufficient time to engage in it seriously. Now a part-time charity worker, she is relishing the opportunity to write the Sam Elsdon series of murder mystery novels and is already planning a new series set in her home town of Milton Keynes.

BOOKS BY THIS AUTHOR

Slaybells Ring

Coming soon! The second book in the Sam Elsdon series, set at Christmas 2021.

As the town prepares to celebrate a much-needed more relaxed festive season, a wealthy businessman donates money for more impressive Christmas lights.

But the benefactor soon makes himself unpopular, tensions rise and Sam is involved in another murder inquiry ...

Printed in Great Britain
by Amazon

84760383R00128